PRAISE FOR

THE RARE EARTH EXCHANGE

SHORTLISTED FOR THE
2015 QUAIS DU POLAR SERIES PRIZE

"From Paris to Malaysia, once again Besson's fast-paced prose uncovers the deepest, darkest and most violent realities of our times."

—*Le Monde*

"A scary book about a globe-spanning confrontation that seems altogether plausible."

—*Big Thrill Magazine*

"With a sharp sense of what is at stake in today's world of espionage and global economic warfare, Bernard Besson has written a fast-paced, intelligent and entirely plausible thriller."

—*Bookseller review*

PRAISE FOR

BERNARD BESSON'S

THE GREENLAND BREACH

www.thegreenlandbreach.com

"Bernard Besson takes the eco-thriller to a whole new level. Masterfully paced and wondrously prescient... Equal parts Clive Cussler and Michael Crichton."
—*Jon Land, bestselling author of the Caitlin Strong series*

"Besson constructs a complex plot and confidently portrays the grandiosity as it unfolds."
—*Publishers Weekly*

"For those who enjoy a rollercoaster of a ride with thrills galore, this book certainly delivers. For the James Bond fan, there are plenty of sophisticated gadgets, fiendishly complex puzzles and clever use of technology. If you look beneath the glossy, high-paced surface, there is a thought-provoking plea to re-examine the way we live and act today."
—*Crime Fiction Lover*

"Bernard Besson clearly doesn't do things by halves. Everything about *The Greenland Breach* is on a grand scale—global powers playing with global stakes, quite literally. A thrilling scenario of a potential disaster on the grandest scale, this book is modern, escapist fiction that entertains while cautioning readers on the importance of climate awareness."
—*Book Lover Book Reviews*

The Rare Earth Exchange

Bernard Besson

Translated from French by Sophie Weiner

LE FRENCH BOOK

SUNDAY

1

The plane's antivirus program froze the download for thirty seconds and then authorized installation. The computer software on the Airbus A340 was as secure as the technology protecting nuclear power plants and the Élysée Palace, the official residence of the president of France.

"Air France operations are reporting fog," the copilot said as he entered an access code. "I just downloaded an updated CAT3 landing procedure."

The pilot was completing the approach briefing, checking minimum safe altitude, pattern entry, flap settings, headwinds, and crosswinds.

"Control, Air France 912 from Kuala Lumpur."

"Pass your message."

"How's the fog over Orly?"

"Not a cloud in the sky."

It took the pilot a half second to register the contradicting information. Then he shifted into emergency mode, reviewing the instruments and looking for anomalies. The copilot was already putting in a call to Air France operations.

"Why did you send a fog procedure when the skies are clear?"

Tension filled the cockpit in the silence that followed. At last, someone responded.

"No one here sent you anything."

The pilot transmitted a recording of the earlier conversation and waited, his anxiety rising, for operations to give its verdict.

"That wasn't us. Looks like the information system and on-board communications box have been hacked."

"The antivirus didn't pick up anything," the pilot said. He turned to the copilot. "Do a cockpit check."

The pilot called in the head flight attendant. "I want a thorough cabin check—all the doors, bathrooms, baggage holds, the kitchen, and the emergency chutes. Inspect everything that's operated by the information system. Don't alarm the passengers. If anyone asks, tell them it's routine."

"What am I looking for?"

"Anything unusual. We could have downloaded a virus."

"I'm on it."

The pilot looked back at the copilot. "What's our status?"

"I checked the engines, the fuel supply, the electricals, and the AC. Everything seems fine."

"Call headquarters and ask them if they can upload something to track down this virus and destroy it."

"Yes, sir."

The pilot flipped the switch that allowed him to speak to the 213 passengers.

"This is Captain Charles Meillan speaking. We're approaching our final descent to Paris-Orly. We'll be touching down in six minutes. It's twenty-six degrees Celsius on the ground with clear skies."

2

"Alexandre, I baptize you in the name of the Father, the Son, and the Holy Spirit."

The priest dripped holy water on the forehead of Victoire Augagneur and John Spencer Larivière's child as sunlight streaming through the stained-glass windows painted the interior of the church in vibrant hues.

John's Franco-American family was occupying the pews on the left, while Victoire's small Franco-Cambodian tribe—survivors of the Khmer Rouge genocide—was on the right.

Alexandre would never know the family members who'd been bludgeoned to death in the rice fields by child soldiers ordered to reform the bourgeoisie.

"You may take your pictures," the priest said before moving on to his third baptism of the day.

John's cousins from New Jersey and Victoire's handful of blood relatives crowded around the beaming couple and their baby, ordering the parents to smile this way and that for the cameras.

For two days, both families had been staying at their home, between the Rue Deparcieux and the Rue Fermat in the fourteenth arrondissement of Paris. The home, actually two connected buildings, was large enough to accommodate a dozen guests. It also served as the headquarters of Fermatown, a private intelligence agency run by John, Victoire, and Luc Masseron.

Luc walked up the altar to fulfill his duties. He proudly signed the papers proving his godfatherly commitment. He was even a little teary.

Once outside the church, John reminded their guests that they had a reservation for lunch at La Bélière, the restaurant at the corner of their street. He ambled over to his wife, who was cooing at the baby they had tried so long to have. The infant had given Victoire her wings and him a new vitality.

The sky over Montparnasse was silvery blue, with the chalky traces of jet planes. The party headed toward the restaurant, crossing the boulevard and strolling by the string of theaters along the car-free Rue de la Gaîté as if nothing had changed in recent years, as if climate change hadn't accelerated and geopolitical upheaval weren't destabilizing the balance of powers.

3

Captain Charles Meillan and his copilot, their eyes glued to the instruments on their control panel, listened to the flight attendant's report as she leaned between their two seats.

"I didn't find anything."

"Thanks, Cathy," Meillan said. "Join the others now. We're going to land."

When she left, the two men did a quick assessment. Headquarters had sent an emergency antivirus. But the director of security had warned that the virus could be a Trojan horse.

"The engines are turning like clocks," Meillan said. "All that's left is the landing gear."

Without its wheels, the Airbus would land on its belly. Its guts would be shredded, and the plane would erupt in flames. How many would perish?

Meillan thought about his wife and his new home on Lac des Settons. With sweaty hands, he gripped the manual control. He'd do it without the computers. It was early, but if there was a problem, they could regain altitude.

"Now!"

Meillan released the gear lock and examined the indicator lights. The landing gear engaged in a beautifully oiled and reassuring operation.

"We got 'em!"

Meillan nodded to his copilot. "We're on final approach for landing. Let traffic control know. What do you think the SOBs could do *now* to screw things up for us?"

"I'd mess with the brakes," the copilot said.

"Have control prepare the nets."

They held their breath until the plane grazed the runway. All the braking systems responded perfectly. The two men high-fived each other and directed the aircraft toward the terminal.

"Air France 912, Orly control. Taxi to gate 26. Way to nail that landing!"

4

At Paris Orly Airport, Pierre-André Noblecourt looked up from his travel bag and saw the red flashing lights of a fire truck and the yellow glow of a heavy-equipment vehicle. The two trucks were heading toward one of the runways. Several other vehicles, including a police car, soon followed. His scalp started tingling with sweat. He took off his baseball cap with the logo of the Olympique de Marseille soccer team but kept his sunglasses on.

Pierre-André watched as the Air France Airbus taxied toward the gate. A phone call from one of his bodyguards served as a rude reminder that he was in the midst of performing one of the worst acting roles of his career. The final act had begun to unfold three days earlier, when he found the photos on his smartphone. Emma had sent them from Kuala Lumpur. The chess match and the clock capable of measuring time down to a thousand-billionth of a second had leaped out at him like wild cats, with more force than his political defeats and the so-called scandals that had marked his overextended career.

"Did you have a safe trip, Mr. President?" It had been a year, six months, and six days since his term in office had ended, but as a former president of France, he would be called Mr. President for the remainder of his life. "The board shows that your flight has landed."

"It was an excellent flight. Thank you." In fact, he had never been on that plane.

A family walked by, and he lowered his head to avoid being recognized. The father was holding a small girl by the hand. Pierre-André thought of Béatrice. His granddaughter would be turning ten in three days and was growing up in a world he no longer understood. It was mostly because of her that, despite all his failures, he still aspired to be Europe's president—the continent's leader in a world that seemed to be spinning out of control.

"Want us to wait for you in the gangway, as usual?"

Pierre-André realized the ridiculousness of the situation. He quickly came up with a lie, as he had so many times before. He'd use his wife.

"Georgette is on her way to the airport. Meet her in the terminal, and wait for me there. I'll be fine. Don't worry."

Pierre-André ended the call and headed toward the arrival area. He paused by a window several feet from a crowd awaiting the flight's passengers and watched as the plane he should have been on approached the gate.

Just as he was about to start walking again, it happened. The emergency-exit chutes shot out from the plane. Pierre-André saw a man throw himself through one of the doors. Other passengers followed, and cries of alarm rose from the crowd. The still-moving plane was dragging all of its chutes on the ground. This couldn't possibly be a drill. Something was terribly wrong.

Then all hell broke loose. An orange ball of fire encircled the plane and hovered around it like a halo. In a matter of seconds, Flight 912 was merely a silhouette engulfed in flames. Men and women, many with children in their arms, streamed down the inflatable slides. A few tumbled down headfirst. Others were shrieking and flailing. Some had even caught fire. Seconds later, one of the chutes vanished in flames.

The crowd inside the building instinctively backed away from the windows, now hot to the touch. As they watched in horror, the plane's wings seemed to melt, and each engine exploded. The plane drifted from its course and crashed into a Saudi Arabian Air Lines A340, which blew up, sending a great mass of debris into the sky. Trucks and fuel-supply vehicles on the tarmac went up in flames.

In apocalyptic succession, one fire erupted after another. Three other planes burst into flames. A blast shattered the terminal windows. Seconds later the terminal itself was ablaze. Panicked, travelers, their friends and family members, concession workers, and all other airport and airline employees rushed toward the exits.

Pierre-André joined the flood of people. Police and private security workers tried to impose order, but it was too much. Men and women in smoking clothes streamed by them, and soon those fleeing the building were stampeding over the bodies on the floor.

His face blackened and sweaty, Pierre-André finally spotted his bodyguards, who, unbelievably, were making their way toward him. The sprinkler system, which had gone off as soon as the building caught fire, had soaked all of them.

"Mr. President, how did you get off that plane?"

"I was lucky. That's all. Let's get out of here."

5

The image of a flaming Orly International Airport looked ready to leap off the plasma screen at La Bélière and into the restaurant itself. The news anchor seemed at a loss for words. Against the fiery backdrop, a reporter was doing her best to describe the scene, but she, too, appeared to be stunned. Only an hour had passed since the late-morning disaster had started to unfold, but the news channels had already gotten their hands on cell phone videos shot by those who had escaped the terminal.

Luc pulled himself away from the images and eyed his two associates. John seemed to be holding his breath. Victoire was clutching the baby and staring at her father, Christophe, who had wrapped a protective arm around his new wife, Dara.

Victoire's mother had survived atrocities, but they had left permanent scars. After her death, Victoire's French father had remarried. Dara was also Cambodian. She was just a child when Phnom Penh fell, but she remembered the brutal regime. Nothing, it seemed, would release the hold those memories had on them.

Luc could see that Victoire was doing her best to stay composed. Motherhood had made her even more beautiful. Victoire's raven-colored hair was lustrous, and her black eyes were radiant. She was tall like her father and had an almost untouchable air. He had never been more in love with his boss's wife.

John, meanwhile, was throwing furtive glances at the street. He was smelling danger—and rightfully so. Luc could see the sweat stains under the arms of the jacket he had just given him. Luc loved John too. Completely. And that was the crux of the problem. Two impossible loves, one unfathomable profession, and three people who were still trying to figure things out. And now they had an innocent kid on their hands. Like John, Luc could see into the future. The fire would come lapping at the walls of Fermatown.

Luc reached over to Victoire and took his godson into his arms. Alexandre smiled, and Luc felt a surge of love. Before he could say a word to the baby he heard the notes of Ravel's *Boléro*—John's ringtone for the agency.

John hadn't even answered when another tune popped into Luc's brain: Glen Frey's "The Heat Is On."

6

John recognized the voice of Hubert de Méricourt, head of the agency at Les Invalides responsible for France's intelligence and counterintelligence.

"John, meet me at Jardin Catherine Labouré on the Rue de Babylone. Bring your team. I know you're celebrating your son's baptism, but we don't have a second to lose. I can't tell you any more over the phone."

John could feel the eyes of his family and friends on him. Victoire's father shook his head.

"Your child gets baptized just once in his life, John. Can't it wait?"

"They need us," John said.

"I suppose it's about Orly," Christophe replied.

"I don't know."

"Do they want all three of us?" Victoire asked.

"Yes."

Luc handed Alexandre to Roberta, a friend who lived at Number 7 on the Rue Fermat. Roberta was a kind of guardian angel in the Daguerre Village. Whenever a resident needed something, she was there, many times without even being asked.

"Do you mind?" John asked as Luc, Victoire, and he got up from their chairs.

"Go," Roberta answered. "And don't worry. He'll be fine with me. Take as long as you need."

The three kissed everyone good-bye and left La Bélière. Less than a minute later, they were in front of their touch-screen wall in the main room of Number 9 Rue Fermat. Each of them grabbed their crisis kit. An invitation from Méricourt was always the prelude to a cluster of shit storms—but it also guaranteed a certified check from Banque de France.

"What do you know about the Jardin Catherine Labouré?" John asked.

"It's a park with a playground and an arbor," Victoire responded. "Every mom in the neighborhood goes there. Kids can play all they want while the mothers talk."

"What's up with this spot?" Luc asked.

"I have no idea. It seems like an odd place to meet. I'll take my motorcycle. You guys take the car. We might need audio and visual."

John was making sure that Luc, the most tech-savvy member of the team—one who had no compunctions about cutting corners—had everything he needed. John had never stopped thanking his stars that Hubert de Méricourt had urged him to hire this lanky man with dark curly hair and skin as white as Carrara marble. Luc was at Méricourt's government agency at the time, but he clearly wasn't cut out for work as a bureaucrat. Méricourt knew talent when he saw it, and he didn't want Luc's to go to waste. Luc was quick, shrewd, and loyal—ideal for Fermatown. And he was game for anything. John and Victoire took to him right away.

"Where's Caresse?" Luc asked.

At that very moment, their Persian cat brushed against Luc's leg.

"She never does that to me," John complained.

"How long have you been married to Victoire? And you still don't know how to treat a female!"

"I beg your pardon! Victoire, set the man straight."

Victoire grinned. "Stop bickering, you guys." She skipped down the concrete staircase to Fermatown's garage. Two motorcycles, one car, and a fake taxi made up the fleet of these French privateers, agents the higher-ups in the French government called on when they didn't want to dirty their hands.

John trailed Victoire down the stairs and shook his head. Just how filthy would they be getting this time around?

7

John spotted Méricourt hunched in the shade of a wall a few feet from the park entrance on the Rue de Babylone. His former boss looked like he was bearing an enormous weight.

John parked his Triumph Thunderbird a few feet away as he scoped the landscape. Everything seemed normal. No undercover agents, no suspicious couples, no fogged-up windshields, no half-closed blinds hiding the barrel of a weapon or a directional microphone.

But he did note the cameras on the apartment buildings across the street. So that was why Méricourt was waiting off to the side and out of sight. John kept his helmet on to shield his face and warned Victoire and Luc, using his embedded mike. Méricourt looked relieved to see him.

"What's going on?"

"Pierre-André Noblecourt was just found hanging by his neck in his home office."

"Our former president?"

"Yes."

John could already see the flood of problems that this news would create. Méricourt cast a furtive glance in both directions before continuing. "His wife, Georgette, discovered the body. His office is on the top floor of their apartment on the other side of the park. Apparently, it was quite a sight."

"I can only imagine."

"She immediately called the president on his private line at the Élysée. He wants to know exactly what happened, and he wants the information *now*. As if there weren't enough to handle already, considering what's going on at Orly."

"Does it look like suicide?"

Méricourt scowled at John, and he felt like he had just walked on the man's carpet with muddy boots.

"His wife suspects something fishy. The president's worried and wants to get to the bottom of this. Noblecourt was a potential candidate for the European presidency, and he had access to strategic information. Georgette hasn't called the police yet. She doesn't trust them—or the judicial system, which would get involved in any investigation. Noblecourt alienated some key judges during his presidency. We'll have to figure out what went down and convince her to call the authorities."

"I'm not sure this is up our alley."

"This job *is* your alley, John. Obviously, no one at the agency can be involved."

"So you called us to do your dirty work."

Méricourt stared at John, who knew exactly what his former boss was thinking. John was a former commando, wounded in Afghanistan while serving a corrupt administration and a lost cause. He had left behind any interest in playing soldier, and not long after that, he had left the agency. Méricourt had told him that a man with his brains and integrity—not to mention his legionnaire face and thick head of hair—inspired too much envy anyway. Like Luc, John was better suited to work on the outside. And that was fine with Méricourt, who used Spencer Larivière's firm for his most sensitive cases.

"I trust your team. We can't have any leaks."

"I know the drill."

John had returned from a recent touch-and-go case in Greenland with quite a few more gray hairs and an even more pragmatic attitude. He was glad to still be alive at the age of forty, and now he had a son to think about.

"What's the risk level on this? I'm getting a whiff of rot here."

"Listen, John, I know you'll handle this with a light touch. If I personally had to take on the police, the public prosecutor, and the entire judicial machine that's going to parade out once Georgette Noblecourt calls the authorities, I'd have a real mess on my hands—a media nightmare for the agency and even for President Jemestre."

"You'd rather have me take the fall if something goes wrong."

"Honestly, yes. You'll get a nice paycheck. Don't worry."

John vascillated between exasperation and excitement. With Méricourt, he always worried, yet this was his chosen line of work.

"And you don't believe my way of doing things will be worse? I'll terrify them. In their eyes, I'm a mercenary. Those people hate us."

"You're right. This country's afraid of everything. France has turned into a nursery. That's why I'd rather see a woman at Georgette's side. What do you say, John?"

"You think Victoire doesn't have anything better to do?"

"Georgette Noblecourt is involved in charity work. Victoire will meet with her under the guise of discussing one of the charities. No one will know why she's really there. Victoire's a clever woman. You know that. The president told Mrs. Noblecourt that someone would come by. He told her not to do anything before speaking with that person. I'm basically handing you a page in the history books, John. You'll have an amazing story to tell little Alexandre."

"You'll say anything to persuade us. You're horrible."

Hubert de Méricourt glanced down the sidewalk. Luc and Victoire were leaning against the wall, just out of earshot.

"I know I can count on you, John. You got rid of a hornet's nest by going to Greenland for me. You can certainly weed out what happened during the final hours of the former president's life."

John didn't have time to respond. He watched his former boss slip away and dive into the backseat of a car with tinted windows. The car pulled out from the curb. Victoire and Luc walked over, both of them looking curious.

"So?" Luc asked.

"I need you to look around the building where Pierre-André Noblecourt lived," John said, pointing across the park. "That's right. I used the past tense. His wife found him hanging from the rafters this morning on the top floor of their place. See if you can find anything. The authorities haven't been notified yet."

"Got it," Luc said. He nodded and sprinted off.

8

Victoire turned to John, wondering what her role in all of this would be. Since Alexandre's birth, she had been feeling energized and positive. The birth itself had been easier than expected, and the baby was sleeping through the night. After losing so many members of her family, she was grateful that she would finally be able to pass on her heritage and at least tell her little boy about his forebears. No, Victoire wasn't experiencing anything close to the baby blues.

John took her elbow and guided her toward a grove of trees.

"So what do you need me to do?"

She listened while her husband explained her end of the assignment.

"And what about you?"

"The first order of business for me is calling the Protection Service, which was supposed to be ensuring his security. Every former French president is assigned two bodyguards for life, and I want to know more about his."

"Do you think you'll get someone to talk to you?"

"I know the man in charge—let's just say he owes me one."

Victoire nodded. How many other people were indebted to John? He was a genuine good guy. His career with the intelligence agency had been a monumental mistake, but

Fermatown was a perfect fit. The two left the stand of trees and walked toward the park entrance.

Victoire pulled out a pair of sunglasses and slipped away from her husband. The mothers were beginning to gather up their broods. It was too hot. Victoire walked past the benches, the slides, the swings, and a toolshed with a wet-paint sign on the door handle. How quaint, she thought. It looked like a little house.

She then headed toward the Noblecourt residence in the low-rise apartment building about two hundred yards away, a traditional-looking structure shaded by horse-chestnut trees and a tall stone wall. Reaching it, she pushed the metal gate and turned around to see if anyone was following. No one. For her, Pierre-André Noblecourt was a series of televised images. His wife and he had never really interested her. She thought she remembered them having a grown child. Was it a son or a daughter? Had to be a daughter, she realized, recalling the mention of a son-in-law in a news article.

A camera above the entrance was directed at the doormat. Victoire lowered her eyes, turned her back to the lens, and slipped on a pair of surgical gloves while she examined the directory. The Noblecourts occupied the second, third, fourth, and top floor. She found Pierre-André and Georgette Noblecourt, their names written in antiquated calligraphy, and pressed the bell. A wary-sounding woman answered.

Victoire hesitated. "The president sent me."

"Thank God. Come quickly."

The door clicked and opened half an inch. Victoire pressed down on the gold handle. The black-and-white tiled hallway led her to the bottom of a staircase. An outdated and attentively polished elevator fit the refined ambiance and the well-maintained silence of the house. She walked past a Chinese-blue door on her right, and through her tinted shades checked for cameras as she stepped onto the red carpet.

Georgette Noblecourt was waiting for her at the top of the stairs. The petite and elegant woman with meticulously coiffed hair watched as Victoire climbed each step. The ex-first lady, who appeared to be in her late sixties or early seventies, stood firmly in place, eyeing her with an air of suspicion. She was wearing a gray suit with black-velvet lapels. Victoire thought back to the televised appearances where the former first lady talked about her charity work. It all came back in a flash. On screen, the woman seemed nicer and more approachable.

"You can remove your glasses. I've turned off the cameras. No one will recognize you."

Victoire complied, noting that the former first lady didn't lack composure. She quickly climbed the stairs. In one hand, Georgette Noblecourt was holding an embroidered handkerchief. In the other she had a cell phone.

"I've told no one, aside from Alain."

Victoire knew the Noblecourts were close to Alain Jemestre, the current French president. In fact, they had furthered his career.

Victoire peeked through the half-open door. The apartment was filled with mahogany furniture, and the walls were covered with old pink wallpaper. The overall effect was banal. Through the living room windows she spotted the little toolshed in the Jardin Catherine Labouré.

"He's on the top floor. It used to be an attic, but Pierre-André turned it into his office. It's hideous."

Despite Georgette Noblecourt's in-control voice, her eyes were red and her hands were shaking. Victoire nodded in sympathy and followed as the woman climbed the stairs to the next floor. They reached the hallway and walked past a door painted Cantonese yellow.

"This is where my daughter, Apolline, and her husband, Serge, live. They're not here at the moment. Béatrice, my granddaughter, is at her piano lesson on the Rue Vaneau."

Victoire mentally recorded the information and followed the former president's widow as she climbed still another flight of stairs. By now, the woman was wheezing.

"My husband never wanted us to go anywhere. He was a homebody."

Victoire watched her bring the handkerchief to her face. They stopped on the next floor in front of a door that was just as polished as the others. This one was another shade of red. Mrs. Noblecourt took a deep breath before speaking.

"This is his office, and down the hall is where our guests stay, as well as Pierre-André's two bodyguards."

"Where were they this morning?"

"They usually have Sundays off, but they went to the airport this morning to pick him up. Then they went home to their families."

"The president was at Orly?"

"Yes. He was coming home from Kuala Lumpur."

As soon as John's phone had rung at La Bélière, she had been sure it was about Flight 912.

"He was one of the survivors. That is, I mean… He was on that flight."

Victoire could detect anger in the woman's eyes, and she was certain now that the airport disaster was connected to Noblecourt's death. But how?

"You can go on ahead. I can't look at him again. I'm the one who opened the door, but I didn't touch anything. You're the expert."

Victoire hesitated and then placed a foot on the first step, telling herself that she was making a foolish mistake.

"I'm anxious to hear what you think," Mrs. Noblecourt said. "This is very important for me. For the president too—the current one, I mean."

Victoire looked up. Sunlight streaming through a round window lit up one of the walls and the red carpet on the steps leading to the top floor—the fourth floor. Her head started buzzing, and an age-old superstition came flooding back. All over East and Southeast Asia, the number four brought bad luck. The Chinese word for four sounded like the word for death. John teased her about this tetraphobia, but it ran deep.

She started climbing, taking the steps one at a time and inhaling the polish to stay in the here and now. She approached the black lacquered door. It was ajar. Her throat was dry as she pushed it open.

Hanging from a rope, Pierre-André Noblecourt stared at her with two bulging eyes and a grotesque tongue hanging out of his mouth. His body was twirling slowly beneath the crossbeam of his large attic office. One of his feet was missing a shoe. His pants were about to slip off, and his shirt was flapping over his belly, which was as white as a codfish.

Despite the sweltering heat, a breeze from an open window made Victoire shiver. The window—one of several in the room—offered a view of the seventh arrondissement's gray rooftops. Towering over them was the dreadfully boring Tour Montparnasse. She walked past the former president's body and craned her neck out the window. Beneath it was a courtyard.

Victoire looked back at the body. How had he managed to hang himself so high without any help? She was eye-level with his shoeless foot, which was swaying gently about five and a half feet above the impeccably waxed wooden floor. His desk was off to the side and too far away. He couldn't have used it to reach the crossbeam. There was no overturned chair, no ladder, no stool. Victoire inspected the ceiling. The rope, which looked new, was securely attached to the beam. She moved around the body and examined it from the other side. The noose had been carefully knotted.

"How could he have gotten up there?"

Victoire jumped when she heard Georgette Noblecourt's voice behind her. "That's what I'm wondering. Alain wanted someone trustworthy to see this before the police, the journalists, and the lawyers started making their ridiculous speculations."

Victoire looked out the window again—and went white when she spotted Luc's silhouette behind a dusty glass window in the building directly across from her. She spun around. Georgette Noblecourt was right there, absolutely still.

"So you're thinking the same thing, aren't you?" Mrs. Noblecourt's voice revealed a fierce will.

Victoire didn't know what to think. Yes, some things were evident. But what had really happened here? And why?

"What do you mean, Madame?"

"I mean he couldn't have hanged himself up there all by himself. He obviously needed help. That person had to get in through the window, since the door was locked. I needed the key to open it."

Victoire looked out the window one more time. Luc had disappeared. Relieved, she examined the ledge in search of a hint or a clue. She didn't find anything, but figured a well-conditioned man could have climbed the building and entered the top floor. Assuming the window was open.

"Was this window open?"

"Whenever it was nice out, like today, Pierre-André kept it open. He hated being in a stuffy room, even in the middle of winter. There's no heating up here."

"That apartment building across the way—I'm wondering if anyone could have seen someone climbing into the window."

"The building's being renovated. It's been vacant for several months. So he was murdered, wasn't he?"

"Who would do that?" Victoire asked.

"I have no idea. A president has more enemies than friends. Pierre-André made many decisions that didn't please everyone."

Victoire felt the woman's worried but determined eyes on her. She turned around to look at her and thought again about the news footage of the Orly disaster that she had seen at La Bélière.

"How did he get off the plane?"

"I don't know."

"What did he tell you?"

"All he said was, 'Someone tried to kill me.'"

"What was he doing in Kuala Lumpur?"

"He went to see our son-in-law. Serge is working there."

The woman's eyes darkened. Victoire had just touched a sore spot. Noblecourt's widow handed her the smartphone she had been holding.

"He left his phone in our apartment downstairs. I figured it might be helpful."

Victoire hesitated, knowing full well that she'd be concealing, at least temporarily, what could be a crucial piece of evidence. Too late. Her hand closed around the device.

"Why didn't he take it with him to the attic?"

"I have no idea. He usually kept it with him. Hold on to it. I don't trust any magistrate who might be following up on this. Everyone in the judicial system was bent on bringing him down. I want you to find out who did this."

"I'll need some time."

Victoire was already regretting her involvement in a matter that wasn't her problem and what would surely become a corrupt case. Damned Méricourt! Mrs. Noblecourt looked around the attic and dabbed her nose with her handkerchief.

"Did you notice anything else that was unusual?" Victoire asked.

"No."

"Is anything missing? Maybe a stepladder someone could have used to climb up there?"

Mrs. Noblecourt walked over to the practically empty desk and did a full circle around the room. She came back to Victoire a few moments later and stared blankly at her husband.

"I never come up here," she finally said. "I don't even know if we have a stepladder. I'm going to call the police in half an hour. That'll give you enough time to collect anything you need. Come back later today. We'll talk then. If the police are still here, tell them I invited you."

"And how are we supposed to know each other?"

"I run a foundation that helps children in the Mekong region. You're from Cambodia, I've been told."

"Yes," Victoire answered, getting the uncomfortable feeling that her privacy was being violated, along with her past. For a freshly bereft widow, the woman was quite well informed.

"Now get to work."

Pinned in place by the abruptness of Mrs. Noblecourt's parting sentence, Victoire nodded. The woman of the house closed the door behind her, leaving Victoire with the former French president. Using her phone, she photographed every angle of the crime scene. She estimated that the floor area of the attic was a little more than a hundred and twenty square meters. No closets or crawlspace.

Five windows—one of which was open—on the courtyard side, five more on the garden side. The president's large desk was near a wall. Behind it was a large leather office chair. Facing the desk were two club chairs, also leather. No dressers, no armoires. Shelves on two of the walls held an impressive number of books and photographs. An entire life dedicated to politics and international relations.

Victoire walked over to the computer on the desk and inserted a USB drive containing the agency's latest data-retrieval program. In a few seconds, all of the former president's digital secrets would be copied, with the police being none the wiser, in theory, at least. In the realm of technology, nothing was a given.

She opened the desk drawers and took pictures of every document she could get her hands on. Having finished her rush job, she walked back down the staircase with Mrs. Noblecourt's final words resonating in her head like an executioner's ax in the bones of his victim.

"What am I getting myself into?"

9

John took off his sunglasses and entered the blissful shade of the Saint Philippe du Roule Church. It was 3:10 in the afternoon and too hot to be outside.

As he looked around, he thought back to the modest stone church of his childhood in New Jersey, his mother at his side—in a crisp cotton dress in the summer and a wool suit in the winter, always scented with the same perfume. But this wasn't the time for memory lane. He walked down one of the side aisles. The two officers in charge of protecting the former president had been called in by their boss, Jean-Claude Possin, who had instructed them to meet John at the church, near the Joan of Arc statue. They had been told to sit and wait. They weren't to look at the man, and they were to forget the conversation ever took place. That was Possin's cloak-and-dagger style.

John spotted the officers and slipped into the pew directly behind them.

"Was Noblecourt on the plane from Kuala Lumpur that blew up this morning?"

"Yes," the bodyguard to the right answered.

"How did he make it off?"

"He got lucky. He was one of the few to escape."

"What state was he in?"

"Shock."

"What was he doing in Kuala Lumpur?"

"I don't know."

"Why weren't you with him?"

"We don't go on every trip. The president takes us along when he wants to. The French embassy in Kuala Lumpur assured us that he would have protection. He left at the end of the week and returned today. We called him as soon as the plane landed. That's protocol. He asked us to wait with Mrs. Noblecourt in the terminal. Everyone was in a panic and trying to get out of the place. We saw him in the crowd before we found her."

"What did he tell you?"

"He said his wife had called to tell him she wouldn't be coming to the airport after all. We left immediately."

"Did he tell you what happened to the plane?"

"He said the engines caught fire."

John knew that planes sometimes made crash landings at airports, and every once in a while, one plane would clip another on the ground, but he couldn't remember anything on this kind of scale. In any case, a four-engine explosion was inconceivable without an outside trigger. But if it *was* an attack, why didn't they destroy the plane while it was in the air? He had no explanation.

"Where did you go next?"

"To his studio."

"What studio?"

"All former presidents have an apartment on the top floor of the Palais de Chaillot at Trocadéro. They call it their studio, even though it's much larger."

"What did he do there?"

"He went up, dropped off his travel bag, and came back down."

"You didn't go up with him?"

"He was in and out in five minutes. Then we took him back to his residence on the Rue de Babylone."

"Did he meet with anyone on the way?"

"No."

"Did he make or get any phone calls?"

"No."

"You didn't stay at his residence with him?"

"It's Sunday, which is usually our day off. Then Possin called and told us to come here and answer your questions."

"How did the president seem to you?"

"He looked rattled, and considering everything that was happening at the airport, that was no surprise. But I'd have to say it was more than that. He seemed worn out and worried. He looked over his shoulder two or three times, like he was afraid he was being followed."

"The president's dead. His wife found him hanging from a crossbeam in his home office."

The two men cringed. According to Possin, Pierre-André Noblecourt had always been considerate of his bodyguards and staff. He was a good boss. John realized he had broken the news rather harshly and he should apologize. But he had never minced his words. He didn't say anything.

"That's horrible," said the bodyguard on the left.

"What do you think happened?" John asked.

The bodyguard looked up at Joan of Arc, her face illuminated by a spotlight.

"It must have been awful on that plane. Just about everyone else died. Maybe he was in shock. But suicide? It doesn't make sense. A man like that wouldn't kill himself. He was committed to becoming the first president of Europe. He talked to us a lot and told us what he wanted to accomplish."

"Was he sick, or did he have any emotional issues?"

The two men shook their heads. The Republican Guard officers who provided security for the nation's presidents were known for their discretion. John respected that.

"Have you ever been in his top-floor office?"

"Once or twice," the bodyguard on the right said. "We haven't spent much time at his residence. We have rooms there, but we've hardly ever used them. How is Mrs. Noblecourt holding up?"

"You can imagine. She's the one who found him."

"My God…"

"Is there an access code to get into the Trocadéro studio?"

The two men hesitated. John would have to do some convincing. After a few seconds of silence, he spit out the only rationale that could get the bodyguards on his side.

"I don't think it was suicide either. Your boss was murdered. You know how the investigation and prosecution systems work in France. It'll take them twenty years to uncover the truth. And that's the best-case scenario."

Hunched over in the half-light, the two bodyguards said nothing. Just as John was about to give up and walk away, the man on the left broke the silence.

"Go to the Musée de l'Homme like an ordinary tourist. There's an exit by the bathrooms. Take it. At the bottom of the stairs, there's a hallway leading to a private area. Follow the hallway until you reach a metal door with a sign that says 'private.' Go through that door, and you'll find another hallway with a heavier door. There'll be a keypad. The first code is Verdun 843. Enter it. Once you've made it in, you'll find an elevator. It doesn't need a code. Take the elevator to his floor. The door to his studio will open with Verdun 844."

John thanked them. "You two will be the first to know the truth."

"Good luck."

10

Luc looked over Victoire's shoulder at the patrons at Café Les Mouettes. The fashionable *bobos* of the neighborhood had paid them no notice when they walked in. Their eyes were glued to the television screens. Four hours had passed since the disaster, and the local news channels were sending feeds around the world.

Victoire was telling Luc about her encounter with Georgette Noblecourt. Although she loved John with all her heart, she could talk with Luc in a way she couldn't talk with her husband. Luc was like her best friend from school. But she had long ago lost touch with everyone she had known there.

"She wasn't putting on an act, but there was something about her that didn't seem right."

"What do you mean?"

"She was incredibly composed, almost too composed. If something like that ever happened to John, I'd be devastated. Speechless even."

"I certainly hope nothing happens to John. He's been through enough already. But as for you losing your tongue— it's not likely." Victoire withheld comment. Luc was irresistible and impossible to put up with at the same time.

"You think she's lying?" Luc asked.

"She knows things, but she's not ready to tell me. She's a woman in pain, but she's got this super-intense determination. It's scary."

"Do you think she killed him?"

"I don't think so, but I did see anger in her eyes."

"Obviously toward the murderers, don't you think?"

"I don't know. I have a feeling it's more complicated than that."

Victoire sipped her hot chocolate. The smell reminded her of her first time in Paris with her parents. She was eight years old. The same hot chocolate had made her feel at home on the Rue d'Ulm when she was a student at the École Normale Supérieure. She had worked so hard—all to forget a past that wasn't even hers, but her parents'. Victoire caught herself. The scene at the former president's home was triggering memories. She had to shake them off. She banished the images and replaced them with a vision of sipping hot chocolate one day with her little boy.

"Why are you smiling?" Luc asked.

"Oh, nothing. Mrs. Noblecourt didn't think there was any way he could have gotten up there by himself. She's positive someone helped him hang himself. I think she's right. But at the same time, I can't say that I trust her."

"Why's that?"

"I got the feeling that she didn't love him. She'd been crying. Her eyes were red. But she was too cool. Actually, it gave me the shivers."

"They were a political couple. People in that world don't have the same feelings that you and I have. They have alliances and agendas."

Victoire changed the subject. "I saw you in the building across from me. What did you find?"

Luc pulled out a digital tablet and a mini camera. He placed them on the table and pushed them toward Victoire.

"I've got proof that someone else was in the room," he whispered.

"I *knew* it."

"Look."

Luc turned on the screen and pressed play. Victoire saw herself in front of the attic's open courtyard window. Behind her, Noblecourt's legs were swaying in the breeze. She could clearly make out his two feet—one shoed and the other shoeless. She watched herself step in front of Mrs. Noblecourt to block her from seeing Luc.

"Now I'm gonna show you the footage in reverse."

Victoire watched as she backed out of the room in sync with Mrs. Noblecourt.

"You're not in the room yet. I only had a minute before you came in, but that was long enough. The camera's in standard mode right now. Look closely."

Noblecourt's body—hanging from the rope—was twirling slowly far above the floor.

"I've switched to high-sensitivity thermal mode."

A red ring appeared around Noblecourt's body.

"He's giving off heat, so he hasn't been dead long," Luc explained. "And the camera captures it perfectly. Then I directed the camera toward the space under his feet, and it recorded heat impressions that basically tell us what happened after he was hoisted up."

Victoire stared at a vague orange form close to the former president's feet. It was pulling away from Noblecourt's body.

"What on earth is that?"

"A second source of heat."

"A second person?"

"Noblecourt wasn't alone. And the heat traces go right through the window. It looks like someone gave Mr. President a helping hand."

"I thought of that right away. So did Mrs. Noblecourt. That doesn't mean she's innocent. But I can't picture her helping him kill himself and then climbing out a window and down a wall."

"Someone either hanged him or helped him commit suicide and then made sure any investigators would know it. Whoever it was took the stepladder with him. Did you see Noblecourt's missing shoe?"

"No. If Noblecourt's hanging was a solo act, the shoe would've fallen to the floor. I would have seen it."

"Exactly. That proves he had help."

"So the guy who was with him left with the shoe? Why?"

"Maybe the murderer wanted something that was in the shoe—an object or a document. Maybe he was trying to send a message."

"Or a warning," Victoire suggested.

"For our current president?"

"We're doing this at his request. He needs to know."

"But he won't tell us anything."

Victoire took Noblecourt's smartphone from her handbag and handed it to Luc.

"Mrs. Noblecourt gave me his phone. She made a point of telling me that he didn't usually leave it lying around. She wanted us to have it instead of the police. She doesn't trust them. She's putting us in a very uncomfortable position—withholding evidence. I don't like this."

Luc flashed a grin. "'Fasten your seat belts. It's going to be a bumpy night.' You know I've always had a thing for Bette Davis."

"You're all excited about this, aren't you?"

"Yes, I am."

"You're ridiculous."

"That's what makes me so likeable."

"And what gets on my nerves."

After glancing around, Luc put on a pair of latex gloves and tried opening the incoming and outgoing call log on Noblecourt's phone to download the information to his own device.

"This has some serious protection on it. I'll need to take it apart to get anything out of it. But walking around with this phone is not only interfering with a police investigation, but also making us vulnerable. It won't be long before the phone gets triangulated right here. Starting now, anyone tracking Noblecourt's phone will begin at Café Les Mouettes."

"We definitely can't bring that thing back to the house."

"Don't worry. It's a godfather's duty to protect his godson from his parents when they're acting insane."

Luc pulled a pouch from his backpack and put the phone in it. "Ta-da… Now no one will be able to track the phone."

"I knew you'd find a use for your little portable Faraday cage. And just think—you had it with you."

"Right you are, ma'am. You're not the only psychic at Fermatown. Thanks to this thing, nobody will know we have the phone."

"Forget Bette Davis and *All About Eve*." Victoire said, shaking her head. "You're a regular Inspector Gadget."

"Yeah, I just need the bionics," Luc said, standing up. "Now let's get out of here."

11

John sped up after crossing the Alma-Marceau metro intersection and soared past a slow line of cars heading toward Trocadéro. He looped around the esplanade and then swung past the Carette pastry shop, where he had taken Victoire on their first date.

Confident that he wasn't being followed, he parked across from a chic bedding store. Happy people in air-conditioned and comfortably lit stores were enjoying their late-afternoon shopping excursions. He, on the other hand, was chasing a boogeyman. What Luc had just told him about the presence of someone else in the former president's office wasn't good news. He crossed Boulevard Wilson and reached the museum. Instead of joining the visitors line at the Musée de L'homme, he headed toward the museum's café.

The stairway to the bathrooms was wide and well lit. At the bottom, he found the hallway leading to one of the museum's private areas. He reached into his backpack and pulled out a woman's stocking. They didn't call it a crisis kit for nothing. He tugged it over his face to distort his features and prevent any biometric restoration programs from recognizing him. He started down the hallway and arrived at a metal door. A sign read "private." He pushed the door open and found himself in a dark, silent hallway. He took a few steps and came upon a heavier metal door.

The access panel had the usual numbers and letters. As he pressed V-8-4-3, he suddenly remembered the gruesome Treaty of Verdun, which had separated the Franks of Germania from the Franks of Gaul. The Rhine River had served as a boundary for a thousand years. But why had they chosen *that* as a mnemonic device? He filed the question away as the door clicked and opened. He followed the hallway and found the elevator.

John pressed the only button next to the elevator. The doors slid open to a roomy space that could hold at least ten people and several large objects. The ride up lasted a few seconds. When the doors opened again, he stepped into a hallway with a marble floor and recessed lights. He found the door with the access panel. Without hesitating, he entered V-8-4-4 and stepped inside, bringing a hand to the Smith and Wesson beneath his jacket. He walked through the foyer and into a spacious living room. To his right, a picture window provided a stunning view of Paris. Under the window was a row of small silver trees. A dozen metal bonsais no more than eight inches tall were shimmering in the light. They were perfectly sculpted—actual works of art.

He turned away from the window and walked quietly toward the hallway leading to the other rooms. The spick-and-span kitchen hadn't been used in a long time. He glanced at the three bedrooms and their adjoining bathrooms. Everything appeared deserted. He guessed that Pierre-André Noblecourt hadn't spent much time here. Back in the living room, he spotted the blue travel bag that the former president had brought back from his trip to Kuala Lumpur. It was on a display case protecting a model of a landscape that was about two meters long and one meter wide. John paused to examine it. The juxtaposition of urban and suburban areas intrigued him.

On the left, the artist had replicated La Défense, Paris's major business district, with pinpoint accuracy. On the right, instead of fashioning the Seine and Neuilly, the model-maker had recreated the downtown of a city that John instantly recognized: Kuala Lumpur. Its Petronas towers were the tallest twin skyscrapers in the world.

Farther to the right was a futuristic city that didn't remind John of anything he was familiar with. At the far end there was a coastal region with a port and a long pier jutting into the sea. And behind some hills overlooking the city, there was an industrial area surrounded by a tropical forest. The lack of continuity was evident, but the large model had to mean something to the person who created it. John took out his smartphone and photographed it from all angles.

Before leaving the apartment, he recorded every item in the drawers and closets. Then he grabbed the travel bag.

Back on the museum's ground floor, he bumped into a woman as she was leaving the lady's restroom. Upon seeing him, she hurried away, and he realized he still had the stocking over his face. He pulled it off and stuffed it into his pocket, making a beeline for the front door before the woman alerted security. He rushed to his motorcycle and sped away.

"What a fucked-up profession."

12

On her way back to the Noblecourt residence, Victoire was obsessing over what the former president's widow had said. What did she mean—*we'll talk*? Had she deliberately neglected to tell her something? That had to be it. Why have her come back so soon, and why invent the whole charade about the Mekong kids? Why put her at risk of being seen by the police?

She had discussed this with John on the phone, and he seemed blithe to her concerns.

"If she asked you to come by, she has her reasons. I wouldn't read into it what's probably not there."

Victoire didn't like being dismissed. She shot back, accusing John of throwing her into the lion's den. She didn't like this case.

Now that she had Alexandre to care for, she wanted more reasonable assignments.

Victoire yearned to be back at Fermatown, where the ever-cheerful Roberta was filling in for her. She felt guilty over leaving her father and stepmother, who had come all the way from Lyon, but Roberta had reassured her that everyone was fine. Roberta's vanilla Labrador, Rainbow Warrior, was keeping a protective eye on the baby, and the dog seemed to delight Alexandre. Victoire actually wished they weren't doing so well. Then she'd have an excuse to go back home and forget about Georgette Noblecourt.

She turned onto the Rue de Babylone and put her sunglasses back on. A few moments later she spotted a commotion at the entrance to Jardin Catherine Labouré. Some police officers had roped it off, and gawkers had gathered on the sidewalk. Joining them, she bumped into a man who looked like a detective.

"You can't go through there, ma'am."

"I have a meeting with Georgette Noblecourt. Why is the park closed?"

The man looked at her and melted the moment she removed her shades and flashed one of her radiant smiles. Victoire knew how to use her almond eyes and seductive lips to full advantage.

"I'll find out," the man said as he brought his phone to his mouth.

Victoire maintained her composure as the detective spoke into the phone.

"There's a woman here who says she's got a meeting with Georgette Noblecourt."

"That's my grandmother!" a child cried out.

Victoire looked down and locked eyes with a little girl. She was about eight or nine years old. She looked like she had been crying, but her tone was confident.

"I live in that apartment building, and I need to go home."

"What is your name?" one of the officers asked.

"It's Béatrice," the little girl replied. "I just came back from my piano lesson, and they won't let me in. What's going on? Is my grandmother okay?"

The detective examined the child.

"There's also a kid saying she's Mrs. Noblecourt's granddaughter."

"I'm not a *kid*. I'm Béatrice."

A minute later, the barricade opened up. Victoire felt a rush of emotions as Béatrice latched onto her hand.

"Is Grandpa dead?"

"Why would you ask that?"

"Something bad has happened. There're so many policemen."

"I'm just here for an appointment with your grandmother. I'm completely out of the loop."

"She won't be able to meet with you."

"We'll see about that."

Victoire glanced down at the sweet little munchkin next to her. Behind her round glasses with pink rims, Béatrice's eyes were clear—verging on blue—and intelligent. Her white embroidered blouse and pleated plaid skirt were the perfect schoolgirl outfit. And her long chestnut-brown hair was tied in a ponytail at the nape of her neck. Victoire's heart tightened. The girl was looking at her like she was the bearer of bad news.

"Who are you?"

"I'm a friend of your grandmother's."

Béatrice squeezed Victoire's hand. At the entrance to the apartment building, a police officer let them in. Georgette Noblecourt, who was waiting, gave her granddaughter a blank look.

"Where's Grandpa?" Béatrice asked.

"Did you tell her?"

"She knows something has happened," Victoire replied.

Anger flashed in Mrs. Noblecourt's eyes as she broke the news to the little girl in a dry tone. "He's dead. Béatrice, come here. You, go see Apolline."

Mrs. Noblecourt took the child by the hand and disappeared inside the apartment, leaving Victoire by herself. She overheard a hushed conversation in the living room and couldn't help thinking it was all an act as she started climbing the stairs to the office.

Two paramedics were bringing down the former president's body wrapped in a heavy plastic bag. She stepped aside to let them by and continued climbing. Just then, she came across a beautiful Nordic woman in leather boots and a lavender-blue suit. Her icy blue eyes cut through Victoire. Two women of the same breed, but not necessarily members of the same team.

"Who are you?" the blonde asked.

Standing two steps lower and annoyed by this, Victoire feigned a submissive and affable persona. It was difficult but tactical.

"I'm a friend of Georgette Noblecourt. I just arrived. She's deeply upset over her husband's death, but we had an appointment, and she wants to keep it. I found her granddaughter, Béatrice, on my way here. She was coming home from a piano lesson."

"We know. We were informed of your arrival. I'm Claudine Montluzac, police chief on duty. Tell Mrs. Noblecourt that the crime scene investigators have finished and the room has been sealed. No one is to go into the president's office without permission from the investigating magistrate or me."

Her eyes were still boring through Victoire.

"Was it suicide?" The question was a calculated risk.

"That's for us to determine. We're stationing an officer upstairs. The place will be guarded night and day. No one is allowed up there."

Victoire judged it wise to draw back, before getting asked too many questions.

"I'll let Mrs. Noblecourt know."

"Please do."

As the police chief continued down the stairs, Victoire got a whiff of her perfume. It smelled like a men's cologne she'd

given John. Luc helped himself to it too. How strange. She was
now standing in front of the door to the third-floor apartment,
unable to move. She gave the bell two enthusiastic rings as the
police chief threw her one last suspicious look.

The door finally opened. In the semidarkness, Victoire could
make out a woman's face. Her skin was pale, almost translu-
cent. She looked like some kind of ghostly spirit in a dress that
was too big and not especially flattering. Suddenly Victoire
recognized the deceased president's features in the face of his
daughter, Apolline. A few TV appearances and magazine photos resurfaced from her memory. Apolline wasn't much taller
than her mother. But her eyes were softer and sadder. Victoire
could sense that she was fatigued.

"Who are you?" the apparition asked in a subdued voice.

"I'm a friend of your mother's. We had a meeting in regard
to her foundation. It sounds like she's very busy. Please tell her
I'll come back another time."

"Were you the one who brought Béatrice home?"

"Yes."

The apparition's lips loosened in a smile.

"I'm Apolline, Béatrice's mother—and the president's daughter. My mother had to speak with the police and answer their
questions. She's very upset. Can we meet in a little bit in the
park? I have some things to tell you, and I think we'll have
more privacy there"

"Of course," Victoire said. She took note of the irony: a private conversation in a public park.

13

Having left Trocadéro, John Spencer Larivière was riding
his old Triumph Thunderbird down the A6 Highway, the
main route to Orly. A stream of ambulances, their lights flashing, was still shuttling the injured back to Paris. The air smelled
smoky and metallic.

When John finally reached the airport, he couldn't believe his eyes. The entire Orly-Sud terminal had caved in. It was a gigantic U-shaped ruin, the bottom of which was belching black fumes. The control tower, however, seemed to have been spared. How had it managed to survive? As he marveled at this, John came across a police barricade and slammed on his brakes. His tires skidded on a bed of cinders, and his cycle almost toppled over. He lifted the visor of his helmet and, after turning off the engine, was met with an incredible silence. He looked down and saw that his motorcycle was covered with soot as gray as the gloves that Luc had given him for Christmas.

"What are you doing here?" an officer asked.

"I'm meeting with the director of Paris airports."

John held out his phone and showed him the contact screen for the director of airports' private line. John had met Sebastian Graffon at an antiterrorist drill for intelligence freelancers like Fermatown and the supervisors of potentially vulnerable institutions.

After speaking with the director, the officer nodded.

"Mr. Graffon is expecting you at the top of the control tower. I'll inform the officers guarding the entrance."

"Thanks."

John continued on to the tower. A riot-control officer opened the door, and John followed the arrow on a sign that read "crisis committee." A second officer directed him to the elevator. He didn't know what to make of the bottled water on a table and the stack of paper towels. But then he understood. He uncapped a bottle, poured some water on a paper towel, and did his best to wipe his face and hands clean.

John felt like he was in a scene from a sci-fi film: a solitary motorcyclist passing a mass exodus before arriving at the ruins of a city spewing smoke. Once he would have smirked at such a goofy plot. But not today. It was real. John thought of Alexandre and silently asked for forgiveness for his part in creating a world gone amok. Then he took a deep breath and headed toward the elevator.

The members of the crisis committee were in the main room. Sebastian Graffon walked over to greet him. He was a bulky guy with an incisive stare, which John judged appropriate for the situation.

"I told them you were an observer from the Élysée. Does that work for you?"

"Yep, perfect."

John took a look at the air-traffic controllers and engineers from the investigation and analysis bureau who made up the crisis committee. Men with tired eyes and sooty faces stared back at him as though he were the bearer of more bad news. The full extent of the disaster became obvious when he walked over to one of the windows and saw the Air France Airbus. It looked like the scorched remains of a gigantic prehistoric bird. First-aid workers—masked and dressed in protective suits—were wandering through the debris in search of blackened bodies.

While all the planes on the tarmac were covered in gray ash, he could make out the bright colors of a Lufthansa Boeing parked three hundred feet or so from the tower. It seemed out of place.

"How did this happen?"

"Come, I'll show you."

John followed Graffon to a table filled with screens and devices of all kinds.

"We have the recorded conversations with Flight 912," Graffon said. "And we were able to recover the black box with its cockpit voice recorder right away, so we can hear what was going on in the cockpit. Listen. You'll understand."

An engineer activated the device, which was actually orange, not black. John stared at it, expecting the devil to pop out at any moment. Gathered around him, the members of the committee were as still as stones as they listened once again. The pilot's voice sounded. "What's that? The fuel jettison's starting to go off on its own… We're dumping fuel onto the runway! Open up the emergency exits… I'm cutting the engines… This was their plan! In this heat, all it takes is a spark!"

The shouting and crying that followed left no doubt as to the nature of the events.

"How could the plane empty its reserves on the runway all on its own?" John asked.

In response to a gesture from the director, the engineer started playing a conversation between the copilot and the control tower. It didn't take John more than a minute to understand that the copilot wasn't actually talking with the control tower. The plane's security system had been hacked.

"The software they downloaded set off the fuel dump," Graffon said. "Their system used standard antivirus procedure and detected nothing."

John couldn't believe what he was hearing. His piloting skills were still fresh enough to rouse doubt about the attackers' methods.

"I'd like to buy your theory, but something had to ignite the fuel. Even in that heat, you'd need one or more triggers."

"They're here," Graffon said.

"What do you mean?"

"Your triggers have flown back from Frankfurt."

Sebastian Graffon waved over two men in Lufthansa uniforms.

"This pilot and copilot were in command of a Lufthansa Boeing waiting on the tarmac. It was the right engine of their plane that ignited the trail of fuel left by the French plane."

"Explain."

"We were waiting to get on the runway when the control tower asked us to accelerate," the pilot said. "That's when one of our engines ignited the fuel. It wasn't until we had taken off that we saw the disaster below. The people in the control tower told us to keep going, and so we went on to Frankfurt. We've come back at the request of the French authorities to help with the investigation."

"You said you sped up quickly at the request of the control tower."

"Yes, that's the truth. We've brought the recording."

The engineer activated the device, and John heard the control tower address the Boeing: "This is Orly control to Lufthansa 8545. Speed up your entry to runway Number 1. We're trying to avoid a problem."

"When a control tower tells you they're trying to avoid a problem, you don't ask questions," the pilot said. "You do what they say."

"Do you know which air-traffic controller gave the order?" John looked at Graffon.

"No one here asked the Lufthansa Boeing to speed up," Graffon answered. "The order didn't come from Orly. The controller was an imposter, just like the people who communicated with the Airbus."

"So someone wanted to destroy that plane by misinforming the two teams."

"Yes. This was intentional—an act of terrorism."

John motioned to the director to follow him to a corner of the room where no one else could hear them.

"The former president of France was on that plane."

"Now I see why I was asked to speak with you so quickly. Do you think they wanted to kill him?"

"That's a possibility. Do you have the passenger manifest?"

"I should have it very soon. I'll make sure my assistant gets you a copy."

"That would be great."

John gave Graffon Luc's cell phone number and left.

His ride back on the A6 highway was especially difficult. All the ash was making the pavement treacherous, and the stream of ambulances was painfully slow—almost funeral-march slow. Winds from the south were pushing a huge gray cloud toward Paris. John sighed and inched his way along, having decided against speeding past on the berm. There was no point in adding himself to the pile of victims.

14

Victoire found a bench facing the Noblecourts' residence and sat down. She'd have a few minutes in the Jardin Catherine Labouré before meeting with the deceased president's daughter. She entered Roberta's number. Picking up on the second ring, her friend assured her that all was well back at Fermatown.

"I can't thank you enough, Roberta. I feel terrible about having to leave you with everyone. You've been there for hours already, and I don't know when I'll be able to break away."

"Victoire, honey, don't worry. Alexandre is fine, and everyone else is fine. They're all in the yard now. Your family understands that you were called away because of what happened at Orly. The television reporters are saying it was an accident. Thank God it wasn't an attack!"

"Have they named any of the people who died or any of the survivors?"

"No, why?"

"I'll explain later. Thanks again, Roberta."

Victoire made sure she hadn't received any messages during her conversation and checked the entrance to the park, which the police were still blocking. Despite the arrival of the investigation team, along with the paramedics, it didn't seem that news of Pierre-André Noblecourt's suicide—or murder—had gotten out.

Alone in the deserted park, Victoire studied the plants, which were withering in the dry heat, and the nearby apartment buildings. Their closed shutters sealed the mood. Thick storm clouds were coming from the south. A little cooldown would do everyone some good. Suddenly Victoire sensed that someone was staring at her. She turned her attention to the Noblecourts' building. Apolline was walking her way.

The woman, who looked like she was in her late thirties or early forties, had a face like her father's. Apolline wasn't as well put-together as her mother, and she exuded less confidence.

"The police chief questioned me," Apolline said, taking a seat next to Victoire. "She wanted to know if my father had any enemies. How naïve of her."

"I imagine he did," Victoire said.

"Politics is a dirty profession. You make enemies from day one, especially in your own party. When you're starting out, they watch you, suspicious of your motives. Those above you think you're after what they have. If you're not rich, you're beholden to your contributors. It's even worse for female politicians. Women are criticized for ignoring their families, while men aren't. Then there're the enemies from other camps. The reporters and other influential people who hate you. They show you messing up at the first opportunity. My father brought all that on us. He wrecked our lives."

Apolline turned a distraught and tearful face toward Victoire, who didn't know how to respond.

"Dad didn't see me grow up, and I wasn't there for him when he needed someone. We failed each other. But he was a good man. Why would he do this to us? I just hope I'm a better parent than he was. Do you have children?"

"Yes, I have a sixth-month-old son. He was baptized today."

"People still do baptisms? That's surprising."

Victoire tried to size up the woman. Apolline, distraught over her father's death and remorseful because she couldn't prevent it, was indifferent to the fact that her family had torn Victoire away from one of the most important celebrations of her child's life. Apolline was lost.

"Your Béatrice is very sweet and full of energy. Do you have any other children?"

"No. My husband and I are separated. We have been for some time. Serge is on assignment in Kuala Lumpur."

"That's where your father was coming back from?"

"Yes."

"Is Serge on his way home now?"

"No."

"Why not?"

"The Élysée asked him to wait for your team in Kuala."

"For me?"

"No, for a man who works for you."

Victoire couldn't put her finger on what it was about the woman, but she liked Apolline better than her mother. She chalked up Apolline's insensitivity to grief and stress.

"Béatrice misses her father," Apolline said. "It's been six months since she saw him last. But Serge isn't easy to deal with. You'll see."

The case was taking still another weird turn. Méricourt had thrown them into both a legal affair that was totally out of their league and a family that was as strange, in its own way, as her own.

"Why does your husband need to stay in Kuala Lumpur?"

"Our president thinks Serge might have some important information. He wants him to stay where he is. I'd be surprised, though, if Serge knew anything."

"Why's that?"

"Because he only cares about himself and poker. When he was still working at the Élysée, my father got him a do-nothing job in Kuala Lumpur. He spends his days tanning by the pool and his nights gambling in the casinos. I never understood why Dad got along with him so well."

Apolline stared at her hands for a few seconds and then turned to Victoire.

"You seem happy despite your profession. What exactly do you call yourself? A presidential spy?"

"I'm no spy," Victoire said, annoyed at the way the woman had spit out the word. "You could call me an observer."

"Well then, keep your eyes peeled. You haven't seen everything yet."

Victoire looked up at the trees. The leaves, like the annuals in this park, were beginning to turn brown. Then she looked back at Apolline. She had collected a few scattered memories of Pierre-André and Georgette Noblecourt's family, but she had to face facts. She didn't know anything about their lives.

Luc, with his way of ingratiating himself, would have been a better person to send here. Immediately, she rejected the notion. He was too unpredictable.

"I'm assuming the police chief wanted to know if you thought it was suicide," she said.

"I told her it wasn't a suicide. He was murdered. Their first attempt—destroying the plane—failed. But they got the job done at his house. I'm sure she agrees with me, although she wouldn't say."

Victoire nodded. The woman next to her was staring at the wet-paint sign on the doorknob of the little wooden toolshed. She was as white as an apparition.

"You think I'm crazy, don't you?"

"I didn't say that."

"I'm used to people with ulterior motives. I've seen them hanging around my parents for so many years. That police chief knows more than she's saying. I don't trust her."

"We'll see."

"You went upstairs, didn't you? Did you see Dad? What did he look like?"

"It's better that you don't know. It wasn't pretty."

Apolline didn't seem to know much about what was going on. Why hadn't Georgette filled her in? The relationship between Apolline and her mother seemed just as off as the relationship between the deceased president and his wife. It was too soon for Victoire to make any sense of it.

"Did you go up to the office after they removed your father?" Victoire asked.

"Yes. The police chief asked me to see if anything was missing. She wanted to know…" Apolline's voice was breaking.

"Know what?" Victoire asked.

"If I noticed anything strange in the room."

"Did you?"

"No, nothing. Everything was like it was before."

Victoire saw a desperate plea for help in Apolline's eyes.

"You didn't see anything strange either, did you?"

"No, I didn't see anything."

Why was Apolline so insistent that she hadn't seen anything out of the ordinary? Victoire, no longer able to look Apolline in the eye, diverted her gaze to the toolshed. She noticed that the paint was peeling. And now there was something else she couldn't figure out: Why had someone hung a wet-paint sign on the doorknob?

15

John parked his motorcycle outside the Gaîté metro station just as a downpour was starting. Some tourists were getting soaked as they hurried toward the Montparnasse train station. He removed the ex-president's travel bag from his cycle's storage compartment and entered the Indiana Club. He headed for the billiards room in the back. After La Bélière, the retro Indiana Club was Fermatown's favorite hangout. The redbrick and portraits of Native American chiefs reminded John of his childhood in the United States. All the bartenders knew the trio. Their rowdy rounds of pool were almost legendary.

John registered an amused look in Luc's eyes and realized he was covered in mud and ash. He turned around and saw his shoe prints on the floor.

"Did you just leave a steel mill?"

"No, I was at Orly."

John placed Noblecourt's travel bag on a bench near the pool table. Thin and lithe like a picador, Luc leaned over the bag with hungry eyes.

"That's Noblecourt's bag?"

"Yep."

"What's in it?"

"Some dirty clothes—nothing exciting there. Also a Paris-to-Kuala Lumpur ticket stub, a seventeen-hour flight with a layover in Oman."

"And I'm guessing the return flight was Air France 912?"

"I couldn't find a return ticket."

John handed Luc the bag.

"Why didn't he have a return ticket?"

"I've got a hunch. Keep the bag and watch the room."

John went to the men's bathroom to clean up and then slipped into one of the club's storage rooms. Through the window he could see the rain washing the tombstones in the Montparnasse cemetery. He pulled out his cell phone and called Méricourt's department at Les Invalides. He knew they'd all be there, given what had happened at Orly. After speaking with a cabinet minister's personal assistant, an old pal who'd been relocated from Niger because of malaria, he was put through to Nicolas Mortemar de Buzenval, the French ambassador in Kuala Lumpur. Going the official route was the most direct way to save time. No point in making any detours.

"Do you know what time it is here, Mr. Spencer Larivière?"

"I know it's one in the morning in Kuala. But I'm not calling to discuss the time of day, Mr. Ambassador. I'm working at the president's behest."

"What can I do for you?"

"Which Air France flight do you usually take to Paris?" John knew that Air France always set aside a business-class seat for ambassadors to use as they pleased.

"I'm partial to the late-night Saturday flight, which arrives at Orly at eleven forty-five on Sunday morning. It's very convenient."

"Unfortunately, it wasn't convenient for the people on this weekend's flight."

"What happened is horrible."

The ambassador fell silent for several seconds. Finally, John picked up the conversation.

"Do you know what Pierre-André Noblecourt was doing in Kuala?"

"He arrived Friday and slept at the embassy, but other than that, I don't know what he was doing. It was a personal trip. I think he saw Serge Roussillon, his son-in-law. You should ask

Benoît Dutreil, your colleague at the embassy. He may know something."

"I'm going to meet with him. I'll pay you a visit too."

"You'll be most welcome. I've already been informed of your trip."

"See you soon, Mr. Ambassador."

The man knew his schedule better than he did. Put off, John gave Méricourt a call.

"You've already told the ambassador that I'm going to Kuala. You should have spoken with me first."

"John, I wasn't the one who told him."

"Who did then?"

"I have no idea. But it appears the ambassador is fairly well informed—even better informed than he's letting on."

"I can't believe it. You were listening in on my conversation with him. You've bugged the embassy."

"You shouldn't be surprised, John. We're dealing with an attack, one that's killed hundreds of people. When you get to Kuala, don't be too quick to trust that colleague of yours. He's a decent public servant, but he's not an easy-going kind of guy. If you ask me, Dutreil's a bit paranoid."

"Thanks for letting me know."

"I'm counting on your expertise. Honestly, I feel better knowing that you're the one who's going."

"I'll need a plane for Kuala. It's too late to buy a commercial ticket."

"Go to the air base in Villacoublay. I've already made the arrangements."

"You've thought of everything."

"You know me, John. I anticipate."

"Yeah, unfortunately."

"All right, relax."

Vexed but also flattered, John ended the conversation and went back to the poolroom, where Luc was waiting. John shook his head and grinned as he checked out Luc's tight designer jeans and navy-and-white polo that was just as form-fitting.

Luc knew how to turn women's heads. But he also had a way with men.

At the moment, the two of them couldn't have looked more different. John was all grubby, and Luc was magazine-cover polished. But despite appearances, they were thick as thieves. The two brought each other up to speed. Then John opened the former president's bag. He pulled out Noblecourt's Marseille soccer cap and an old rust-colored sweater, along with a heavy pair of sunglasses.

"Why would a former president of the French Republic be packing these things for a trip abroad?" Luc asked.

"Maybe he was trying not to be seen."

"Why?"

"Great question, Little Luc. For all we know, he was meeting secretly with someone very important in Kuala Lumpur. I'm going there, and maybe I'll find out."

"You're leaving the country, and you want me to be the one who tells Victoire?"

"Yes."

"Coward," Luc said. He picked up the bag and brought it to his nose.

"This Louis Vuitton smells like it came straight off a display, not a flaming plane. Take a whiff. And for that matter, I'm amazed that he thought to grab it in the rush to get off."

John breathed in the travel bag's scent. The pristine leather had no trace of Orly's hellish fumes. "You're right. We'll have to clear up those details. Also, I've asked Graffon to get me a list of the passengers. Maybe Noblecourt wasn't the target."

"What makes you say that?"

"It's possible that you and Victoire aren't the only psychics at Fermatown."

Luc placed his antitracking, signal-blocking pounch containing the ex-president's phone on the pool table.

"I haven't had time to play with its contents yet. I'll take the components apart tonight and separate them from the motherboard. I'll have access to all of its memory."

John nodded. This kind of work was outside his wheelhouse. Luc, on the other hand, loved figuring out how gadgets ticked. In his lab at Fermatown, Luc had put together an autopsy room where he stripped and dissected telephones and other devices. Then he used the latest tools to examine their contents.

"How's everyone at home? Is Alexandre okay?"

"Everyone's okay, John. Between Roberta and Victoire's parents, Alexandre can't let out a peep before someone rushes over to pick him up."

"Thanks. I'm going over there to say hi and pack for Kuala Lumpur. Méricourt is holding a plane for me at Villacoublay. No flights are leaving Orly, and Roissy is a clusterfuck."

John gave Luc an apologetic look. "I hope you understand. I'd feel better if you were here with Victoire and Alexandre."

Yet he knew that Luc didn't understand. Luc was so much more than a techie. He was a master investigator, and no one could worm information out of someone better than he could. He'd be invaluable in Kuala Lumpur. But the baby had brought out all of John's protective instincts, and if he couldn't be with his wife and child now, when he didn't know what to expect next, he wanted Luc to be with them.

"Don't worry. I'll live. Roberta can watch the baby when Victoire and I have to work. I need to go to the Musée Édouard Branly on the Rue d'Assas anyway. We'll be fine."

"For Noblecourt's phone?"

Luc glanced at the cloaking pouch securing the phone.

"It's a walking bomb. I can't autopsy it at Fermatown. Too dangerous."

"Be careful. I want to find you in one piece when I get back."

16

L uc walked through one of the main buildings on the campus of the Catholic University of Paris and veered left. Although it was Sunday evening, several students were out and about. Probably on their way to the library or study groups,

Luc figured. The university had the feel of an American college dropped in the heart of Paris. Its stone corridors and vaulted ceilings reminded him of the photos he had seen of Princeton University.

Outside, he continued toward the Musée Édouard Branly. The museum was named after the father of telecommunications, a man who had dedicated his life to science. Before his death in 1940, he had asked that a school be built above his laboratory on the Rue d'Assas. His wish was granted after the Second World War, when the Institut supérieur d'électronique de Paris was founded. Luc had done a portion of his academic and emotional education at this school. Each building reminded him of a celebration, a discovery.

He entered the building and greeted the guard on duty.

"Denis told me you were coming," the guard said. Denis was his last comp-sci professor and his first student—the apprentice had become the master.

Luc stepped into a square room with glass display cases housing an array of devices instrumental in the development of the radio-wave detector, generators, electrical contacts, and so much more. Each object had something to do with Édouard Branly's experiments. Luc's heart swelled. He entered this space with respect and gratitude, and found it conducive to discipline and meditation.

It was in this museum that faculty members decided who would be admitted to the institute, and master's degree students defended their theses. The door's digital security pad was where it had always been. Thanks to Denis, he was able to enter the four digits and two letters granting him access to Édouard Branly's famous Faraday cage room.

The room was a large cube lined with copper. No interference could get in or out of this place. Luc felt like he was in a submarine.

In the center of the room was the experiment table, which was anchored to a marble column that extended more than twelve meters underground so that nothing, other than an earthquake, could move the table. In Branly's day, vibrations caused by horse-drawn carriages on the Rue d'Assas could compromise his trials in telemechanics.

Vibrations, however, were not Luc's concern. Signals were. He needed to keep the cyber spies off his trail. They were in back rooms all over the world.

He dug into his backpack and pulled out his disassembly kit, along with the tools needed to isolate the components of Noblecourt's smartphone. After arranging the instruments, he removed the phone from the portable emissions-blocking pouch.

He put on his headlamp and latex gloves and used a scalpel to open the device. After extracting the SIM card, he placed the phone on an infrared plate and slowly raised the heat. When it reached 250 degrees Celsius, he unhooked the microprocessors, the flash memories, and the data buffers. With great precision, he then went after the black parallelepipeds corresponding with the antenna and the GPS, Wi-Fi, and Bluetooth functions. He noted the two separate tracking devices nonnative to the phone—presumably related to his position as former president. Luc surmised that they allowed French intelligence to know the former president's whereabouts at all times.

If Pierre-André Noblecourt could no longer talk, his phone would speak for him. Any moment now, Luc would have access to the man's private life. His fingers cast gigantic shadows on the walls around him, and he felt a little like an Egyptologist in one of the Great Pyramids. He took out a pirating device designed to extract data from micro-memory chips. The device, of his own engineering, left no traces behind—one could never be too careful—but did give off signals in the process, which could alert observers if it was operated in the wrong place. The information transfer took a few minutes. He would analyze the different memory splices later.

Luc carefully cleaned up his material, as well as the pieces of the phone. He put the disassembled phone inside his Faraday pouch and thanked the temple guard on his way out.

17

Hannibal Montangon, owner of Café Les Mouettes, said good-bye to his last customer as he watched the coverage of the Orly disaster on the restaurant's television. A reporter noted that the former president had narrowly escaped the disaster while saving a mother and her baby. With the flames pursuing them, he had guided the mother and infant down an emergency chute.

"Good Lord…"

Hannibal had crossed paths with Pierre-André and Georgette Noblecourt several times at the Bon Marché department store. The last time he had seen them, the former president and his wife were purchasing picture frames for their apartment on the Rue de Babylone.

"Noblecourt was on the plane!" Hannibal yelled to his wife, Jocelyne.

"Close the shutters, Hannibal. It's time to go home."

Hannibal pressed the control switch without taking his eyes off the screen. Maybe he'd see the former president leaping out of the fire. There was no shortage of footage.

He didn't notice the briefcase that had stopped his metal shutters twenty inches from the ground. Two men as nimble as wild cats slipped under the gate. The second one pulled out the briefcase, and the two of them sat down at a table Hannibal called Number 4. As far as he was concerned, it was jinxed. Foul-mouthed patrons always seemed to wind up there.

"The bar's closed, gentlemen."

The men with chocolate-brown skin responded with sneers. Hannibal knew right away that he was dealing with take-charge guys—men capable of being far more convincing than any police officer he had ever encountered.

"Have a seat," said the man in a white shirt with a stiff collar.

Hannibal read something in his face that sent shivers down his spine. There was no point in resisting. These two men could slit his neck on the spot. And they would relish it. His legs turned to jelly, and his throat dried up as he fell into a chair, incapable of uttering a word. At that moment, Jocelyne emerged from the kitchen.

"The bar is closed. Who are you?"

"Tell her to shut it."

Hannibal shot a desperate look at Jocelyne as she threatened to call the police. He watched her lips form an "oh" in shock when she saw one of the men pull out a gun with a huge silencer. Before she could say another word, her head exploded, sending blood, hair, and brain matter all over the walls. She slumped to the floor like a rag doll, still spurting blood.

"The lady was lucky. Very lucky."

Jocelyne's murderer had just placed a pair of pruning shears on the table. Hannibal felt his guts rushing to his throat. He vomited them out on table Number 4. After two minutes, one of the men handed him a napkin. He wiped himself. Through tears that burned his eyes, he saw a finger with silver rings pointing at him.

"One question. One."

Hannibal could barely make out the killer's dark eyes. He wanted to speak, but couldn't. Something had short-circuited in his skull. The man locked eyes with him.

"Where is Noblecourt's smartphone?"

18

Luc stopped in front of the Backstage Café on the Rue de la Gaîté to take stock of the day's events. It was just eight in the evening, but Alexandre's baptism felt like a lifetime ago. Eight hours earlier, he had been walking back from the ceremony with friends and family members. Life was good. The Bagad Lann Bihoue—a Breton bagpipes band—had come down to join them. Then they had found themselves plunged into the heart of one of aviation's biggest catastrophes.

Suddenly, a thought crossed his mind like the blade of a shiny sword. If someone was out to assassinate Noblecourt, and had no compunction about taking down all those people at Orly in the process, then the possibility that France was a target, along with the former president, seemed obvious. This was a political crime. After waging war in every corner of the globe, France had made many enemies. Shaken by his realization, Luc looked over his shoulder. Nothing suspicious. Shorter-than-usual lines were forming at the street's theaters. The tables of the Backstage were filling up with people, but they were sober tonight. The bars' glowing TV screens had garnered more attention than the performances at the Théâtre de la Gaîté.

One of his phones was ringing. He answered. It was Victoire. She was whispering, and she sounded frustrated.

"I'm at Noblecourt's place. The police just questioned Mrs. Noblecourt. They want the president's phone."

"What did she say?"

"She said she hadn't seen it. She acted surprised, but the police chief didn't seem convinced."

"So? What happened?"

"Georgette wants me to return her husband's phone. She's changed her mind."

"Oh, so you're calling her Georgette now?"

"I'm in character. A friend of hers, remember? So what about the phone?"

"It's in a bunch of pieces. You didn't tell me you'd need it back."

"Figure something out."

"Like you've got a million ideas!"

Luc ended the call and looked up at the sky, with its clouds drifting above the Theatre Bobino, for inspiration. And inspiration he got. Of course he would come up with a plan. Who else at Fermatown had his kind of creative intelligence?

At the Avenue du Maine, he walked past the Indiana Club and then veered left onto the Rue Froidevaux. He walked past both the Rue Fermat and the Rue Deparcieux as he continued along the Montparnasse cemetery wall to the Rue Émile Richard and the cemetery entrance. No one to his right. No one to his left. A long stretch of pavement cut through the cemetery from north to south. A few loners were walking their dogs, while men leading double lives strolled alongside their mistresses.

Luc entered the cemetery, making his way along the familiar tomb-lined cobblestones. Soon he spotted the large rectangular structure, whose story he knew well: a cenotaph abandoned by the descendants of a once well-known family. The city's cemetery-management department was using it for storage now. For Luc's purposes, the structure was ideal.

A staircase descending from the crypt led to a metal door. Luc put on his headlamp and took out the key that opened the gate. He soon found the tunnel leading deep under the city of Paris. The catacombs were no secret. The Gallo-Romans had used limestone from the underground quarries to build the city of Lutetia, as Paris used to be called. The quarries were turned into a massive bone depository in the eighteenth century, when the inhabitants of central Paris complained about disease from the age-old Les Innocents cemetery. The city's underground labyrinth had always attracted illustrious visitors, from King Charles to Napoléon III. And now every Tuesday through Sunday, the curious gathered at the Place Denfert Rochereau and paid twelve euros each for guided tours through the city down below.

Luc headed toward a chamber below the Denfert Rochereau square. If he went deep enough into the limestone, the catacombs would act like a Faraday cage of sorts. And then he got an even better idea.

He stepped over a chain guarding a UNESCO archeologists' work site and wandered until he found the perfect chamber. After setting up his lab, he carefully removed the pouch containing the parts of Noblecourt's cell phone. He reconstructed the device, meticulously returning each piece to its proper place. Georgette would soon have her husband's phone, and no one would discover the traces of his operation. In theory, and assuming his technique was solid.

Before leaving the catacombs, he dropped what looked like a two-euro coin on the ground. In fact, it was a Fermatown tracking device. A team with a geolocation on Noblecourt's cell would be able to pinpoint here, and perhaps if they came to check it out, they'd pick up the coin.

Then he turned the phone off and tucked it into his protective pouch.

He quickly fled the area before fear clouded his judgment. Unlike John, he wasn't made for hand-to-hand combat. At least not the kind that ended with a screwdriver jab to the throat. The only wrestling matches he enjoyed were in the bedroom.

19

Victoire had slipped into the foyer of the Noblecourt residence, where she could give John a piece of her mind and not be overheard. Although he had asked Luc to deliver the bad news, he had been forced to do it himself.

"Let me get this straight. You're going to Kuala Lumpur and leaving me in Paris with Luc and Alexandre? And on the day of his baptism!"

"Luc will be right there with you."

"But you won't."

"I've got to go, Victoire. I need to find out why Noblecourt went to Malaysia."

"Who's paying for your trip?"

"Méricourt's taking care of everything."

"Yeah, right, with lots of strings attached and expenses reimbursed six months from now."

"Better late than never."

"Keep me updated."

"Love you."

Victoire ended the call. She was mad at John for his unilateral decision. She was worried, too—and not just about the case. The disaster at Orly had everyone spooked. Something else could happen, and in that event, she wanted her husband home with her. Victoire called her father, hoping to get some support. No luck.

"We'll stay a little longer and help Roberta with the baby," he told her. "Now get back to work."

"But Dad—"

"Go on now."

"This is ridiculous," Victoire muttered as she slipped the phone into her purse. "He's treating me like a child."

Muffled voices coming from the living room reminded her of the reason she was at the Noblecourt home. She was about to rejoin the adults when Béatrice came out from the kitchen. She was holding a container of strawberry-flavored milk.

"My mom says milk makes you strong. Would you like some? We've got other stuff in the fridge, too, if you're hungry."

Victoire smiled and followed the Noblecourts' granddaughter into the kitchen. The girl closed the door behind them and turned to Victoire.

"Why did they hang Grandpa?"

So Béatrice knew what people were saying. Victoire felt a knot in her stomach. She didn't want to discuss this with the child.

"What makes you think someone killed your grandfather?"

"The police lady seemed to think that. I was hiding when she was with Mom. I heard everything."

"Oh really?"

"Is it bad that I listened?"

Victoire wavered. A lecture was the last thing the little girl needed now, and she certainly wasn't the appropriate person to deliver one. She changed the subject.

"Do you think someone could get into and out of the top-floor office through the window that overlooks the courtyard?"

"Yes, someone could do it, but it would take practice."

"I imagine that anyone who'd do that to your grandfather would have to be strong. He had to lift your grandfather off the floor."

Béatrice poured herself more strawberry milk and paused, looking pensive. She was probably a very good student, Victoire thought.

"Maybe there were two of them. Grandpa's heavy."

"That's possible."

"Why are you here?"

"I'm working with a foundation that helps children in Cambodia. I had a meeting with your grandma."

"Grandma never has people over on Sunday."

A good point, but Victoire bounced back.

"People make exceptions."

"I don't believe you. I know who sent you here."

"You do? Who would that be?"

"The president. He wants to know what happened. You work for the Élysée. The police lady thinks the same thing, and I could tell she was mad."

"What makes you say that?"

"She asked questions about you. Grandma said you were from that foundation, but the police lady kept asking questions. I think she knew Grandma lies. My mom doesn't. Mom says it's because she's a scientist, and the truth is always important to scientists."

"Is that so."

"Plus there's the picture."

"What picture?"

"I listened to the police lady when she was talking on her phone in the stairway. She was asking someone to send her a picture of the Chinese centerfold model. Are you the Chinese model? Are you actually Chinese?"

"I'm Eurasian, but my features are more Asian."

"Either way, the police lady doesn't trust you. She wants to know more about you."

"You don't think I had anything to do with your grandpa's death, do you?"

"I don't think you killed my grandfather. But I'm like my grandma. I don't always tell the truth. I only tell the truth to the people I like."

Victoire put her hands on her hips and observed the mischievous and very clever child. Her smile reminded Victoire of something, but the memory vanished.

"Maybe the people who sent you here are the real killers," Béatrice said. "They want you to keep them clued in."

"Why would you think that?"

"I listen to what people are saying. I already told you."

Béatrice got up from her chair and skipped over to the fridge. Her ponytail and Scottish kilt disappeared behind the door.

"Guess what," she said, rummaging through the refrigerator. "My birthday's next week, and I get to go swimming all by myself!"

Béatrice reappeared, holding a package of Laughing Cow cheese.

"Here. Want some?"

"No, thank you."

Victoire was feeling thrown off by the girl. Behind that sweet and expressive face, there was a shrewd ability to watch, listen, and put things together. And her eyes had a strangely familiar quality.

"So you're allowed in the pool all by yourself. That's great! But I want to know more about the police lady. Do you think she believes I had something to do with your grandpa's death?"

"Maybe, and if she does, she'll start looking for the other two."

Victoire flinched.

"What other two?" she asked, trying to control her rapid heartbeat. This kid knew exactly what buttons to push.

"To lift Grandpa up. There had to be at least two strong men. You're a woman."

"I am."

"Are you a mom?"

"Yes."

"How many kids do you have?"

"One."

"That's good, but it's not enough."

"Why's that?"

"If the first one dies, you'll need a new one."

"That's one way of seeing things."

"So what's your kid's name?"

"His name is Alexandre."

"That's a good name, I guess. I'm not sure I want children when I grow up. You don't know how long the world's gonna last."

"I think I will take that piece of cheese."

The little girl handed her a wedge, and Victoire started unwrapping the foil, all the while wishing she were home with her baby.

20

Back at Fermatown, Luc put together a spread of brioches and croissants for the following day and went to retrieve Caresse from the garage. The Persian cat, whose fur stuck to every piece of furniture, was a celebrity in the neighborhood—as well-known as Rainbow Warrior, Roberta's Labrador.

"How's it hanging, little kitty?"

The animal purred and rubbed against his jeans.

Luc put his backpack in one of the secure cabinets. "Come on, Caresse," he said, getting ready to leave the garage. "Let's go."

In the main room, Victoire's father and stepmother were busy pampering their grandson and paying just as much attention to Luc as they were to the images on the touch-screen wall. Fermatown was one of the very first private intelligence firms to have this invaluable piece of technology, thanks to Méricourt. These days, interactive walls were more common—they could be found not only in investigative firms and intelligence agencies, but also in businesses and museums—but Fermatown's was still an indispensable tool, and Méricourt provided all the necessary updates. Standing in front of it, the three members of Fermatown had round-the-clock access to an overwhelming amount of information.

Luc updated the grandparents on John and Victoire's status, getting only smiles and nods in return, and went back to the kitchen, where Roberta was tidying up.

"Everyone's left except Victoire's parents," she said.

"I just saw them. Thanks for everything, Roberta."

"No problem. It's almost nine, way past Alexandre's bedtime. I'll put him down as soon as I'm done in here."

"Thanks again."

Luc left the kitchen and climbed to the top floor. This was where he had his lab, next to the exercise room. He closed the door and double-locked it, with Noblecourt's phone resting in the off position in his Faraday pouch.

The contents of the various memory chips were quickly analyzed, synthesized, and restored, based on several modes of presentation—outgoing, incoming, e-mail, and text message, and sorted by theme, geographic location, chronological activity, language, conversation, enclosure, attachment, download, data analysis, and so on.

For this first test, Luc requested a display by date and examined what the former president had received in the days leading up to his trip to Kuala Lumpur.

He had made his Air France reservation the day of his outgoing flight. No trace of a return reservation. If the former president had planned to travel free of charge in the French ambassador's seat on Flight 912, this made sense.

Georgette had told Victoire that her husband had flown to Malaysia to see their son-in-law, Serge. Was that the real reason for the trip, and if so, was there more to it? Going back in time, Luc discovered that on Thursday morning, the former president had received three attachments sent from another cell phone.

The e-mail had arrived at three in the morning, and it didn't have a subject, message, or signature. Noblecourt most likely knew the sender. A few hours later, he reserved his seat on the plane.

Luc tried to open the three documents, one of which was much larger than the others.

"Yeah, right."

The attachments were encrypted. It took two minutes and change for his decoding software to do its work. Finally, Luc opened the first document. What he found was a chess match viewed from above. He couldn't make out the players. Other photos in the file were similar to the first, all of them documenting the match as it progressed.

At some points, the camera angle widened, and Luc could see more tables, as well as quite a few spectators. Many of them appeared to be Asian. Luc surmised that he was looking at photos of a chess tournament in an Asian country.

Luc opened the second document and discovered a photo of a rectangular metal apparatus the size of a dresser with a series of numbers. The first number was zero. A period and about a hundred other numbers followed. Luc had no idea what this was or what the numbers meant.

The third document pinned Luc to his chair. It was a photo of a gorgeous hunk, maybe five or six years older than he was. The man was blond, and he was gazing at the sky with eyes so intense, Luc felt himself getting aroused. He blushed and checked the skylight to make sure no one was watching. That was just a reflex, he knew, because they had installed powerful motion sensors after an intruder had used the skylight to get into Fermatown.

He turned back to check out this sexy creature and found a caption in white ink: 123751-ETI-CHRONOSPHERE.

There was no doubt in Luc's mind that the documents had spurred Noblecourt to leave for Kuala Lumpur and meet up with the mysterious correspondent.

Luc put the blond demigod out of his mind and continued his time-travel adventure. He noted all telephone calls made from

Kuala Lumpur. Surprisingly, he found only two—both under a minute to normal-looking numbers in Paris.

In a few seconds, a Les Invalides identification program provided the names of the two recipients: Titus Polycarpe and Béatrice Roussillon.

Pierre-André Noblecourt had called his granddaughter right after speaking with Titus Polycarpe, CEO of the Martin and Polycarpe Bank at 43 Rue de Monceau. It took him a couple of minutes to find out that Titus Polycarpe was Georgette Noblecourt's older brother.

Before leaving for Malaysia, Noblecourt made a call to a switchboard. Luc would track it down later.

He sent Victoire the pictures and called her immediately.

"I'd bet those photos are the reason he flew to Malaysia," he said.

"Who's the man candy?"

"I don't know. Fine-looking, isn't he? Wouldn't mind meeting him, but I don't know how much luck I'll have identifying him. Also, you should know that the former president didn't use his phone much. But someone else had access to that phone."

"What are you saying?"

"I've analyzed the data, and I've noticed that on several occasions someone accessed the phone, even though it was turned off. Even in off-mode, a cell phone can be hacked and turned into a GPS and microphone. Someone was tracking Noblecourt—from city to city and building to building—and listening to his every conversation."

"That's crazy. I thought turning off a phone protected you from hackers."

"That's coming from a woman whose husband is *allegedly* the most informed man in France."

"Quit it with the sarcasm."

"The only surefire way to protect a phone is to take out the battery. Anyway, Noblecourt didn't get a call from Georgette when he landed in Paris—as his bodyguards said."

"Why did he want his security men to think Georgette was meeting him at Orly?"

"So they'd wait for him in the terminal," Luc said.

"You're right. Noblecourt arranged it so that his two body-guards wouldn't see him getting off the plane. Do you think he had a traveling companion? Maybe he didn't want any-one to know."

"Unfortunately, the plane caught fire," Luc said.

"You'll have to find out which passengers were sitting near Noblecourt."

"That's what the boss asked me to do," Luc replied.

"Oh my God, you're such a pain!"

21

John waved to one of the gendarmes at Villacoublay Air Base and sped off in the rain toward a plane at the end of the runway. It wasn't until he entrusted a second gendarme with his motorcycle that he realized just how important this mission was. The plane was the president's Airbus A330. That it had been freighted for him was flattering but worrying.

A steward welcomed John and took his bags. The pilot and copilot shook his hand.

"We'll be taking off for Kuala Lumpur International Airport at 9:25 p.m., five minutes from now," the pilot said. "You are our only passenger. Let us know if there's anything you need."

"Thanks."

"This plane will be at your disposal for as long as you need it."

"I hope it won't be *too* long."

The steward led John to the presidential bedroom. He scoped the huge bed, the walk-in closet, and the bathroom and then followed him to the office-living room.

"Feel free to make use of the presidential desk, telephone, and computer. You'll be connected with the outside world at all times, and everything's encrypted."

John nodded. The steward opened another door, and they walked into an even larger room.

"This is the meeting room. It can comfortably seat twelve people. Louis Vuitton did the interior."

"Very nice."

"We've had two cabinet meetings here. The first was over the Atlantic, and the second was over Mongolia. Come, there's more."

John followed his host.

"This is the medical center. We have a small operating room, but there aren't any doctors onboard today."

"Here's hoping we don't have to use it."

"Behind that door is the communications room."

The steward led John into that room, and he admired the screens, scanners, and radar securing connections with every French official in the world.

Next was the area reserved for the president's guests.

"We have sixty business-class seats for people flying with the head of state: anyone from cabinet members to friends of the president. This part of the plane was recently renovated. Not bad, huh?"

"Not bad at all."

A light flashed, and a ding sounded behind them. The two men sat down. The A330 accelerated and rose into the sky, whipping the rainwater off its wings and fuselage. John could tell the ascent was faster than an ordinary passenger jet's. As soon as they were allowed to unbuckle their seat belts, John returned to the presidential bedroom. He wanted to take a shower and get some sleep.

He was half naked when the phone on one of the bedside tables rang. He picked it up and recognized the voice of President Alain Jemestre. After all, he was on the man's plane. A call from the owner was no surprise. Ten years earlier, he would have stood at attention—even in his boxers. But that was another life. John sat as Jemestre apologized for disturbing him and asked about his comfort.

"Everything all right?"

"Yes, Mr. President. Thanks for the ride."

"Enjoy it. Méricourt told me all about you and what you're doing. I'd like to thank you and let you know that I was the one who asked the Élysée's secretary general to tell the ambassador about your visit. He'll take care of anything you need."

"Thank you, sir."

"Be careful in Kuala Lumpur. Pierre-André sounded rattled when we spoke before he left for Malaysia. We have reason to believe that his death could be connected to some kind of kickback scheme. Wherever there's a government, there are people willing to pay for favors and politicians who'll take their money."

"What kind of kickbacks, Mr. President?"

"We don't know yet. But let me give you some background. After leaving the presidency, Pierre-André served as our representative at the G20 Summit, and he was instrumental in the creation of an international organization called G.Terres. Maybe you've heard of it. G.Terres regulates the rare-earths market. It's based in both Paris and Malaysia and uses the absolute latest in high-frequency algorithmic trading, a system that initiates orders based on information received electronically at a speed human traders couldn't dream of matching. The organization has done some good things, but it has also put a number of speculators and traders out of work. Pierre-André was passionate about G.Terres. It was his baby."

"I'm no expert in financial affairs, Mr. President."

"It's not complicated. Serge will explain everything."

"That's little Béatrice's father, right?"

There was a microsecond of hesitation. The president cleared his throat. "Yes."

"I'll make sure I see him."

"You know I owe everything to Pierre-André and Georgette."

"I know, Mr. President."

John mentally reviewed Alain Jemestre's political career. It was common knowledge that he was close to the former president and his wife.

"I can't believe Pierre-André is gone. I'm heartbroken."

John sensed some hesitation.

"If you find anything—anything at all—that could be a threat to the family's peace of mind, please let me know."

"Of course."

"On the back of the phone you're holding, there's a number. It's my direct line. Please call me whenever you need to, day or night."

"Will do, Mr. President."

"Speaking of phones, Georgette told me that she entrusted Pierre-André's phone to a woman who works with you."

"That's correct. Actually, she's my wife, as well as my associate."

"Did your firm find anything?"

"Just before Pierre-André left for Malaysia, he received an e-mail with three attachments. The documents were encrypted, but we've decoded them."

"What's in them?"

"Photos of a chess match, a machine, and a man with blond hair. The photo of the man has a caption with some letters and numbers and the word Chronosphere."

"What's Chronosphere?"

"I don't know yet."

"Anything else?"

"Mr. Noblecourt used his phone just twice while he was in Kuala Lumpur: once to call his granddaughter, Béatrice, and the other time to contact his brother-in-law, Titus Polycarpe, who's a banker. I'm thinking that he might have had access to another phone while he was in Kuala Lumpur."

"Do you think the documents are related in some way to his trip?"

"Yes."

"Send them to me. I might be able to make sense of them. Good luck. And remember, call me anytime. Anything else?"

"A few hours before takeoff, Mr. Noblecourt made a call to a switchboard. We don't know who it belongs to yet."

"Give me the number."

John did as he was told and thanked the president for his help. He looked at the phone for a long time after the call ended. Alain Jemestre had seemed friendly but tense. Where was all this headed? At this point, there was no telling. John lay back on the bed and stared at the ceiling. The subtle swaying of the cabin was the only reminder that he was on a plane.

22

Victoire was taking deep breaths in the Noblecourts' living room as she waited to be questioned by the police chief. The woman had called Georgette and Apolline back into the dining room. Meanwhile, Victoire mapped out her story. Why would someone from a Cambodian foundation be at this crime scene—on a Sunday, no less, and on the day of a huge disaster at Orly Airport? If Georgette and Apolline's explanations matched her own, she'd have a slight chance of getting the chief to believe her.

As she sat there, the TV droned on. It seemed that every political, aviation, and medical expert in Paris had been asked to weigh in. Had Pierre-André Noblecourt died from injuries suffered on Flight 912? When would the Élysée release a statement?

Even though it was nine thirty, no one had turned on the lamps, and the light from the television was giving the room an eerie feel. The apartment breathed order and comfort, but she had to disagree with the reporters. It wasn't as ritzy as they always made it out to be.

"When they find out Grandpa was murdered, they'll ask questions about what happened at Orly. Don't you think?"

Victoire was startled by Béatrice's remark. She had forgotten the little girl was sitting next to her in the living room. She answered the question with one of her own.

"Do you think Orly was an attack?"

"It's a hypothesis. A hypothesis is something you think but don't know for sure. Right?"

"Yes, something like that."

"If Grandpa was murdered here, it means they messed up at the airport. That's my hypothesis. In math, you'd call it conjecture. But I know something for sure."

"What do you know for sure, Béatrice?"

"That there's no difference between a hypothesis and conjecture, which means they messed up at Orly."

"Who's *they*?"

"The bad guys."

"What bad guys?"

The little girl placed her hand on Victoire's arm and inched closer.

"You'll never catch the murderers."

"Why?"

"Because they're far away. Malaysia is on the opposite side of the world." The little girl grinned. "You have to dig a hole in the Earth to get there."

"Very funny, Béatrice. Don't tell your parents, or they might think twice about all the money they're spending on your education. But tell me: What makes you think the bad guys are in Malaysia?"

"I have a secret. But you can't tell Grandma. Promise?"

"Promise," Victoire replied. Her breathing exercises weren't doing the trick. Her nerves were taut—as taut as the strings on the piano John had brought to Fermatown, but no one ever played.

"Grandpa called me before he got on his plane to Paris," Béatrice whispered in Victoire's ear. "He always calls me when he's coming home from a trip. This time he told me something strange."

"What did he say?"

"I didn't really understand, but I'm sure he was talking about the blue book."

"What's the blue book?"

"It's a story about pirates on the Indian Ocean. Grandma gave it to me."

Victoire heard the door open. She looked up and recognized the face of the police chief, Claudine Montluzac. The woman looked determined.

"I've just finished questioning Mrs. Roussillon. I'd like to speak with you too. As a witness, of course."

Victoire nodded and got up from the couch. In the dining room, Apolline reached for her arm.

"My mother's exhausted," Apolline said. "I have to go to the Élysée. Everything's in turmoil there, and I need to take care of one of Dad's files. Could you drop off Béatrice at her uncle's place? She can spend the night there." Apolline's tone was almost pleading.

"Of course," Victoire said. "The questioning shouldn't last too long."

"Thank you so much."

Apolline left, and Victoire took a seat at the table, hoping against hope that the police chief sitting across from her would believe that she and the grieving family were on the same side.

"Can you show me some ID?" the chief asked.

Victoire searched her bag, wavering between her real ID, which bore the name Victoire Jeanne Augagneur, and one of her doctored passports.

She still hadn't decided between the two bad options when the police chief's phone rang. Montluzac spoke a few words and leaped to her feet. A fresh situation demanded an urgent response. Something had happened in the neighborhood. Was it connected to Noblecourt's death? Victoire heard sirens. Montluzac told the person on the other end that she'd be there right away.

"I won't be able to question you tonight, ma'am, but I would like to see you tomorrow at 8 a.m. at police headquarters. Bring real documents with your real name, if that's possible."

"Of course," Victoire replied, thanking the police chief with the silliest smile of her career.

The chief tossed her beautiful mane of hair over a shoulder and grabbed her laptop. Victoire breathed a sigh of relief and shook her hand. Georgette showed her out and closed the door behind her.

"I'm expected at police headquarters tomorrow," Victoire said, joining Georgette at the front entrance.

"These are the risks of the profession, my dear."

Victoire hated it when people called her "dear." Since their first encounter she'd been distrustful of Georgette, and the feeling was turning into distaste. Under the guise of a well-educated grandma, the widow was a cold machine, a political beast. The elderly woman glanced at her blood-red nail polish.

"She doesn't believe Pierre-André misplaced his phone. She's suspicious of me. I told her the president would leave it in his car sometimes. As soon as you bring it back, I'll give it to one of the bodyguards. He'll give it to the police. Did you find anything interesting?"

Victoire sighed. She didn't want to divulge anything. She told the woman that they hadn't found anything special. Now they'd have to explore other avenues.

"Did you call your husband just before his plane landed at Orly?"

"No," Georgette answered, still staring at her painted nails.

Victoire didn't like the way the woman wouldn't meet her eyes.

"And yet he told his bodyguards that you'd be coming to Orly. He asked them to meet you in the terminal."

"He said that?"

"Yes."

Victoire could tell Georgette was vacillating between lies—as she herself had vacillated with the police chief. Still in her fine gray suit with black lapels, Georgette seemed to shrink. Victoire tried another tack.

"Do you know if he was traveling with someone who might have information?"

"I do not."

"You seemed to be familiar with the police chief. Had you met her before tonight?"

Georgette took Victoire's elbow and led her back into the dining room. Her cheeks were red, and her smile was tense.

"Let's have a seat," she said, pointing to a chair.

Victoire sat down across from the Noblecourt widow—in the chair the police chief had chosen for herself.

"I must say, my dear, you have keen observation skills. Claudine Montluzac chased after my husband for years. You saw how stunning she is, and everyone knows Pierre-André loved beautiful women. Is it so hard to believe that the president of France would help her get ahead? And isn't it an interesting coincidence that she happened to be the chief on duty the day my husband was killed."

Victoire digested this new piece of information. The situation was already bad. Now there was reason for even more suspicion.

"If an important figure dies in a questionable way, it's the chief on duty at police headquarters who leads the initial investigation," Georgette continued. "And this initial inquiry is decisive for the rest of the investigation. You can understand why I have my concerns."

"So Claudine Montluzac knew that her lover was in danger and made sure she'd be at the scene."

Georgette Noblecourt bore the blow of Victoire's harsh words, which she quickly regretted saying.

"Victoire, dear. You're not going easy on me. You're a strong woman, and you enjoy your job—just as I take pleasure in politics. Deep down, we're the same. Claudine Montluzac's official position is with the white-collar crimes unit. She's the police chief on duty just one weekend a year. I looked into it. I'm friends with the interior minister. He's just as surprised that she happened to be on duty the day that her *lover* was murdered—as you so delicately put it."

"I didn't mean to offend you."

"Don't worry. My skin's as thick as an old cow's. I'd like to get rid of that little tart, but since I can't, I'd like you to look into how she happened to be in charge today."

"I'll consider it,"Victoire replied, noting the hateful glare in the former first lady's eyes. What other secrets was this family hiding? Victoire wasn't sure she wanted to know.

The former president's widow paused and put up a finger, wordlessly telling Victoire to stay quiet. "Come in already, instead of listening behind the door. I know you're there. Don't try tiptoeing back to the kitchen."

Béatrice opened the door and came up behind her grandmother. The little girl wrapped her arms around the woman's neck.

"Did you do your homework, honey?'

"I finished my math. For history, I'll just tell my teacher that I couldn't concentrate because of Grandpa. He'll definitely believe me."

"I'm sure he will."

"When I go into politics, he'll vote for me. I'll get all the history teachers' votes."

"And the math teachers'," Georgette said. "You're very good at math, like your grandfather."

Georgette patted her granddaughter's arm, and Victoire knew she was watching two clever ladies—ladies who were rivals and accomplices at the same time.

"I really did love Grandpa. So did you, Grandma. I know you're not mean, even though that's what all those people are saying."

Finally, Victoire saw the emotion that had been missing. Tears streamed down Georgette's and Béatrice's cheeks. The two of them were united in grief. Georgette took the child's arm and pulled her from behind the chair. Then she tenderly drew her granddaughter onto her lap.

"You do want to spend the night at your uncle's, don't you?" she asked, wiping Béatrice's face and smoothing her hair.

"If Victoire comes with me, although she's probably had enough of us. It's not very much fun with a family like ours, right?"

Victoire stood up and registered the fatigue weighing on the grandmother. "Come with me," she said. "We're going to your uncle's."

Béatrice grabbed her schoolbag and led Victoire out of the room. As soon as the door slammed shut behind them, the heat hit Victoire. She pulled out a tissue and mopped her forehead. She was thinking about her morning appointment. She didn't want to go, but she had no choice, and she didn't intend to lie. Claudine Montluzac probably knew who she was anyway and why she was at the crime scene. The entire legal and media machine would wind up accusing Fermatown of obstructing the investigation. They'd be ridiculed and come off as amateurs who had taken a case that was out of their league.

As Victoire and Béatrice walked by the little toolshed, she noticed that the wet-paint sign had been taken down. That was odd. Park workers usually had Sundays off.

"You're so quiet," Béatrice said. "What are you thinking about?"

"And you're very observant. I'm thinking about my meeting tomorrow with the police chief."

They had reached the park entrance on the Rue de Babylone. A police guard gave them a nod. Victoire could see swarms of mosquitoes hovering above the cars parked along the street. A species of genetically modified mosquitoes had recently traveled from La Marne to the capital.

"Where does your uncle live?"

"At the end of Rue de Babylone, across from Le Bon Marché."

"Is your mom working with the president tonight?"

"Yes, she's a scientific advisor. She has an office across the street from the Élysée. She's there because she's not a politician. Otherwise, she'd be at the Élysée with everyone else. She's not brainwashed, like Grandma."

Béatrice was staring up at Victoire. In the streetlights' illumination, her eyes held a strange sparkle. Victoire slowed down to get a better look at the child, who was perceptive and intelligent beyond her years.

"Mom's a chemist. She used to work for Rhodina. When the Chinese bought out the company, Grandma told Grandpa to ask Alain Jemestre to give her a job. Mom didn't want to take it. But since she couldn't find work anywhere else, with the economic crisis and all, she accepted the offer."

"What about your dad?"

The sparkle in Béatrice's eyes disappeared. She gave Victoire an incredulous look, as if the answer were obvious.

"He's in Kuala Lumpur."

"And what's he doing there?"

"He's pretending to work. My dad has a fake job."

"Did that have something to do with your grandfather's trip to Kuala Lumpur?"

"You got it. When I grow up, I'm going to run a secret agency and work in international politics, like you. I'm learning Chinese and Arabic."

"You can probably do better than that."

"That was a test to see how you'd react. I don't know what I want to do when I grow up. My grandpa said I have lots of time to decide, but I don't know. What do you think?"

"Your grandfather advised presidents and prime ministers all over the world. I think any little girl would be smart to listen to a grandpa like that."

"You have a point there."

23

Victoire felt Béatrice's hand tighten as they approached the intersection of the Rue de Babylone and the Rue du Bac. A second later, she understood why.

"Look!" Béatrice cried out. Victoire picked up her pace.

Police cars and an ambulance, their lights flashing, were parked in front of Café Les Mouettes, and paramedics were wheeling out two gurneys. Atop each was a body bag. This was where Luc had put Noblecourt's phone inside his signal-blocking pouch. She too held Béatrice's hand tighter. Someone had tracked the former president's smartphone to Café Les Mouettes.

Why had Georgette entrusted her with her husband's cell phone instead of handing it over to the authorities? Questions bounced in Victoire's head as they approached the passersby congregated behind the police barrier.

"You're hurting me."

"I'm sorry." Victoire loosened her grip.

Two people had died, and she knew it was because of the cell phone. It was her fault. Claudine Montluzac was the next person to emerge from the bar. Once on the sidewalk, she froze in place and looked straight in Victoire's direction.

Victoire stared back and saw accusation on the police chief's face. The interrogation would be hot and heavy. Had Montluzac guessed that she had the phone? But instead of approaching her as Victoire feared she would, the police chief climbed into the passenger side of a police car. She turned toward the driver, and the car sped off toward the Sèvres-Babylone intersection.

"I thought she was going to take you in," Béatrice said softly.

"Me too. One second—I have an important call to make."

Béatrice put both hands over her ears.

"I can't hear anything *at all*. I promise—I'm not lying now."

Victoire stepped away while keeping an eye on Béatrice.

John answered.

"Are you free to talk? I've got news."

"Yep, I'm all ears."

Victoire knew they could speak freely, thanks to their en-cryption technology, so cutting-edge that even Les Invalides couldn't listen in. Trust had its limits. She told John about the scene unfolding at the corner of the Rue du Bac and the Rue de Babylone, and he immediately made the connection with Noblecourt's cell.

"Montluzac has called me in for questioning. I'm sure she knows who I am, and she'll hold me for obstructing justice and evidence tampering. So tell me, John, who's going to take care of Alexandre? This is bullshit!"

"Who's Montluzac?"

"She's the investigation's police chief on duty. Her name's Claudine Montluzac."

"That's 'M' as in Marcel Marceau?"

"Yeah, John. 'M' as in Marcel Marceau. Stop trying to placate me. Georgette thinks she was screwing her husband."

"Sorry, hon. Doesn't that seem strange, how she was there on the very day he was murdered?"

Victoire said nothing. She continued watching Béatrice, who hadn't missed a second of the activity across the street.

"Stay calm," John replied. "She's got no proof that you and Luc have the phone. Don't worry about the meeting. You'll do great, like always. Just don't let her bully you."

"Right now, I'd like to bully you, John."

"I get it, but that won't be necessary. The president's behind us. This Claudine Montluzac is the one who should be scared."

"Easy for you to say. I'm the one who could be detained."

"If she holds you, call Charles Simon. He's an excellent criminal lawyer, and he loves political scandals. And remember, you're friends with the former first lady—right?"

John's optimism was disarming and incredibly ballsy. Victoire couldn't help smiling. In less than two years, her good-looking husband with eyes as blue as an Afghan sky and the hair of a Viking warrior had become as Machiavellian as his employers. His flight on the presidential plane had apparently put him in a euphoric state and disconnected him from reality. He was like all men—symbols of power impressed him. He was still a kid inside. Victoire told him what Béatrice had said about her father in Kuala Lumpur and her grandfather's trip.

"That could help," John said. "Guess what. The president just called to ask me how everything was going on his plane. He mentioned you too."

"I don't find that cute."

"How's your dad doing?"

"He's having a blast with the baby. Your cousins from Princeton left."

"And how's our little angel?"

"He's a babbling brook. To be on the safe side, I'm going to ask Roberta to take him to her place. I'm sure there's a team tracking Noblecourt's phone."

"I hope Luc didn't do anything stupid with it."

"Don't worry. He opened our Pandora's Box inside the catacombs to send them on a wild goose chase."

"That's such a Luc idea!"

24

John indulged for a moment in the gentle purring of the plane. Then he re-opened the documents Luc had sent him, which he had already forwarded to the president. After consulting his reference for acronyms, he learned that ETI, the letters on the photo of the metal apparatus, stood for *entreprises de taille intermédiaire*, middle-market companies. Thanks to his subscription to BEIC, Europe's premiere resource for business information, he learned that Chronosphere was a Paris-based company specializing in precision industrial clocks. Their headquarters were on the Rue du Montparnasse. He had passed it with his family after the baptism. How crazy—that very morning they had been right in front of the company that had something to do with the former president's trip to Kuala Lumpur.

It didn't take John more than a minute to realize that the metal device was an atomic clock, the most accurate time-keeping device known. This kind of clock, which used the microwave signal emitted by atoms, had a number of sophisticated applications, including GPS navigation systems. John was willing to bet a year's fees that the clock in the photo was Chronosphere's, and the guy with the killer looks was the company's boss. John grinned. Luc was probably drooling the second he laid eyes on him.

John scrolled through the forty-three frames from the chess match. He concluded that the person who had taken the pictures was more interested in the people in the background than the chess players, whom he couldn't make out at all. The spectators had been photographed without their knowledge. Whoever sent this series to Noblecourt was clearly trying to draw his attention to one or maybe more of these faces. Or perhaps to a strategic meeting organized during the chess tournament.

Jemestre hadn't gotten back to him yet with any information about the switchboard number. John didn't want to wait any longer. He called Luc. Minutes later, Luc was back on the phone with him.

"This is gonna blow you away, John."

"Okay, let's hear it."

"Before his flight to Malaysia, Pierre-André Noblecourt called the landline of the police chief on duty at police headquarters, 36 Quai des Orfèvres."

"Are you saying he called Claudine Montluzac?"

"Well, he called the duty chief's desk. I double-checked, Claudine Montluzac had just taken up duty."

"Hmm, it may mean something, but then again, it may not. According to Victoire, Noblecourt and Montluzac had the hots for each other. Maybe he was just calling to tell her he'd be gone for a couple of days. But who knows?"

The last image John looked at before falling asleep was of Victoire and Alexandre. She was holding the baby in front of the hollyhocks planted by his aunt at 9 Rue Fermat.

25

Major Adil Paniandy scanned the horizon once more with his powerful binoculars. All seemed normal above the banks of the Arabian Sea. Some clouds masked a portion of the stars, but the sky was mostly clear. The peninsula of Nava

Bandar stretched into the sparkling waters. Offshore, a tanker from Kuwait slowly moved southward toward Sri Lanka.

Paniandy turned around. He greeted the sentinel and headed for the antiaircraft battery's bunker under the mountain. Two Akash-2 missiles delivered a month earlier promised to perform much better than the previous missiles. The two rockets were operated remotely from an army camp outside Bombay. They were part of a new and sophisticated arsenal designed to intercept any attack from Pakistan or China. With this kind of intelligent weaponry, every minute—every second—mattered. Only a highly complex computer could coordinate such an effective response.

Paniandy greeted Havildar Dahana Opoula. The sergeant was hurrying to meet him.

"What is it?"

"We've received another order from Bombay. Shooting position in ten minutes."

"Execute," Paniandy commanded.

Opoula ran off to rouse the men in the bunker. In less than five minutes, the soldiers would leave the shelter with their machinery and arsenal, which could ward off the most powerful armor-piercing bombs. The two missiles would be positioned on their site, and Paniandy would have a stronghold with a clear view of the Indian Ocean and the Nava Bandar coast.

Paniandy and his men practiced this exercise every two to three days, at all hours. The major had to make sure his team was ready for anything. During his training in Bombay, he had seen firsthand the diabolic capabilities of the two new missiles. The first antiaircraft missile could attack an enemy plane by locking onto the engine's heat source and the target's image photographed by the missile's cameras. The second missile, programmed for launch twenty-five seconds after the first one went up, received ballistic, visual, and thermal settings, which allowed it to correct the course of the attack in case the first burst failed. The engineers had refined the program with systems that adapted to each type of enemy aircraft. They even factored in the individual characteristics of enemy pilots, based on information provided by India's intelligence service.

Adil Paniandy's pride grew every time he watched the two missiles emerge from the bunker.

26

Titus Polycarpe ushered Victoire and Béatrice into the foyer of his apartment on the Rue de Babylone. The little girl's great-uncle was wrapped in an embroidered dressing gown. The retired president of Martin and Polycarpe, the commercial bank on the Rue de Monceau, was in his eighties. He looked very much like his sister.

"Georgette told me you were coming with Béatrice. But I didn't expect you this late." He looked at his great-niece. "It's almost eleven, child, way past your bedtime."

"This isn't an ordinary day, Uncle Titus. Grandpa was murdered." She went straight into the living room, where the TV was recycling footage of Orly.

Titus turned to Victoire. "If Béa says it was murder, it's probably true. What do you think?"

Victoire was wary. "Béatrice thinks whatever your sister thinks."

"Come into the living room. Have you had dinner?"

"Not really."

Titus led Victoire into the massive living room and motioned to a Filipino woman.

"Laura, please get us something to eat."

The woman disappeared into the kitchen.

"I haven't eaten either. I've been glued to the news since this afternoon. My sister called to tell me that Pierre-André was on the plane. He got out just in time, only to be murdered in his own home. I can't believe it."

The man seemed sincerely shocked. He invited Victoire to have a seat across from him. "You're the expert. What do you really think?"

"I'm no more an expert than your sister, but I do believe he was murdered. I don't see how he could have hoisted himself up on his own. There was no stepladder. He was missing a shoe, and I couldn't find it. That means someone else was there. And this someone else took the shoe."

"That doesn't make sense. If someone helped him, how did he get in, and why would he take the shoe?"

"They came in through the courtyard window and left with the stepladder," Béatrice said, still watching television. "And maybe they took the shoe as a souvenir. Killers have been known to do weirder things."

"True, honey."

From the pocket of his dragon-embellished dressing gown, Titus took out a pair of sunglasses and put them on.

"I have to keep the rooms dim because of my eyes. Poor vision is one of the Polycarpe family's weaknesses. Among others."

The banker turned to Béatrice. Next to her was a large stuffed panda bear. Nice, Victoire thought. How many great-uncles kept toys for the youngest members of their families?

"Grandpa was healthy and happy. He called me just before he left Malaysia. There's no reason he would've hanged himself. Right, Uncle Titus?"

"Right, Béa."

Outside, at the Sèvres-Babylone intersection, the Lutetia Hotel towered in the night. The Boulevard Raspail rose up a gentle slope toward Montparnasse. The headlights of cars and the neon signs of cafés blinked in the darkness. But Victoire couldn't hear any of the outside noises. The owner of this home had paid attention to every detail, including the soundproofing.

On the television, a softly lit commercial broke the monotony of the news. The servant brought in sandwiches and iced tea. At that moment, John was flying over the dark waters of the Indian Ocean. At Fermatown, Roberta and Luc were caring for Alexandre. Victoire reflected on the day's events and shook her head. It was all overwhelming, and she was fatigued. She sipped her tea, hoping it would keep her alert, and looked around the room. On a large credenza there was a display of silver bonsai trees. She hadn't seen them when she entered the room.

"Your trees are beautiful."

"They were a gift from the Malaysian government."

"For services provided by your bank?"

Titus Polycarpe smiled in the semidarkness.

"Let's just say they were a thank-you gift to a banker and member of the former president's family. Béatrice, I see you weren't too embarrassed to tell the nice lady I was a banker."

"You don't embarrass me, Uncle Titus. I don't let any of you embarrass me."

Victoire took note of the unspoken collusion between the great-uncle and his grand-niece. This kid exercised a playful and troubling authority over the adults in her life.

Titus turned to Victoire. "Call me the family's odd duck. I've always preferred numbers to campaign speeches."

"I understand. So you do business in Malaysia?"

"Right. I forgot you have an investigation to lead for the Élysée."

Victoire nodded and took a bite of her sandwich.

"My bank helped finance a trading room where shares in companies that mine and produce rare-earth elements can be bought and sold."

"I've heard of rare earths, but I don't know what they are."

"Yes, rare earths are elements—or, to put it simply, minerals that we find in deposits that can be mined and used in various applications. Cerium oxide has been used for many years as a lapidary polish. But since the start of the twenty-first century, demand for rare earths has surged. Their chemical and electromagnetic properties make them indispensable in high-tech and other vital industries. Without rare earths, computers, radar, semiconductors, missiles, scanners, cell phones, electric cars, wind turbines, renewable energies—none of them could exist. For example, they're used as phosphors—or luminescent materials—in cathode-ray tubes, X-ray screens, and florescent lamps. The rare earth that's especially important in this application is europium, which is mined in China, India, the United States, and Russia. Another rare earth, lanthanum, is largely responsible for the rechargeable battery. Oh, don't get me started. I could go on and on. I'd bore you to death."

"Oh no, it's quite fascinating. Tell me more."

"Not too long ago, China controlled the market. Some even say they had a stranglehold. But the market has experienced some dramatic changes in recent years, and other countries, including the United States, India, Russia, and even Malaysia, have stepped in to meet the demand."

"When he was president, Grandpa developed the strategy to manage the supply of rare earths. You know, they're really important for the future."

Victoire looked at Béatrice. "So you know all about this?"

"Of course. Like I said, Grandpa told me things."

"Béatrice is right," Titus said. "My brother-in-law developed a strategy. He knew that rare earths are indispensable in our modern-day world, that all our infrastructure depends on them now. Whoever controls them controls everything, from phone technology to power grids and smart cities filled with sensors and meters. In a word, they control humanity's future. And when anything is precious, unscrupulous people and even governments can become threats. They can cause prices to spike or plummet and arbitrarily control supply. My brother-in-law wanted everything to be aboveboard and transparent. He wanted to avoid unbridled speculation. So he convinced the heads of the G20 nations to create an organization that would oversee the buying and selling of rare earths."

Béatrice's arm shot up. "Ssh, Uncle Titus. They're talking about Grandpa!"

Titus Polycarpe focused on the screen. A reporter was double-checking the information he had just gotten.

"We've learned that the body of the former president of France, Pierre-André Noblecourt, has been transported to the Forensic Medicine Institute of Paris. According to a source with close ties to the police, President Noblecourt committed suicide. His body was found hanging in his Rue de Babylone residence."

"She's a liar! They're protecting the bad guys. Grandpa didn't commit suicide!"

Béatrice ran over to her great-uncle. He put his arm around her and pulled her close. As Victoire looked at the pair, a chessboard just beyond the banker's shoulder caught her eye. It reminded her of the photos of the chess match in Malaysia. Victoire filed it away and checked her watch. She needed to get going.

"It's late, Béatrice. I have to go home. Would you like me to come by tomorrow and take you to school?"

"No, you don't need to do that. I'll ask Ninjutsu and Aikido."

"Who are Ninjutsu and Aikido?"

"They're Grandpa's bodyguards. They're really nice. They're martial-arts champs. Ninjutsu and Aikido are just their nicknames. I'm the only one who calls them that. I like martial arts, but I like swimming better. Have you ever gone scuba diving?"

"No, I haven't."

"If you want to come get me at five o'clock, that works for me. Mathilde, who lives on the Rue Vaneau, can't give me my piano lesson."

She moved closer to Victoire and spoke in a quieter voice,

"And we can talk while I have my snack. I really like the cookies from the pastry shop at the corner of the Rue Notre-Dame-des-Champs and the Rue de Rennes."

"I'll see what I can do."

Victoire left Titus Polycarpe's apartment, wondering what to make of the family. The night was even hotter and stickier, and it wasn't until she reached Denfert-Rochereau that she could let her mind relax. By the time she reached the Rue Deparcieux, through, she was worrying about what awaited her at police headquarters.

One day, and I'm already sick of this. John's been sent off to Malaysia and I'm under police scrutiny, she thought, quickening her pace as she neared home. Then, she weighed her frustration against the two innocent café owners who were murdered, the hundreds of deaths at Orly, and the near-certain connection with her assignment. They needed to get to the bottom of this. And quick.

27

Thrown from his bed, John hit the wall of the presidential plane like a billiard ball. The A330 was bringing its engines up to full speed as it made a dizzying ascent over the Arabian Sea. He watched as blankets and other objects came hurtling toward him.

A warning siren added to the commotion. John managed to grab the bed frame, which was bolted to the floor, and began crawling toward the front of the aircraft. The plane shuddered as he reached the hallway. Through one of the windows, he saw that the right wing was in flames. Then, in a burst of fireworks, a burning engine flew off. John had a visceral vision of Victoire and Luc tossing flowers at the crash site.

The engine on the left wing exploded, piercing John's eardrums. Still, the plane continued its ascent. Suddenly it leveled out, and just as quickly it began a tight turn. Already banged up, John was thrown once more against a wall. He waited for the plane to stabilize, then asked the pilots for an explanation.

"What's going on?"

"We're getting missile strikes from an antiaircraft battery on the Indian coast. They probably think we're Pakistanis."

The pilot pointed to two white dots on the radar screen.

"I thought the engines exploded."

"Those are countermeasures. They're pyrotechnic effects to confuse the enemy. Our engines are intact. We're expecting a hit in ten seconds. You should sit down and buckle up."

Following the steward's lead, John returned to the hallway separating the presidential suite from the cockpit and buckled himself into a seat.

"The pilot launched the decoys to trick the missiles," the steward said. "We'll be stabilized soon."

John nodded and stared out at the night sky. The fireworks show was entering its final phase. Two spinning tops were shining in the darkness. John guessed they were a half mile away. Suddenly, the contrail of one of the missiles indicated a troublesome trajectory. Unperturbed by the decoys, the rocket was charging right at them. John braced himself for the worst. The plane took an abrupt nosedive toward the sea, causing his seat belt to dig into his stomach. The missile reacted just as fast and performed a tight turn to keep its target from escaping. In the distance, the two useless balls of fire were drifting off in the night, lighting up a bed of clouds.

John could sense the pilot's maneuver as his first presidential meal came spewing out of his mouth and nose. The sources of heat created by the decoys were having no effect on the state-of-the-art missiles designed to outflank this type of countermeasure. The plane was now plummeting at what seemed like a ninety-degree angle and at a speed so terrifying, John feared the wings would break off.

John dared to take a breath when the missile lost its lock on the plane and zoomed off in another direction. But the moment of relief was painfully brief. The second missile corrected the first one's mistake and came rushing at them. John grasped onto an image of Victoire and Alexandre in his mind as the sky, the moon, and the stars all disappeared. The plane was flopping like a salmon in a fisherman's net. It was bound to burst into pieces before reaching the water or getting pulverized by the second missile.

The engines idled, and the precipitous drop became a trip to hell. The plane was now a tomb rushing headlong toward the sea.

John was whipped back in his seat as the A330 quickly leveled off again. He realized the pilot had made a desperate maneuver. To escape the second missile, the pilot had plunged toward a cloud bank. He had brought the plane upright once they were out of the enemy's sight. John heard the engines rev up, coinciding with the deafening sound of an explosion. The second missile had lost track of its target and exploded in the exact spot where the plane had been seconds earlier.

The Indian rockets were equipped with an incredible memory that could visually reproduce the plane's exact shape. Even rendered blind, the second missile had been able to calculate where and when to explode. The pilot had factored that in before cutting the engines.

John had lost his whole meal by now. But he didn't care about his clothes or the sullied seat. The steward and he burst into laughter. The gentle sway of the A330 was having a euphoric effect. Just as he was beginning to breathe normally again, the pilot emerged from the cockpit, his shirt drenched in sweat. He planted himself in front of John.

"Who the hell are you?" he demanded.

"John Spencer Larivière, citizen of France and the United States, currently on assignment. That was some impressive maneuvering. I had no idea the Indians had missiles like that. How did you guess?"

"Six months ago, we received a message from Paris Air Base BA 117 warning us about this sort of missile. If I hadn't had that cloud bank or the thirty meters above the water to level off, we wouldn't be having this conversation."

"Nice work."

"You'd better get changed. You're a mess."

John didn't need to look at himself. He could smell it—just like he could smell the shit storm Méricourt had gotten him into. This was no longer just a Méricourt job. It was personal now.

MONDAY

1

John watched as the two Indian Air Force fighters that had been following them from Sri Lanka swirled into the distance.

Two minutes later, the A330 grazed the runway at the Kuala Lumpur International Airport, accompanied by a stream of police cars and fire trucks. The Malaysian authorities were sparing no expense with their safety measures, but it seemed like a big performance.

The plane taxied toward a hangar that was isolated from the other buildings. John studied the insignias on the building and concluded that it belonged to the Malaysian Air Force. Gathering up his things, John felt his cell phone vibrate in his pocket.

"It's Jemestre. Congratulations on dodging those missiles. How are you?"

"Relieved," John answered. "But your pilot is the one you should be congratulating—not me."

"I've just spoken with the prime minister of Malaysia. His security forces and interior minister are at your service. You'll be treated like a head of state. I'm making sure of it."

"There's no need for all that."

"I insist. You are on an important assignment there, and you're working as my representative. Don't hesitate to ask for their assistance. And I have the information you wanted. We've identified the number that Pierre-André called before leaving Kuala Lumpur. It belongs to the police chief who was on duty at Quai des Orfèvres. And we know who that was. See how I'm working for you? What do you say to that, Larivière?"

"I believe her name is Claudine Montluzac. Apparently the woman's quite a looker. Do you know her, Mr. President?"

Jemestre was silent.

"Yes," he finally answered. "Somewhat."

"Can you tell me anything else?"

"Later. Keep me updated. I'm expecting an explanation. Good luck."

Jemestre had ended the call as soon as things took a delicate turn. John looked at the phone. So the president was familiar with Claudine Montluzac.

John met back up with the flight crew in the cockpit. A former helicopter pilot, he always enjoyed interacting with fellow pilots and their teams. They were like kin.

"What's the weather like?"

"Thirty-eight degrees Celsius and very humid. It's going to be quite a shock."

"Haven't we had enough shocks?"

"The Élysée has asked us to stay here for the remainder of your trip."

"Thanks for the ride. I hope I don't keep you waiting too long. It's been a pleasure."

As the pilot finished taxiing to the hangar, John scrolled through the news on his smartphone. The major sites had moved on from the fire at Orly, which was under control. Now they were focused on the former president's mysterious death. On Twitter, people were questioning Noblecourt's presence in Kuala Lumpur the day before his suicide. A few British sites were hypothesizing a sex scandal linked to a suicide that was really a murder. Very French.

John put away his phone and walked over to the exit. As soon as the door opened, he was bathed in sweat.

At the foot of the stairs, a limousine as long as a tramway awaited him. It was the middle vehicle in a convoy led and trailed by police cars. Guards armed with machine guns were stationed all around the plane. John noticed cameras and directional microphones. The heavily armed and equipped presence made for remarkable theatrics.

A round-faced Malaysian woman in a black uniform walked up the staircase. She beamed as she welcomed John in perfect French. Meanwhile, the door to the limo opened, and a man in a white suit got out. He walked over to the bottom of the stairs and looked up at John.

A female police officer made a discreet announcement just as John reached the last step.

"His Excellency Amir bin Muhaimin, minister of home affairs for the Federation of Malaysia."

Struck by the power of the man's crafty black eyes, John extended his hand. "John Spencer Larivière."

"I wanted to personally greet you. Please, be my guest."

The minister gestured to the limousine, and John hopped into what looked like a luxury cabin on the Orient Express. Feeling the effects of the AC, he instinctively straightened his jacket. As soon as the minister and the driver joined him, the convoy began gliding toward the exit. The armored vehicle's bulletproof windows were as thick as bricks, and the way the limo rocked on its wheels meant it weighed two to three tons.

"Help yourself."

The minister of home affairs raised the top of a minibar filled with juices and mineral water.

"We have no alcohol. Most of us here in Malaysia are Muslims."

"Of course, Your Excellency."

John would have preferred coffee but opted for an apricot juice, which he poured into a Baccarat crystal glass.

"As soon as your president informed us of the attack on your plane over India, I launched an investigation. I'll show you the results later. First I would like to know what really happened to Pierre-André Noblecourt. I had a lot of respect for your former president. He loved Malaysia and even thought about retiring here. His son-in-law moved to our country not too long ago. You knew about that, right?"

"Yes, Your Excellency."

"What happened at Orly?"

"The plane caught fire, but Mr. Noblecourt managed to escape. He was found hanging in his home soon afterward."

Amir bin Muhaimin repositioned himself on the green leather seat and looked at John skeptically.

"And you believe this story?"

"It's the official version."

"It's a false version. Pierre-André Noblecourt was not on the plane that blew up at Orly."

John digested the news. The Malaysian government seemed better informed than the high-level officials in France. If this man was telling the truth, then Noblecourt lied to his bodyguards. And if that was the case, was he waiting for rather than traveling with someone?

"May I ask how you know this?"

"Your former president returned to Paris from Singapore on the Singapore Airlines flight that landed at Orly three hours ahead of Air France Flight 912. So, of course, he was not on the Air France plane. How can you explain that, Mr. Spencer Larivière?"

John was dealing with a wolfish local politician who was doubling as Malaysia's highest-ranking police authority. There was no point in playing wise guy.

"To be honest, I can't explain it."

"There's more that's off with what the French authorities are—and aren't—saying. I talked with your interior minister just fifteen minutes ago. He didn't know about your trip to Kuala Lumpur, and he certainly didn't know about your plane getting attacked last night over India. I get the feeling that your government doesn't disseminate information very efficiently."

Despite his six-foot rugby-man build, John was feeling smaller than a little person. French intelligence was obviously an international embarrassment.

"Don't beat yourself up, my friend. Information between ministries doesn't flow much better in my country."

"Any theories about who may have killed Mr. Noblecourt, Your Excellency?"

"I think that whoever killed him has some connection with Malaysia. Coming here was a good idea."

"Do you have any names?"

"Not yet, but we've got a lead. I'm about to share it."

Amir bin Muhaimin took a sip of water and glanced at his watch with diamond inlays.

"We're arriving in Putrajaya, our new capital."

Looking out his window, John could see brand-new buildings and avenues alongside pristine man-made lakes. Many of the buildings had futuristic architecture, a startling contrast to the old mosques. In the distance, the silhouettes of a Disneyland-like park loomed, and the skeletons of incomplete skyscrapers rose toward the sky.

"We're correcting Brasília's mistakes."

A line from Proverbs came to John's mind. "Pride goeth before destruction, and a haughty spirit before a fall."

He had seen it with his own eyes, and he knew, without a doubt, that he would see it again.

2

The driver veered onto a small street lined with tropical trees. After coming over a hill, it pulled into a parking space.

"We're at the site of the future police academy. I'd like to introduce you to someone whose confession will be of great interest to you."

A young woman in uniform opened the door of the limousine, and the powerful scents from nearby gardens assailed John. Amir bin Muhaimin and John got out, and the two headed down a walkway. The luxuriant grounds accentuated the black-and-silver uniforms of the police officers, who were lined up by rank to welcome Bin Muhaimin and his guest. One of the officers stepped out of the group and approached the minister. His face still bore the scars of acne.

"Are you ready for the performance?"

"Yes, Your Excellency."

"John, this is our commissioner of police."

The police commissioner turned to John with a smile that suggested an apology. "Come with me."

John trailed behind the minister, the commissioner, and several officers as they passed through a guarded gate and a tall hedge, finally arriving in a huge courtyard surrounded by ultramodern buildings. The procession then continued toward a Buddhist pagoda. Against these futuristic buildings, the pagoda was an anachronism.

"The academy is opening in two days. Its first class will have 360 officers in training. We're also admitting fifty French students, who will learn the most up-to-date techniques in fighting cybercrimes. Your interior minister is delighted."

John nodded. As they drew closer to the pagoda, he saw that it served as an entrance to an underground space. John followed the group down the steps and into a hallway beneath the academy buildings. Amir bin Muhaimin continued his spiel.

"We teach our students the most modern techniques in criminal interviewing, what you call interrogation. We use hypnosis, graphology, and the latest research in neuroscience to draw information from a suspect. We don't use any psychotropic drugs or synthetic products. Malaysia wants a sustainable police force."

Once again, John nodded. A sustainable police force. Who'd be against that?

After walking another sixty meters or so down a hallway lined with posters that boasted success in the war against drugs and pedophilia, the group came to an amphitheater capable of holding some three hundred spectators. A metal curtain hung across the stage. John looked all around. This place was as impressive as a Chinese corporation's boardroom.

The minister pointed to seats in the front row. John sat down, and Bin Muhaimin took the seat next to him. The others filed in behind them. The lights dimmed, and the curtain went up.

On stage there was a large room with ultramodern décor. In the center, two police officers—one of whom was a woman—sat on each side of a young man in a Hawaiian shirt. The scene looked like a swanky bar at a beach club.

John picked up a simulcast translation kit, which he put over his ears.

"The man we see here is an air-traffic controller at the International Airport of Kuala Lumpur. Our anticybercrime unit arrested him this morning at his home."

Despite his exhaustion from the turbulent flight, John was savvy enough to understand their little performance. They were trying to reassure Paris of Malaysia's desire to cooperate fully with France.

"He gave us a detailed confession when we showed him files from his computer. We didn't have to resort to any extreme methods. You'll now see a live reenactment of his criminal interview."

John watched as the two police officers and the air-traffic controller waved to the audience. The woman, who apparently ranked higher than the male officer, initiated the interview.

"Asrul, you acknowledge that you downloaded the flight plan for President Alain Jemestre's plane, which was taking Mr. John Spencer Larivière from the Villacoublay air base in France to Malaysia?"

"Yes."

"You acknowledge that you gave the flight plan to an accomplice."

"Yes."

"Who?"

"He didn't give me his name. I didn't know him. He contacted me during a break and offered me money. He had a suitcase full of cash."

"Was he Malaysian?"

"Yes."

The confession proceeded, with the main characters exiting the stage like disciplined actors. After several trips to Iran and Libya, John couldn't be fooled. Asrul had most certainly told the police a lot more.

Amir bin Muhaimin, clearly pleased with the performance, turned to his host.

"My people will continue the interrogation, and I will personally keep you up to speed. If it's all right with you, I'll take you to the ministry now. The ambassador of France is sending you a diplomat."

"Thank you."

John was certain that Bin Muhaimin knew who the air-traffic controller's accomplices were—and a lot more than that. He was behaving like a strategic politician. The man was merely a pawn, positioned between Paris and Kuala Lumpur.

And John was feeling much the same. He didn't like being played with.

3

Claudine Montluzac gave Victoire a steely look as she pointed to a chair.

Victoire sat down. A uniformed officer sat next to her, his computer ready for note-taking.

The musty interrogation room at Paris police headquarters was separate from the rest of the criminal investigation unit. Its barred windows overlooked the Seine. Victoire assumed this was to deter suicide and escape attempts.

The police chief's blond hair, lavender-blue eyes, and overall BCBG look clashed with the room's austerity. Montluzac might have been fooling around with the former president, but Victoire couldn't tell by her attitude. Was the head of the financial crimes unit even upset over her lover's death?

Despite John's counsel, Victoire was on the edge of her seat. She had decided to give the former president's phone back to

Georgette. Victoire had considered tossing it into the Seine. But instead, she and Luc were keeping it safely tucked in its pouch at Fermatown until it could be returned to the Noblecourt residence. Georgette had said she'd get the bodyguards to bring it in.

Victoire looked her adversary over. She was unquestionably beautiful, despite her distrustful glare.

The uniformed officer started reading from his computer screen. "Your name is Victoire Jeanne Augagneur. You have spent a portion of your career working for the French intelligence agency."

"That's correct."

"You are now an associate at Fermatown, a private agency at 18 Rue Deparcieux in the fourteenth arrondissement of Paris."

To Victoire, it sounded like he was spitting out a rotten piece of fruit. So what was wrong with having your own business?

He continued.

"Why do you have a different address listed on your website? That's unusual."

"We have two addresses because our adjoining buildings face both the Rue Deparcieux and the Rue Fermat."

"That will have to be fixed. You can only have one address."

"Yes, officer."

The officer entered her response and turned to the police chief, who continued the questioning.

"I am aware, Ms. Augagneur, that until your visit to the Noblecourt residence yesterday, you had no dealings with Mrs. Noblecourt in regard to her Mekong children's foundation. So what was the real reason for your visit?"

Victoire gave Montluzac her most confident smile.

"I'm a friend of the family. That's the simple truth."

"A friend of the family, you say?"

"That's right. I was there to do what I could to help, and I offered to take Béatrice to her Uncle Titus's house."

"Her Uncle Titus?"

"Yes, actually it's her great-uncle. Titus Polycarpe is the former head of Marin and Polycarpe Bank. I offered to take her to his place because Béa's mother and grandmother were exhausted. They needed some rest."

Victoire could feel the tension creeping into her shoulders. Okay, so Montluzac probably knew that she wasn't exactly a family friend. She could handle this.

The uniformed officer peeked over his computer. "Mr. John Spencer Larivière also worked for Les Invalides, and now he's an associate of yours at Fermatown," he said. "Where is your associate at the moment?"

"He's in Kuala Lumpur."

"How strange. And what is he doing in Kuala Lumpur?" Montluzac asked.

"Let me clarify. Mr. Spencer Larivière is not only my associate, but also my husband. As for his trip to Kuala Lumpur, he's assisting Apolline Roussillon's husband, Serge. He needs to come home."

"Mr. Roussillon can't come home on his own?"

Victoire hit her stride. "John and Serge have known each other for a while. John can help him avoid all the reporters and their questions about the former president's suicide. They'll be taking Alain Jemestre's plane back home. That way, they won't get bombarded by the press."

"They're taking Alain Jemestre's plane?"

Victoire registered the surprise on Montluzac's face. She felt a rush of satisfaction at the way she had slipped the president's name in so smoothly. Montluzac quickly regained her composure and continued with her questions.

"What do you think of Pierre-André Noblecourt's suicide?" Montluzac asked.

"Do you suspect it wasn't a suicide?"

"I'm waiting for the report. The medical examiner won't be able to perform the autopsy until this afternoon…"

For a second, Montluzac looked annoyed. "We'll have the results soon enough. But back to Mr. Spencer Larivière. So he has a special relationship with the Noblecourt family?"

"He is a former intelligence officer, as you know."

Victoire was playing off the energy of the back-and-forth without going too far. Her adversary didn't seem to be fooled.

"I just have a few more questions."

"Go ahead."

"I saw you and Béatrice after I was called away from the Noblecourt residence last night. I was leaving the bar at the corner of the Rue de Babylone and the Rue du Bac. The two owners were murdered. You were en route to Mr. Polycarpe's residence, I presume."

"Yes, that's what I was doing."

Claudine Montluzac turned to the officer who was taking notes.

"Théo, could you please bring us some coffee and croissants? I'm starving. You can have them charged to my account."

She waited for him to leave before continuing with her questions. "I received a phone call yesterday from the counter-cybercrimes bureau. They had just tracked down the former president's cell phone."

"Where was it?" Victoire asked, forcing herself to sound dispassionate.

"Believe it or not, Mr. Noblecourt's phone made a cameo appearance at that bar yesterday afternoon."

"Really?"

"Without a doubt. Did Mrs. Noblecourt say anything to you about her husband's phone?"

"No, she didn't say anything. But she was so shaken up, I wouldn't blame her for overlooking something like that."

Montluzac nodded.

"We happened to pin Mr. Noblecourt's phone to another location in the evening."

"You're tracking his phone—that must be difficult. I'm assuming the Élysée is helping you in your search."

Victoire could almost see the woman fidgeting. To access the geolocation system on the former president's phone, the criminal investigation unit would have had to circumvent the top-secret classification, which hadn't been lifted yet. Montluzac was taking a calculated risk in sharing the information about the phone. She sensed that the police chief didn't even want her colleagues in the unit to know.

"The second geolocation was at Place Denfert-Rochereau, in the catacombs."

"You don't say."

"Since your agency is on the Rue Deparcieux, which is quite close, I was wondering if this might mean something to you."

"I'll think it over."

"I mean, maybe you could tell me why the phone would be in the catacombs, of all places. Any light you could shed on this would be helpful. The contents of that phone are undoubtedly crucial in retracing the murderer's route."

"So you don't think it was a suicide. You think the former president was murdered?"

"Yes."

"If I think of anything, I'll let you know immediately."

Claudine Montluzac gave Victoire her business card.

The compliant Théo returned with the croissants and coffee, and the questioning continued, with no pertinent questions or answers. Montluzac, however, seemed to be preoccupied. She was glancing at her watch. Was she waiting for someone?

Just as Victoire was about to answer another irrelevant question, a blast sent shards of glass flying across the room. The walls and floor of the building shook violently. Victoire, Montluzac, and the uniformed officer dived off their chairs and covered their heads. They heard people outside screaming for help.

Finally, Victoire and the two others rose to their feet and left the room. They made their way to the smoking and debris-strewn stairwell, where they encountered bloodied police officers and civilians, who, like them, were trying to get out of the building. Reaching the ground floor, Victoire realized the explosion hadn't occurred at 36 Quai des Orfèvres, but at the left-bank entrance to the Saint Michel bridge.

The fiery remains of a car or truck—Victoire couldn't make out which—were sending up black plumes of smoke. The area surrounding the vehicle was shimmering in the heat from the blaze. She heard the sirens of fire trucks and rescue vehicles, and nearby, injured people were trying to help each other. No sooner had she figured out what to do next than two cars near the first vehicle exploded.

Montluzac grabbed the arm of an officer emerging from the building. The man's eyes were distraught, and his face was covered with soot.

"Were they in that car?"

He nodded.

Victoire turned to Montluzac.

"You knew who was in the car?"

"Yes. The former president's bodyguards. We called them in this morning to ask about Mr. Noblecourt's itinerary. And about your…"

Victoire couldn't take her eyes off the flaming vehicle and thought about the two bodyguards—killed, perhaps, because they knew something they weren't supposed to. Montluzac turned around, and at that moment Victoire realized she was looking at a woman who was grieving, a woman who had dared to love someone else's husband. And not just any husband. Now he was gone. Victoire almost felt bad for her. She steadied herself against the bridge to shake off the thoughts coursing through her brain.

"Are you hurt?" Montluzac asked, examining her from head to toe.

Victoire smiled weakly. The horror had transformed them into comrades, if only for a few minutes. A situation like this wouldn't happen twice. Victoire put a hand in her purse and felt for a two-euro coin. As the two women looked back at the glowing flames, she slipped the tracking device into the police chief's pocket.

"How horrible. I hope you catch the killers who did this."

4

John said good-bye to Amir bin Muhaimin at the police compound, promising to visit him at his country home. His driver and Benoît Dutreil, the cultural attaché for the French ambassador, were waiting for him. The Malaysian barely cleared the Frenchman's belt.

Benoît Dutreil was studying the fog over the canal. Cultural attaché my ass, John was thinking. Why did they even bother with the fake title? The man looked like a spy, had the bearing of a spy, and probably talked like a spy. This was one of the most politically sensitive spots in Southeast Asia, and Dutreil was obviously leading local espionage operations. No one was fooled by the cultural relations cover, especially Malaysia's counterespionage team.

Dutreil was an honest, technically skilled operative. At Les Invalides, he had no known vices or affiliations of the sexual, philosophical, political, or financial variety. This had slowed his career considerably. He was a cold and reserved mystery. Not a fun guy and certainly not a badass. A sort of Jansenist Catholic—a worker bee of the French Republic.

"Hello, Benoît. It's good to see you."

"Good to see you too, John. I hear you almost didn't make it to Kuala Lumpur."

"They're keeping you well-informed, as always."

John shook the Malaysian driver's hand. It felt sticky. The man had a round face and a smarmy expression. John was already speculating. He slid into the backseat, followed by Dutreil. With the AC on full blast, he felt like he had just entered a butcher-shop freezer. Not a good sign. The driver got in too and turned the ignition of the 607 Peugeot.

"The Ministry of Foreign Affairs says it doesn't have the money to build an embassy in Putrajaya. We're still in Kuala. But you'll see that it's not so bad."

"So what's your take on the situation?"

John followed Dutreil's hand as he slipped him a cell phone. He took the device and read the screen: "Can't tell you anything in the car. Don't know who the driver works for. Don't trust him."

"How about I give you a quick history lesson first."

John listened as the agent recounted the story of battling sultans from the Strait of Malacca and their complicated relationships with India and China. There were highs and lows through the centuries, but things always ended up back where they started.

"As you know, Malaysia occupies the Malaysian Peninsula and part of the island of Borneo. Kuala Lumpur is centrally located in the peninsular part of the country. This road is an ancient route. It connects Kuala Lumpur—which is getting too big—with Putrajaya, the new capital, and farther on, with Cyberjaya, a key part of Malaysia's Multimedia Super Corridor. You've heard of it, I'm sure. It's a special economic zone, and online startups from all over the globe have set up operations there."

John remembered the model city he had found in the Trocadéro studio. It was beginning to make sense.

"This country is experiencing an economic boom, John. Malaysia has gone straight from the Middle Ages into the twenty-first century. It's crazy. Kuala Lumpur is unlike anything you've seen before. And you'll like the people. Very friendly."

"I can't wait."

5

Spotting the smoking pillar rising from the heart of Paris, Luc rushed out to the balcony to get a better look. He had been meeting with Sebastian Graffon at airport authority headquarters.

"An explosion?" the director of airports asked, joining Luc on the balcony.

Luc checked his smartphone and learned that it was, indeed, an explosion, and the epicenter was the bridge separating the Place Saint-Michel from the Île de la Cité. He knew that police headquarters were right there on the Quai des Orfèvres. He excused himself and sent Victoire a text. She replied, assuring him she was safe, but the two bodyguards John had talked to the day before were dead.

"A car bomb. Two people died—the former president's bodyguards," Luc told Graffon. "Mr. Noblecourt's bodyguards had been summoned to police headquarters. One of our associates was nearby, but she wasn't hurt."

Luc and Graffon walked back to the table where they had been meeting. Luc finished scrolling through the news flashes and put his phone down. He looked at Graffon, and for the first time he noticed the stiffness in the man's hand and arm. The airport director was wearing a prosthetic.

"Your firm seems to be in the line of fire," Graffon said. "I heard a missile almost took down the plane your boss was on."

"Yes, apparently someone's trying to keep us from getting to the bottom of things."

"I'm sure the people who initiated that remote attack are the same ones responsible for emptying the Air France carrier's fuel. I've been warning the government about cyber strikes, but no one's listening. France isn't the best at anticipating or even making simple projections—aside from elections, of course. And even then we fuck up."

"You weren't alone in your concerns, Sebastian. We've been aware of the threat for some time. Cyber terrorists can take over an air-traffic control center, a hospital ventilation system—you name it. Their capabilities are terrifying."

Luc, usually cool and collected, was having an unusual reaction to the missile strike and the car bomb so close to Victoire. Although he was hiding his anger from Graffon, he could feel it surging through his veins. He was mad as hell that the two people he loved most in the world had almost lost their lives. If he got his hands on the person—or people—behind all of this, he'd settle the score himself.

"President Jemestre was the one who hired you for this, wasn't he?"

"He wants to know who killed the former president."

"So it *was* murder, like the Brits are saying."

"That's what his family thinks. And the police."

"Jemestre clearly has some inkling of who the murderer is."

"What makes you say that?" Luc asked.

"You don't become president of France by accident."

Luc could tell that Sebastian Graffon had something else to say but was holding back. Graffon was known for his supremely effective intelligence network. The director didn't say another word about the president and went back to the missile attack.

"To coordinate that kind of data transfer between the two missiles, you'd need an extremely sophisticated transmission system. The Indians had to be using high-precision technology. They've been training the best computer engineers on the planet."

"Does time calculation need to be considered for this kind of transmission?"

"No clue, but you may be onto something."

Luc nodded and continued his train of thought.

"I'm interested in a company that's not far from here. It's called Chronosphere. They make atomic clocks. In your opinion, could this company be connected to the cyberattacks?"

Using his left hand, Sebastian Graffon composed a couple of messages on his smartphone.

"I'm asking my competitive-intelligence people to work on this," he said, looking up. "I'll let you know what they find out."

"You have your own spy agency?"

"Economic intelligence is nothing like the spooks you're familiar with, kid. It's an open and transparent system that collects information and analyses. Nothing is secret. That happens to be why it actually works. Anyone can participate. And there hasn't been a single issue yet."

Luc wanted to roll his eyes. It wasn't so much that Graffon was calling him "kid," but that he was being patronizing.

"Thanks for your help."

"John told me you wanted the list of survivors. I'm guessing you'd like to know how Noblecourt was able to make it out of that plane."

"We've got to dispel any doubts."

"What doubts?"

Luc saw the twinkle in the director's eye. He seized the opportunity and put his cards on the table.

"I'm wondering if the terrorists were trying to kill someone else. That's why I'd like to see the passenger list."

"John trusts you, doesn't he?"

"Yes," Luc answered. "We keep no secrets at Fermatown."

Graffon smiled. "If he trusts you, then that's good enough for me. John and I met at Val-de-Grace when he got back from Afghanistan. We shared a hospital room in the burn unit for a month, and it's an experience that bonds people, as you can imagine. My injury was a domestic accident—I was grilling meat. Nothing heroic, like his story."

Sebastian Graffon pushed up his sleeve and showed Luc his prosthetic arm.

"You're lucky to be working with him. He's quite a guy."

Graffon pulled his sleeve back down and removed the flash drive from his computer.

"This has all our video footage. It was taken from the terminal. We also have a recording made by a Flight 912 passenger. He died at the hospital—in the major-burns unit. I suggest you pay close attention."

"What do you mean?"

Graffon didn't answer the question. "In addition, I'm giving you a list of the passengers and the flight crew, but we don't have the names of all the survivors. Some of the bodies haven't been identified. Whatever you do, keep this list confidential.

The airlines still hasn't released it. We'll be continuing our own investigation."

Sebastian Graffon placed his good hand on Luc's wrist.

"I had the opportunity to greet the former president at Orly and Roissy on several occasions. Sure, he was a decent man, but that's not what's keeping me up at night. I want to know why all those people were killed at one of my airports. There were a dozen children on that plane. You'll tell me, Luc, won't you?"

Graffon was on the verge of tears.

"Of course, Sebastian."

Luc took the USB drive, and the two men got up and walked toward the door. Just as Luc was about to leave, Graffon stopped him.

"I shouldn't be telling you this, but I got a call from Claudine Montluzac, the police chief on duty when Noblecourt was killed."

"What did she want?"

"She wanted a list of witnesses and hospitalized passengers. I was expecting a call from the antiterrorist unit. That didn't come until later. And then I got a call from homicide, and they said it's their case, not Montluzac's. Three police units in a turf war. Plus you guys. Intriguing, isn't it?"

"I agree, Sebastian."

"I haven't even mentioned the special prosecutors involved in the investigation. I've gotten voice mail from two different special prosecutor's offices that obviously aren't communicating with each another. And then there's the Air Gendarmerie."

Luc cracked a smile. "Good luck with that."

6

A half hour after meeting with Sebastian Graffon, Luc was at Fermatown's touchscreen wall, downloading the drive that the airports director had given him. The video taken from the terminal underscored the scope of the panic. Luc watched the footage. None of the passengers sliding down the plane's emergency-exit chutes looked like Noblecourt, which confirmed what the Malaysian minister of home affairs said. The former president was not on that plane. Why had he wanted people to believe otherwise?

Luc watched the clip filmed by a passenger in the first-class section. Noblecourt wasn't in the ambassador's reserved seat. A large Indian family was occupying much of the first-class section, and both the parents and a flight attendant were trying to calm the children, who were annoying the other passengers. After a few minutes, an attractive Asian woman got up and tried to do the same.

On Luc's command, the touchscreen wall showed the list of first-class passengers Graffon had given him. The names of the Indian family's fifteen members came up. But who was the woman helping the flight attendant? Luc had the screen zoom in and asked the wall to use facial-recognition technology to identify her. The response appeared ten seconds later. The woman was Emma Wong, and from what the touchscreen was telling him, she was something of newsmaker.

Luc set his sights on Emma Wong. He opened up every search engine possible and had the results ordered chronologically. He activated translation and synthesis programs.

"Jesus Christ…"

Emma Wong, a lawyer licensed to practice in Malaysia, was a local celebrity. At the start of her career, she had chased after lowlifes active in the sex industries of Thailand, Singapore, and, of course, Malaysia. But in the last few years, the beautiful lawyer had switched to higher-profile crimes.

Wong had recently been in the news for handling a wrongful death case. She was representing the family of Charikar Abaganda, an Indian marine officer who died while in custody. The stories implicated Abaganda in a blackmail scheme related to Malaysia's purchase of two Scorpène submarines from France. The articles were vague, but Luc got the impression that Abaganda had threatened to blow the whistle on the kickback arrangement involving the submarine contract in exchange for immunity, and somebody inside the police made sure he didn't talk.

"Well, well."

The two submarines had been delivered to Malaysia during the last year of Noblecourt's presidency. A second later, an intriguing photo appeared on the touchscreen. It was of Malaysia's defense minister, Syafiq bin Rodney; France's defense minister, Pascal Massicot; and the French ambassador to Kuala Lumpur, Nicolas Mortemar de Buzenval. They were standing in front of the two submarines with Abaganda, captain of the Zanbaldi, one of the subs. In the background was a frowning fourth man, facial recognition pinned him as a Malaysian citizen of Pakistani origin named Musa Kherrican.

Luc focused on the three top brass. "Now that is an interesting threesome."

He started digging. As defense minister, Syafiq bin Rodnay was a man of power and influence. He had three wives, so he had money and was a Muslim, since non-Muslims couldn't take more than one wife in Malaysia. He had one son. He apparently spent a lot of time on the international political road and got camera time in France for advising the French on how to fight modern-day pirates. That would explain him being buddy-buddy with France's defense minister Pascal Massicot.

Luc pulled up an overview of Massicot's political career—the usual top schools and political backstabbing as he climbed the ladder. He wasn't close to President Jemestre, but had enough clout to be defense minister. He was married to a woman named Ludivine.

Nicolas Mortemar de Buzenval was not married. Luc could only find pictures of him from before his tour as ambassador in Malaysia. Lots of pictures, in fact, shaking hands, patting backs, and licking the boots of people from the entire political spectrum and just about every major business personality in France.

Luc stared at the screen, trying to grasp just how far and wide their assignment could reach. What did Abaganda know that got him killed? Did it have anything to do with these men? Had the captain told Emma Wong everything? Was Noblecourt waiting at Orly for Emma Wong? Did he want to discuss her case in private? Had that case made her the target? What were the consequences going to be?

7

The car was heading down a wide street lined with apartment buildings, shops, and mismatched houses. Unlike Putrajaya, Kuala Lumpur was a mix of skyscrapers and modest homes, shiny glass and moldy wood—buildings thrown up without any attention to urban planning. John didn't mind. Kuala Lumpur had a relaxed feel, and the lush vegetation with flora everywhere was breathtaking. Soon the car stopped in front of the nondescript light-gray wall surrounding the ambassador's compound. John could see rust-colored roofs peeking above the wall. The French flag swayed softly in the humid early-evening breeze.

"Remember the code," Dutreil said as they exited the car and headed toward the door. "It's 1-7-8-9."

"How original. The storming of the Bastille. I feel so protected."

"The guys in charge came up with that one. You'll be staying in the presidential suite that Noblecourt used when he used to come. The ambassador insists on it."

"So what can you tell me about him?"

"Nicolas Mortemar de Buzenval's a man dedicated to advancing his career. He makes friends on the left and the right—and in the extreme parties too. He knows everything related to the political scene in Paris, and he's well connected with all the important multinational corporations."

John gestured to the driver, who was carrying his bags, to go in ahead of him. The Malaysian man smiled as he passed through the entrance, which opened onto a manicured yard with a swimming pool.

"You could go for a quick dip. Grapefruit wouldn't object."

"Who's Grapefruit?"

"That's what the Malaysians call the ambassador. You'll get it when you see him."

They followed the stone path leading to the guesthouse, which resembled a Buddhist temple with a wraparound teak deck. Dutreil tapped out the digital code, and they walked in. The semidark residence smelled like Indian wax and incense, but the oversized plasma screens gave it a more contemporary look.

John smiled at the driver and slipped him a tip. The Malaysian lowered his head as a sign of respect and left.

"You didn't have to give him a tip. He's paid to do that. He's never going to leave you alone now."

John didn't argue.

"Can we talk here?"

"No."

The two men headed into the yard. Although he had just arrived, John was acclimating to the humidity and overpowering smells. The murmuring sounds too—an odd mix of car engines, chirping birds, and distant voices.

"How long have you been here?" he asked Dutreil.

"Three years. I'm returning to Les Invalides at the end of the year."

"What are your thoughts on Amir bin Muhaimin?"

"He's a cunning and ambitious politician. He knows how to suck up when it benefits him. He's also a Muslim, and he goes easy on the extremists."

"He told me that Noblecourt never got on that plane and that he flew to France from Singapore. Do you know why?"

"No, I don't."

"Can you look into it?"

"I'm on it. This all happened so fast. How's your firm doing these days?"

"It could be better. With Europe's debt crisis and slow economy, companies are tightening their budgets. Luckily, we've got a good client base, and we have our ways when it comes to drumming up business. As for this assignment, you and I will be working together. I'll be telling you everything."

John knew he was stepping on Dutreil's toes, and no one at the embassy appreciated his presence. Any member of the agency who switched to the private sector, even if he worked for Les Invalides as a private contractor, was *ipso facto* a renegade and potential traitor. John had to make it clear that he understood this. He needed Dutreil's acceptance.

"I'm here because of Méricourt. He wants to assure you that he has big plans for you at Les Invalides."

"Oh really."

"Malaysia is a strategic spot. You've done an incredible job, despite your working conditions and lack of help from that asshole—"

"You have no idea what he's put me through. It's one humiliating task after another. The guy's sadistic."

"We know."

John put a sympathetic hand on the Dutreil's shoulder. The agency was always hiring competent and faithful servants who wound up being bullied by ungrateful technocrats. Dutreil looked at him with appreciation and seemed to relax. Having seen Méricourt do it, John knew how to deal with agents like this man. Even a tepid compliment could comfort a weary intelligence officer. And in this case, John's complicity had done the trick.

"So Méricourt told you about me?"

"He's very impressed."

"I've only been doing my job."

"That's becoming less and less common, Benoît."

They had been walking slowly around the grounds. Suddenly, Dutreil grabbed his sleeve and pulled him behind a huge bush with garish red flowers.

"We should stop here—or else that jackoff might see us. He spends all his time spying. He's so freaking paranoid. I wouldn't be surprised if he put in extra hours for Internal Security."

"You're right. The guy's a sneaky bastard."

Now was the time to gently extract the information from Dutreil.

"Do they have chess tournaments here?" John asked.

"Grapefruit's got a chess set in his office, but no one uses it. It's just there to impress visitors. Sitting across from that guy is something no one wants to do."

"Do people in Kuala play chess?"

"I don't know."

"It would be great if you could do a little digging and come up with a list of chess clubs and meet-up spots where people play, especially the places that attract photographers. If you can, get any names of the people who come and watch the matches."

"Why the spectators?"

"We're interested in Asians who attend a lot of chess tournaments. Especially this one." John showed Dutreil the photos of the chess match stored on Noblecourt's cell phone.

"I'll look into it."

"Does the French company Chronosphere ring any bells?"

"Not at all."

John also showed Dutreil the photo of the good-looking man. He examined the picture for several seconds before shaking his head.

"Total stranger. He's more the kind of guy that Grapefruit would like. Who is he?"

"He might be related to Chronosphere. They've got an extremely sophisticated time-keeping device. Do you know of anyone here, or any company here, that needs something like that?"

Dutreil looked at John like a sad puppy.

"Sorry, I don't."

"All right. Well, I'm going to get some sleep now. I'll see you later."

Back in the presidential suite, John squashed a couple of healthy-looking cockroaches before sweeping for electronic bugs. He also photographed key spots in the suite, including his bedroom closet, where he found several wooden hangers and a baseball bat. He pulled it out and took a few swings. He had loved the sport as a kid. Funny, he thought, as he returned the bat to the closet, neither Noblecourt nor the ambassador struck him as men who'd be playing much baseball. John closed the closet door and stretched out on the bed. Then he picked up his phone and called Victoire on their secure line. She lifted Alexandre out of his crib so John could coo at him. She put him down again to ask John a question. As usual, it was a good one.

"If Noblecourt flew from Singapore, as you say he did, and he arrived at Orly a few hours early, why was he still there when the Air France flight from Kuala Lumpur came in?"

"Maybe he was waiting for someone," John replied.

"Luc thinks that person was Emma Wong."

"Who's that?"

Victoire told John all about Luc's discovery of the beautiful Chinese lawyer.

"Why blow up the plane?" Victoire said. "None of those people deserved to die."

"And then we have the two bodyguards and the couple from Café Mouettes," John said. "The people behind this are doing everything they can to get their hands on Noblecourt's phone and stop us. They want the photos of the atomic clock, Chronosphere's director, and the chess match because those images are proof of something important. And let's not forget that they almost took my plane down too. Who in Paris knew that I was on the plane?"

It took Victoire a few seconds to respond. "Méricourt, President Jemestre, who may have told Georgette Noblecourt and Apolline Roussillon, and most likely Claudine Montluzac. The damage is done, John. My mother had a saying: the first part of a fish to rot is the head. One of those people may very well have betrayed you."

John thought it over. He had a smart wife who had been blessed with an insightful mother. Witnessing the interplay of savagery and cowardice in Cambodia, Victoire's mother had acquired a surgical and infallible understanding of humanity.

"Here in Malaysia, there's the ambassador, my colleague Dutreil, and Serge Roussillon, Béatrice's father. They're all in the know, and any one of them could have ratted me out. Where is that goddamned phone?"

"It's in Luc's portable Faraday cage, here at Fermatown. I'm giving it back to Georgette. She told me she'd hand it over to Montluzac, even though those two aren't exactly best friends."

"Never trust what's on the surface."

Victoire smiled. "It sounds like my Eastern sensibilities are rubbing off on my New World husband. Do you have any suspicions?" Victoire asked.

"We're keeping tabs on a basket of crabs. But at the bottom of that basket, there's a dangerous beast. I'm gonna try to get some sleep now. I love you."

Before passing out, John called Luc to see what progress he had made.

"Chronosphere's run by a guy named Julien Lanfrey. According to the European Bureau of Commercial Information, he doesn't have much cash flow. The company's on the verge of bankruptcy, in fact. I'm trying to figure out a way to approach him."

"Use your natural charm."

"I don't think that'll be enough. Plus I'm sure a bunch of people are watching and wiretapping him."

"That's highly possible."

"I'm thinking the atomic clock might have something to do with the submarines. Emma Wong is involved in this affair somehow, and I'm wondering if she was the one who sent the documents to Noblecourt and triggered his trip to Malaysia. I'll have to really hit it off with this Chronosphere guy."

Stretched out on Noblecourt's bed, John searched for inspiration while gazing at the ceiling.

"Buy 'em out."

"Are you kidding?"

"I'm serious. You said he has financial problems. Tell him you're working for a Chinese investor. Make him a huge offer. You've got that young-wolf look. You'll knock him out."

"Are you hitting on me?"

"You're such a jerk. I'm serious. Get Victoire to help you."

8

Victoire stormed down the Rue de Babylone toward the Noblecourt residence. The Indian rockets, plus the attack on the Pont Saint Michel, had first fed her anxiety. But now they fueled her anger. Victoire was picturing the most despicable betrayal imaginable.

Politicians and financiers were a big headless chicken that had brought the world to the brink of ruin. And the former president's part in that world smelled of foul meat and rotten tricks. As she got closer to the park, Victoire saw that the crowd near the residence had grown even larger, and scores of news trucks were parked nearby.

Ironically, the former president was experiencing a surge in popularity when he could no longer use it to his advantage. The Twitterverse and other social-media sites were spreading the craziest claims. He had stayed behind on the plane to make sure those who were still alive could get out. He had wrapped a blanket around a passenger whose clothes were burning. He had rescued an infant. A blurry photo of a man holding a child as he slid down the chute was already making its way around the globe.

Victoire greeted the police guard and walked through the deserted park, passing the little wooden toolshed. Everything at the Noblecourt home looked normal. She scanned the other buildings and spotted a few faces at the windows. Word had it that television crews were paying apartment owners for access to their windows. Apparently they were hoping to see something inside the Noblecourt home.

Just as she was approaching the residence, her phone rang. It was Luc.

"Hold up!" he ordered.

"Why? What's going on?"

"The coin you slipped into Montluzac's pocket indicates that our police chief is at the Noblecourt's apartment. You'll be dealing with both women again."

"Perfect. Now I'll be able to get the facts straight and tell the police the truth."

"Still, think about what you're going to say before you say it. Let them show their hands first. Don't reveal anything until you have to. They'll try to grill you. Don't let them. Now put your earpiece in."

Peeved about the trap awaiting her, Victoire slipped a hand into her purse and found the box containing the small audio device. She surreptitiously fished it out and put it in her ear. Now Luc would be able to hear the questions and suggest answers.

Having practiced this kind of exercise twice before, Victoire knew what to expect. It was difficult to listen to two conversations at once. And she feared she wouldn't be able to keep the sharply observant Montluzac from catching her in the act.

"Make your suggestions short."

"You know me. Frugal in all things."

"Cool it with the wisecracks."

She took a deep breath and pressed the doorbell. Georgette's husky voice answered the intercom.

"I'm buzzing you in."

Victoire opened the front door and climbed the steps to the apartment, where the former president's widow was waiting for her.

"Come in."

Victoire followed her into the dining room. In the mid-morning sunlight, the furniture and walls looked dusty. No sign of Claudine Montluzac. Victoire sat in the designated chair. Georgette, her features and expression fixed under heavy makeup, took a chair across from her.

"Did anyone follow you here?"

"I don't think so."

"You came by yourself?"

"Yes."

Victoire heard Luc. "Montluzac's in the other room—not even five meters away."

Victoire instinctively brought a hand to her ear, even though Georgette couldn't possibly have heard. Then she reached into her bag and pulled out Noblecourt's phone, still in the anti-tracking pouch. She removed the phone and set it on the table.

"Here's your husband's phone," Victoire said. "The one you gave me yesterday."

"Did you find anything interesting?"

"Last Thursday, your husband received some documents from an unknown sender. These documents may have triggered his flight to Kuala Lumpur. In addition, your husband called Béatrice and your brother while he was there. My associates believe he may have used other means of communication in Kuala."

Victoire slid the photographs of the chess match, the atomic clock, and Chronosphere's founder, Julien Lanfrey, toward Georgette. "These are the documents."

Georgette picked up the pictures and went through them one by one. Even the thick makeup couldn't mask her clenched jaw. Victoire thought she saw her hands tremble as she placed them down on the table.

"What does this mean?" Georgette asked.

"I don't know," Victoire answered, certain that she did, in fact, know what they meant.

Using a soft-questioning technique, Victoire explained the problem to the former first lady.

"You see, Georgette, it's not the chess match itself that's important—or the names of the players. The person who sent these photos to your husband wanted to draw his attention to the Asian spectators. Look. There are several very clear shots of them."

Victoire stood up and walked around the table. On her way, she glanced at the door to the hallway. Montluzac had most likely bugged the dining room so she wouldn't miss a second of their conversation. John could be right. The two women were possibly accomplices. But how could she know for sure?

Georgette examined the faces and turned to Victoire. "Have you identified them?"

"Our database hasn't been able to do that yet. John is planning to ask the Malaysian intelligence authorities for help. He's using the ambassador as an intermediary. It's absolutely imperative that we know who these people are."

"Yes it is," Georgette replied. "And you'll tell me once you find out, won't you, sweetie?"

"I promise."

Victoire thought she detected a glimmer of relief in the old woman's eyes.

"Let's see the other photos. What's this?" Georgette asked, pointing to the clock.

"We think it's an atomic clock made by the Chronosphere company. The founder is a man named Julien Lanfrey."

"What role does he play in all of this?"

"We don't know yet. If anything comes to you, please let me know." Victoire reached for her purse. "I'm going to your daughter's office now. I have some questions for her."

Georgette's face darkened. "What kind of questions?"

"The president's plane was attacked last night. He was allowing my associate, who's also my husband, to use it. He and the flight crew nearly died. Someone is feeding information to the people who killed your husband and his two bodyguards, and most likely those same people tried to take down that plane last night."

Georgette's face registered shock. It was hard to tell if she was being sincere or disingenuous. "I'm sure Apolline will help you. The president can't do anything. He's—" Georgette stopped in midsentence. "I hadn't heard about the attack on his plane."

"Yes."

Georgette looked back at the table and put her husband's phone on top of the documents. At that moment, Montluzac appeared in the doorway.

"Oh, so you're here already," Montluzac said, smiling. "Georgette said you were coming to fill her in on your progress, and since I was here to go over a few follow-up questions, I asked if I could stay until you arrived. I was just in the restroom."

"You're not going to believe this, Claudine," Mrs. Noblecourt said. "Victoire and I made a remarkable discovery while you were gone. I hadn't checked Pierre-André's coat. Imagine that. And there it was—his phone."

"My, that is remarkable," Montluzac said, still smiling. "Now I won't have to pester you anymore. And while I'm here, I have something for you, Victoire."

She reached into her pocket and pulled out the two-euro tracking device.

"I believe this belongs to you."

9

John stared at the ambassador's male personal secretary, dressed in a tight mauve sweater and white jeans. The man had come into his room without so much as a knock on the door.

"His Excellency is waiting for you," the secretary said in a monotone.

John hoisted himself up. He followed the secretary across the yard. The chirping of the birds wasn't as loud, but the cars had become even noisier. The quiet electric cars getting pumped out of Malaysian factories hadn't yet taken hold here.

The bad lighting in the ambassador's building verged on unsafe. Very few of the fixtures had bulbs. The young man opened a double door before bowing, as though he were escorting John into a temple.

"Mr. Spencer Larivière," the secretary announced.

John tried not to slip on the excessively waxed floor. Behind a massive desk surrounded by tropical plants, a gold-painted Buddha, and a fountain, the ambassador awaited him. The man had blond hair in a bowl cut, and his pale coloring made his red lips and heavy eyeliner look all the more gaudy. How had the Malaysians come up with that Grapefruit nickname? It was an insult to a perfectly fine citrus fruit. John had a vague feeling that the man was not only dangerous, but also disgusting. And he knew that fear-based repulsion toward shadowy figures was often warranted in the world of diplomats.

"Mr. Ambassador, I'd like to thank you for your hospitality." John sat down—without being invited to do so—in one of the wicker chairs.

Grapefruit let out a breathy question.

"Have you had a shower?"

John took a moment to respond, not sure where this was leading.

"No."

"I've got to have the plumbing fixed. Unfortunately, the government provides me with very little money to maintain this compound. If you could use your influence in Paris, I'd be quite grateful."

"I'll see what I can do."

John was trying to make eye contact with his host, but the man was staring at something. John looked around and discovered two mirrors reflecting the ambassador's image. Why hadn't he sent Luc here instead of coming himself? John pulled himself together and got to the point of the trip.

"Pierre-André Noblecourt was murdered shortly after he left your embassy. The president of France is expecting an explanation from you."

Nicolas Mortemar de Buzenval turned away from his reflection and stammered a response.

"I... I didn't know it was a murder. No one told me anything. How terrible. I wasn't given any specifics."

"That's why I'm here."

"Fine… But what can I do?"

"I have confirmation from the head of Malaysia's home affairs that Pierre-André Noblecourt was not on Flight 912. He led me to believe that Mr. Noblecourt's murderers live here. Do you have any idea who in Kuala Lumpur might have wanted him dead?"

John read fear in Mortemar's heavily made-up eyes.

"I don't know who could have hated him that much."

"Who did the former president meet with in Kuala Lumpur?"

"His son-in-law, Serge Roussillon."

"Would you be kind enough to let him know I'd like to see him? As soon as possible."

Mortemar pressed a button on his desk, and the secretary slinked in.

"Inform Serge Roussillon that Mr.—"

"John Spencer Larivière," John said, hardly surprised that the ambassador had forgotten his name.

"He'd like to see him immediately."

The secretary slipped around the tropical plants, the fountain, and the Buddha and whispered something in the ambassador's ear. Mortemar—aka Grapefruit—was staring intensely at John as he lent his ear.

"Lili tells me that Serge is expecting your call."

The young man slithered over to John. He handed him a business card with Serge Roussillon's name on it, as well as his title: "G. Terres French Representative in Putrajaya." John thanked him. This kid from the tropics was starting to get under his skin.

"Now I'd like to ask you a few more questions," John said. "Alone," he added, giving the secretary an icy look.

"Certainly."

The ambassador waved off his secretary, who glared at John on his way out.

"I'm listening."

John took out his phone and placed it on the desk.

"I'd like you to look at this list of passengers on Flight 912 and tell me if Pierre-André Noblecourt may have been waiting for one of them at Orly."

Nicolas Mortemar de Buzenval picked up the device and scrolled through the list, from first passenger to last.

"I don't see anyone who could have been linked to the former president."

"Really?"

The ambassador was shifting in his chair.

"I can tell you, however, that this list is incomplete."

"What do you mean by that?"

"A passenger is missing."

"How do you know?"

"Half an hour before Flight 912 took off, Emma Wong's secretary called to ask if her boss could use the seat reserved for the ambassador. I'm sure you're aware that Air France reserves a seat on each of its large carriers for any ambassador who's flying. Of course I agreed, since Mr. Noblecourt had told me he wouldn't be using my seat. She boarded a few minutes before takeoff. I didn't give Air France her name. It's not required."

"Who is Emma Wong?"

"Emma's a Malaysian lawyer and the daughter of a rich Chinese importer of tropical wood. Her family has roots in Malaysia and Singapore that are generations deep. She's very well known—what we call a Baba Bling."

"Excuse me?"

"A Chinese person who's a member of a rich family here in Malaysia. Lots of money."

"Did she know Mr. Noblecourt?"

"Yes. The former president and his wife had dinner in Kuala Lumpur a couple of times with her and other important Malaysian figures. Georgette Noblecourt is interested in helping the young girls who've been forced to work as sex slaves, and Emma has been working on their behalf for years. She's been trying to put the men who run the prostitution rings behind bars. She's had the support of the authorities here, most notably the minister of home affairs, who welcomed you. Do you think she died in the disaster?"

"I don't have confirmation, but I fear she was unable to escape."

"That's awful."

"Did anyone here have reason to kill her?"

"That might be the case. Emma didn't confine her efforts to children. For six months she had been working on a wrongful death case connected to Malaysia's purchase of two French submarines and some illegal kickbacks."

"Sounds very complicated. Tell me more."

"Yes, it can be complicated. Let me simplify. As you know, commissions are common in the military sector. Contractors pay them to political leaders and military officials who approve their bids. Very out in the open and legal. But sometimes a contractor has to sweeten the deal and make payouts—or kickbacks, if you will—under the table. Two years ago, France sold the navy two top-of-the-line Scorpène subs. Apparently, some people got those under-the-table payouts, and the sub captain was threatening to blow the whistle. His plan was short-circuited when he suddenly died. His family was pushing for a wrongful death suit."

"So why was Emma Wong involved? I thought she was a champion of women's rights."

"Yes, that was unexpected, but stranger things have happened in Malaysia. It's possible that she wanted to use the information to advance a personal agenda."

"So Emma Wong knew about these kickbacks."

"Of course. Consider her client. She probably knew even more than the captain's family did."

"Are you suggesting that someone here was trying to keep Emma Wong from sharing what she knew with higher-ups in Paris? That someone was making sure that she didn't arrive at Orly alive?"

"Someone either here or in Paris, my friend. Greed is a great motivator."

John was starting to piece together the catastrophe's actual narrative. The official version did, indeed, differ from reality. Pierre-André Noblecourt was never on that plane, despite what he had led his bodyguards to believe. Had he been waiting for Emma Wong at Orly? Or was it possible that he was waiting for her to die?

"What do you know about the Scorpène kickbacks?"

Buzenval sighed. He glanced at his reflection one more time before looking John in the eye. "As I suggested, I only know the generalities. Kickbacks and such are not my embassy's concern."

"But they do concern you. You are France's representative in Malaysia. Any misappropriation of French taxpayer money could be embarrassing for the president, who has been keeping you in your prestigious job here."

The ambassador squirmed. "I keep Paris informed at all times. But those submarine contracts were the domain of the Ministry of Defense, not the French embassy. My hands are clean."

"All right. Can you give me the names of some middlemen who can provide me with more information regarding the submarines?"

"Ask your colleague Dutreil. He knows a few wheeler-dealers. That's his job, after all."

"Have you heard any rumors about the former president—or his people—taking any kickbacks?"

"I don't listen to rumors. That's not what I was trained to do."

John saw the ambassador glance at a cube-shaped box on his desk. A silver bonsai similar to those he had seen at the French president's Trocadéro studio apartment was on top of it. Mortemar's box was most likely holding a few incriminating documents. John stood up without waiting to be dismissed.

"I'll let you know how the shower works."

10

Victoire spoke into the intercom, and the door opened at once. She entered and decided to take the stairs instead of the elevator. Since Alexandre's birth, she hadn't had enough time for swimming, running, or yoga. She missed it. There was nothing like a nice jog or a few laps in the water.

After climbing three floors, she was greeted by a gendarme, who directed her to Apolline Roussillon's office. Apolline came to meet her and politely welcomed her into a sun-lit space. Victoire noted that she truly bore a strong resemblance to her father, although her coloring was paler. She had the same somber eyes.

"I know it's close to lunch, but could I offer you some coffee and pastries?"

"Just coffee would be fine," Victoire answered.

Apolline told her secretary to get them two cups of coffee and joined her on the couch.

"I don't know how to thank you for helping Béatrice."

"Of course. You've been through quite an ordeal. It was the least I could do."

Apolline looked tired and on edge. On Sunday, Victoire had assumed it was because her father had just died. But now she sensed that something else going on. Was she anticipating something bad? Like Georgette, might she keeping a secret? Victoire sighed. Like mother, like daughter.

Apolline affectionately took Victoire's hand. "I can trust you since you work for the president."

"Of course."

"I'm pleased that you get along with Béatrice so well. She's a bright and sensitive girl."

Victoire nodded and offered a sweet reply to reinforce the sense of intimacy.

"Yes, she's very smart and seems capable beyond her years. Please let me know if I can help your family in any way this week. But as I was saying over the phone, I've come here to speak with you about last night's attack on the president's plane.

I'm scared to death over what happened to John. Someone wanted to kill him."

"The president was informed immediately. He's been in touch with your husband and the flight crew, and the incident was given priority status. India's government said its missiles were sabotaged. And now I have confirmation from our own government."

"Oh, my God!"

"The president's chief defense advisor just called me. He knew I was meeting with you, and he gave me permission to share some information. Your husband was the target of a cyber attack. Control of the missiles was seized by malware."

"How is that possible?"

"Unfortunately, our civilian and military systems are being infiltrated with disturbing frequency. Factories are being tampered with from a distance. Trains are getting derailed. A month ago, every water purification plant that supplies Paris was shut down for half an hour. Luckily, the real reason never got out. The city just said they were doing maintenance. Can you imagine how people would have reacted if they had known the city's water plant was sabotaged?"

"But missiles—that's a big deal!"

Apolline leaned closer to Victoire and lowered her voice. "We are on the brink of a global crisis. Some sixty nations either have or are developing cyber weapons and tools for computer espionage—countries ranging from Bahrain and Ecuador to France, the United States, and China. Planes, military arsenals, water systems, broadcast networks—you name it—everything's vulnerable."

"This is almost beyond comprehension. So can you tell me who was responsible for the attack on the president's plane?"

Apolline paused.

"To tell the truth, we don't know. We're doing everything in our power to find out, but we're asking you to help. We need to know how this all went down."

"But you have satellites, diplomatic forces, intelligence agencies. How can you not know?"

"Yes, it does seem preposterous, doesn't it? With all our capabilities we shouldn't be so in the dark."

Victoire felt a deep hole opening underneath her. "Since we're speaking in confidence, I'd like to ask you something, Apolline."

"Go ahead."

"Were we hired because of your father's death or because of the attack on the Air France plane?"

"We think there's a connection between the Orly disaster, Dad's death, and one of the governments that has those cyberattack capabilities. Alain asked for your expertise after Mom's emergency call, but things snowballed."

Victoire took note. Apolline had just called the president by his first name. Her familiarity was all too natural.

"Mom told me you paid her a visit. What were you doing at our place?"

"Your mom didn't say?"

"Say what?"

Victoire didn't want to mention the phone. She'd let mother and daughter hash that out.

"Your mother wanted me to bring her up to speed on our investigation."

"And what did you tell her?"

"I told her we haven't gotten very far. So, I'll pick up Béatrice after school today if you'd like. Do you want me to bring her to your place?"

"No, I'm too overwhelmed with my father's arrangements and all the paperwork we need to take care of. And I'm tired. Please take Béatrice to her great-uncle's house. By the way, I got a call from Claudine Montluzac. She wanted to know where my father's phone was. Do you have any idea?"

Victoire lied in the same way the Noblecourts lied—with ease and a smile. "Your mother found it in one of your father's coat pockets, of all places."

"Well, maybe we should have looked there first. Anyway, can I be of assistance to you? Perhaps provide some information that would move your investigation along?"

"Yes, you could help. Your father founded G. Terres with a few other heads of state. My associates and I think his death might be linked to that organization. It's based in Kuala Lumpur."

"The G. Terres headquarters are in Putrajaya. It's a new city. One crops up every day in Asia."

"I believe your husband is more or less in charge of it."

Apolline flinched. The relationship between Béatrice's mother and father seemed as obscure as the relationship between all the other members of this family.

"Your husband will be meeting with Serge soon, and he'll explain how G. Terres works. Serge wanted to come back to Paris, but I suggested that he stay and welcome your husband. After the failed missile strike on the president's plane, we're convinced that Dad was murdered at home because he managed to survive the Orly disaster. Claudine Montluzac happens to agree."

Victoire didn't tell Apolline that her father wasn't on that fated flight. The Malaysian minister of home affairs hadn't yet informed the Élysée. Or maybe the French president was judging it wise to keep the Noblecourts out of the loop. With the media's help, the politicians and police authorities were still pushing the story of a heroic former president who escaped the flames while carrying a child in his arms—a former president who was later found dead in his home.

Victoire was considering the disastrous consequences of challenging the official version. For now, it was better to keep her mouth shut, just as her mother had taught her.

Apolline's secretary arrived with a pot of coffee and two bone-china cups, along with cream and sugar. Apolline poured, and Victoire couldn't help noticing that her hand was trembling. The woman was clearly suffering.

"Can you tell me a little more about G. Terres?" Victoire asked, taking her cup.

"Yes. In creating G.Terres, the G20 member states wanted to deter speculation over rare earths. We're living in a time of speculative bubbles. They're making some people rich, but they're creating hardships for many others. In a worst-case scenario, a bubble can destabilize the global economy. We've seen them in the housing market, the Internet, and oil. China, Japan, and India are especially worried, not only about rare earths, but also about food. China once dominated the rare-earths market, but they got behind Dad's idea, too. In forming G.Terres, though, my dad made some fierce enemies. Certain financial institutions and individuals have a lot to gain when prices skyrocket, and, believe it or not, when they take a plunge."

"What about you—can you tell me what you're working on here?"

"I'm a chemist. Alain Jemestre asked me to spearhead our nation's strategy in the extraction and treatment of rare-earth elements. Basically, I coordinate research and information-sharing among the various private and public institutions working in the field, and I advise the president. Of course, our work here dovetails with what G.Terres is doing. There's someone like me at the highest levels of every member state."

"What about Serge?"

"Officially, my husband is G.Terres's French representative in Putrajaya, although he's also an advisor to the ambassador. He oversees France's participation in the organization. Each member state has a permanent advisor at the group's headquarters. There's a trading room in Putrajaya and another one here in Paris, at La Défense."

Apolline looked at her watch. Victoire asked a final question.

"A lawyer by the name of Emma Wong was on Flight 912. What can you tell me about her?"

Apolline replied instantly. "Do you know if she survived?"

"No, I'm sorry. I don't."

"I certainly hope she's one of the lucky ones. Emma's a wonderful person. She's a well-known lawyer in Malaysia and has worked tirelessly to put an end to sex slavery, especially the prostitution rings offering very young girls. My parents have supported her efforts for many years. I'm not surprised that my dad and she were traveling together."

Apolline seemed sincere and ignorant of the fact that her father wasn't on that plane.

"I heard that Emma Wong was filing a wrongful death charge in the case on behalf of the Malaysian marine officer who died in custody. He was allegedly threatening to blow the whistle on some high-ranking people over kickbacks related to the purchase of two French submarines."

"My father supported Emma's campaign to end sex slavery. He had integrity. If he had gotten wind of any high-level kickback scheme, he would have come down hard on any French involvement."

"Do you think it might have had something to do with his death?"

"Are you thinking a French politician could be behind this?" Apolline smiled and sipped her coffee.

"Yes."

"Our politicians are as corrupt as any others—no surprise there. But they're way too incompetent to commit murder. Don't overestimate them. I see them every day. They're like house cats. They're cool and full of themselves, but they're harmless. That said, avoid them. They shed and claw the furniture."

Victoire smiled. "Maybe it was Malaysian politicians?"

"Now that's something to consider, but still, I don't see it. Why go to the trouble of killing an ex-president? Or a current one, for that matter. In Asia, you don't have to bother. Corruption's a way of life. Are you sure you can't stay for another cup of coffee?"

"It makes me too edgy."

"I can't live without it."

11

Back home, Victoire took in the sight of Alexandre snoring lightly on his grandfather's shoulder. The decimated-car images on the touchscreen wall were a jarring contrast to the calm at Fermatown.

"I thought he was at Roberta's place."

"Roberta brought him back here so she could run to the store for formula and diapers," her father said. "You were out."

Victoire picked up her son, feeling guilty that she hadn't thought to replenish his supplies. "Come here, little man."

In the kitchen, she found Roberta preparing a bottle. She didn't turn around when she heard Victoire come into the room.

"The attack on the Pont Saint Michel—is that your problem too?"

"I know. I'm an awful mother. And I'm so sorry I made you go shopping."

"Not to worry, Victoire. I'm taking Alexandre back to my place. Just please do me a favor. I'm very attached to this little guy. Make sure he chooses a boring career when he grows up. Persuade him be an accountant, or an actuary, or a software engineer."

"Good suggestions, Roberta."

"Luc's back. He seems all worked up about something."

"Okay. I'll go talk with him. But first I'll walk you over to your apartment."

Victoire, Roberta, and the baby went down the stairs to the ground floor, where the garage was located. Victoire opened the door leading to the courtyard abutting Roberta's building. As they headed across the grass, Victoire could hear the muffled sounds of cars heading past the Montparnasse cemetery.

"Thanks again," she said when they reached their destination. "It won't be much longer. I promise."

She handed over the baby and turned around, muttering as she walked back to Fermatown. During her pregnancy, John had promised to work out a schedule that was compatible with raising their child. She was mad at herself for believing him. And why was it that she was the one feeling guilty about foisting Alexandre on a benevolent neighbor? Why didn't he feel bad?

Victoire was in no mood to face her father's and stepmother's judging eyes. She went straight up to the top floor and pushed open the door to Luc's lab.

"So you had some excitement at police headquarters," Luc said.

"You're right. The interrogation was the least of it. The explosion—so much blood. I thought I was going to get sick. And the Saint Michel bridge and square are unrecognizable now."

"I'm so glad you're okay. And everything at the Noblecourts? You gave the widow her husband's phone?"

"Yeah. And guess what, Montluzac returned the tracking device I slipped into her pocket."

"Well, let's give credit where it's due. We're dealing with a smart cookie. Better watch our step. So, how was your visit with Apolline Roussilon?"

"She thinks some foreign government's connected to what's going on. But the question is: what foreign government? You wouldn't believe how many countries have cyber-weapon capabilities and what they can do, Luc. It's terrifying. What kind of world have we brought Alexandre into?"

"Now, now, Victoire. We can't give into our fears. You know that."

Luc, who was ten years her junior, was the little brother she never had. He didn't have to say a word for her to understand how much he cared about her, and she would have been embarrassed if he ever did say anything. Victoire pulled a chair up to the big table cluttered with various gizmos and computer screens and felt herself let go. It had, indeed, been a hard day.

"Shedding a few tears is good for the soul," Luc said, grabbing a tissue and handing it over.

Victoire dabbed her eyes and blew her nose. "Okay, I'm done. What about Emma Wong? Are you on that?"

"I almost forgot. I called her offices in Kuala Lumpur again. I pretended I was from Val-de-Grâce Hospital. I told them we were trying to identify the bodies. I also said there were survivors."

"You're horrible."

"Yep. They told me that her father was coming in after hours, and I should call back. Let's do it."

Luc selected a phone from his never-been-used collection. After turning on the speaker function, he entered the number for Emma Wong's law office in Malaysia.

Victoire could hear the dread in the man's voice.

"Have you found my daughter?" he asked in flawless French.

"No, we can't give you any confirmation. We still haven't identified all the passengers. We have three survivors who are unconscious. Does Emma have any distinguishing features or specific physical attributes that could help us?"

"No, I can't think of anything. My daughter doesn't have any flaws. She hasn't had any surgeries, at least not that I know of."

The man's voice was shaky, and Victoire was getting angry. She couldn't imagine being on the other end of a call like. She stood up and walked away while Luc kept up the charade.

"What was your daughter doing in Paris?"

"She had a meeting with someone important."

"The former president of France?"

"I don't know, sir."

"Where was your daughter supposed to be staying?"

"She always stays at the same hotel near the Élysée."

"Which one?"

"Hold on. I'll ask."

Victoire had turned back around. Luc avoided her eyes. The silence between Paris and Malaysia lasted several seconds.

"Le Bristol on the Rue du Faubourg-Saint-Honoré."

"I'll keep you updated."

Luc ended the call and looked at Victoire.

"You know what I'm thinking, don't you?"

"Yes, and I won't do it. I'm done playing spy girl. I'm sick of your bullshit tactics."

Luc brought up a picture of Emma Wong on the computer screen.

"She's Chinese—kinda looks like you. She's beautiful, not as beautiful as you, of course. You could dress like a fancy lawyer and easily pass for Emma. Then you could pay a visit to her room at the hotel. Who knows what you might find? Maybe somebody's even expecting her. Other than us, that person at her law practice, and her father, no one knows she was on that plane."

"The Malaysian minister of home affairs knows she was."

"John asked him to keep the information a secret. And he agreed."

"You two are the worst! The person who was supposed to meet with Emma knows what happened to that plane. He's not waiting for her."

"It's worth a try. You never know."

"You're going to drive me insane." Victoire stood up. "By the way, did you know that G. Terres has a trading room at La Défense?"

"No, I didn't, although it does make sense. A room in Malaysia and another one here would allow them to trade round-the-clock."

"So what's with your clockmaker?"

"I'm working on Chronosphere. Meanwhile, I haven't found anything on the submarines or the Indian missiles that almost blew up John's plane."

"Find something. I'm anxious as hell."

"Go to Le Bristol. It'll be fun—honest. But before you check out your closet for a lawyer-type outfit, I need you to write me a letter in Chinese for my clockmaker. John wants me to buy him out."

"Yet another scheme. What am I going to do with the two of you?"

"You know we'd be nothing without you. That's why you love us."

"Stop it."

12

John was letting his ex-colleague Dutreil be his guide—in a Peugeot lent to them by Grapefruit. Their destination: one of the best restaurants in Kuala Lumpur, a small gem with colonial architecture nestled in a house ridiculously out of place among all the skyscrapers.

"This is Malaysia—Buddhist temples, mosques with minarets, and pink evangelical churches cheek by jowl with soaring office buildings. It's a shock at first. But you get used to it. Look at all the folks on the café terraces. They're enjoying themselves. Life is good."

John couldn't disagree when he surveyed the restaurant Dutreil had taken him to. Chinese lampshades gave it a romantic glow, and, indeed, couples all over the place were engaged in the art of seduction. Women in long flowing dresses and plunging necklines were sitting across from well-off-looking men wearing Rolex watches and tailored suits. John soon realized that he and Dutreil were the only same-sex diners.

A creature straight off a Bollywood movie set welcomed Dutreil like a prince.

"Follow me, gentlemen."

John and Dutreil trailed the man to the appointed table, where each of the red velvet chairs looked like it could accommodate two people. John unfolded his napkin and got down to business.

"Do you know someone named Emma Wong?"

John saw Dutreil's jaw muscles clench.

"Emma Wong is a famous lawyer here. She's a champion of children who've been forced into sexual slavery. High government officials all over the world support her cause. Lately, though, she's been working on something else, a case that's related to Malaysia's purchase of two Scorpène subs. It's all very complicated, and it's gotten a bit tricky—for her and for us."

"Tell me more."

"Malaysia purchased two French Scorpène submarines two years ago. It was a deal worth more than a billion euros, and the contractors paid out millions in legal commissions. But some higher-ups who thought they didn't get enough or didn't get anything at all started pressuring the contractors. Soon under-the-table payouts were passing hands. You know—kickbacks. A well-connected marine captain who knew all about it was blackmailing the brass. When he got caught, he unexpectedly died in custody. His family brought a wrongful death case, which was threatening to bring all the dirty little secrets out in the open. Emma Wong represented the family."

"What was the embassy's part in the sale and the aftermath?"

"Grapefruit told me to keep my distance. He's such a weak-ling. And to be honest, I get the feeling that he's scared—real scared. He doesn't even go into the city anymore. But I've been keeping Méricourt up to speed."

"You think Grapefruit's involved in this?"

"I don't have the proof, but I wouldn't be surprised if he was."

"Did Noblecourt meet with Emma Wong during his stay in Kuala Lumpur?"

The worker bee cracked a knowing smile and gave his folded napkin an impressive snap. An officer's mess-hall habits were diehard.

"I'm going to find out," Dutreil said before downing his whole glass of water.

"Emma Wong and Noblecourt probably discussed the sub-marine issue," John said. "And maybe the rare-earth-metals situation too. How well acquainted are you?"

"Well enough to meet with her again," Dutreil said, look-ing amused.

"That'll be tough—she died at Orly."

In seconds, Dutreil's face turned flaccid. The man froze for a long, silent minute. Then, without a word, he leaped up, knocking over the table with his knee. As the dishes, the glasses, and the silverware flew with an ear-shattering crash, the worker bee disappeared out the restaurant door, melting into the crowded street.

John leaped up and could feel the eyes of everyone in the dining room.

13

Luc walked into a courtyard. To his right were apartment buildings covered with climbing geraniums and trumpet creepers. To his left were Chronosphere's premises, with assembly space on the first floor and offices on the second.

He found the entrance. A fortyish woman sat behind a reception desk, surrounded by plants and vintage grandfather clocks. A showcase displayed the most beautiful collection of pocket watches Luc had ever seen. He walked over to the display to get a better look.

"These are amazing," he said, turning to the receptionist. "Are they real?"

"The real deal. Each and every one."

"Well, you're someone who never has to ask for the time," he said, grinning. "So, I'm Luc Racine, here to see Mr. Lanfrey."

"He's not here. What is this regarding?"

"I represent the Hoang Ho firm from Shanghai. We're interested in a business arrangement with Chronosphere."

The secretary nodded and gave Luc a once-over. He was sporting a two-button Brioni jacket in lightweight woolen silk—a splurge Luc had chalked up as a business expense. His aim was to present himself as wealthy, confident, and on trend—a man from a firm with the means and discernment to acquire a company like Chronosphere, which was richer in talent than cash.

"Mr. Lanfrey is busy at the moment, but I'll see if we can squeeze you in. Perhaps sometime next week? Have a seat. Would you like some coffee? Maybe some water? Our AC's broken."

"I'm fine. Thanks."

The Shanghai name, packaged in the promise of a much-needed cash infusion, had the effect of shaking up the most set-in-stone schedule. Luc heard the receptionist whispering on the phone and kept one ear perked while he examined the posters on the walls, which featured Chronosphere's products: precise measuring instruments, athletic stopwatches, metronomes, and atomic clocks. Luc immediately recognized the yellow atomic clock. It was the same one he had seen in the photo—a photo that he now believed was sent by Emma Wong. The clock he was looking at had been photographed in a different location.

"Sir?"

Luc tore himself away from the atomic clock and turned to the receptionist.

"Yes?"

"Mr. Lanfrey is waiting for you on upstairs. I'll take you."

Luc followed the receptionist into the factory area, where workers in white lab coats hovered individually and in groups over timekeeping devices in various stages of development and assembly. Everything was spotlessly clean, worthy of the high-precision mechanisms that had earned Chronosphere worldwide recognition. The receptionist and Luc walked up a set of stairs and down a hall to the director's office. When the door opened, Luc laid eyes on the same angelic face that Emma Wong had e-mailed to Noblecourt.

Julien Lanfrey looked like he'd come straight out of a Venetian fresco. Blond-haired, blue-eyed—and very comfortable in his own skin and clothes. So what was his connection to the former president of France? The head of Chronosphere rose from his chair and walked around his desk to greet his visitor.

Luc guessed that Lanfrey was no older than he was, but when he shook his hand, Luc realized that he wasn't dealing with a neophyte who had gotten in over his head. His handshake had energy and authority. This engineer would be harder to convince than Luc had assumed.

"Mathilde tells me you're from the Hoang Ho firm of Shanghai. I figured this must be serious, so I pushed back another meeting. Please, have a seat."

"Thank you for meeting with me on such short notice."

Luc sat down in a brown-leather chair across from Julien Lanfrey. He placed his briefcase on his lap and took out two documents—a Chinese version and its English translation—which he handed to the head of Chronosphere.

"I didn't have time to ask for a French translation."

"No worries."

Luc felt nervous as he watched Lanfrey put aside the English translation to focus on the Chinese text. Victoire could speak and write in several Asian languages, but business jargon wasn't her specialty. The phone number on the cover page was a real number in Shanghai. In the event he called, a bypass would direct him to Victoire's cell. She could speak French with a lovely Chinese accent.

"I see you read Chinese."

"I started studying it after my last trip to Beijing, but I'm not fluent yet."

Lanfrey put down the documents and looked at Luc with a strange smile.

"If I understand correctly, your firm wants to buy me out. Why do you want Chronosphere?"

"You have an impressive reputation. Your company produces some of the most precise and advanced time-keeping pieces in the world. Perhaps *the* most advanced and precise."

"What will happen to my employees if I sell?"

"We'll pick up the best ones, after consulting with you, and offer them a promising future with us."

"Some of our production is in strategic sectors protected by the French government. I'm talking about our most-advanced products. There's a *savoir-faire* law that covers output that France wants to retain control over."

Luc gave him a cheeky smile.

"The Hoang Ho firm is very familiar with French law and dynamics. We'll receive exemptions in due time. But more important, we want you to know that it's not your machines, your patents, your name, the building, or your lab that intrigue us. We're focused on something else."

"So what do you want?"

"We acquire ideas, imagination, experience, a vision of future applications, ways to diversify and differentiate. We're looking well into the future, and your company can help us do that. These are far more valuable assets than your books would lead others—those with no insight or creativity—to believe."

"That's what I keep telling our accountants."

Luc tried to contain his rising excitement. It looked like he had the head of Chronosphere on the hook.

"The Hoang Ho firm doesn't pay much attention to the accountants of this world. Your financial situation is evident, but that doesn't mean anything."

Julien Lanfrey turned to one of the walls and pointed to a photo of two French swimmers wearing gold medals.

"I know why you're here, Mr. Racine."

"You do?"

"You see those two athletes?"

"Yes."

"Those French swimmers were both awarded gold medals for the hundred-meter backstroke at a meet in Shanghai. They finished within a hundredth of a second of each other. That's never happened before. Chronosphere was in charge of the timekeeping. I'm sure it grabbed your firm's attention."

Luc nodded as he inwardly kicked himself for doing a half-assed job of studying the Chronosphere file. He shrugged it off.

"Nothing gets by the Hoang Ho firm. We keep abreast of all the news."

"Unfortunately, it didn't get the kind of coverage that we would have liked. Marketing just isn't one of our strong suits. We know how to invent, but we can't sell. Technically, of course, we can do much better than a hundredth of a second. We've exceeded a thousand-billionth, and you couldn't begin to comprehend the applications we've come up with—in our minds, at least."

Julien Lanfrey glanced at his watch and looked at Luc with passion in his eyes. "It's two already, and I've got a very busy schedule this afternoon. What do you say we have a chat at my place after work? Maybe seven o'clock? I live at 18 Rue Vaneau. Does that work?"

"That works perfectly, Mr. Lanfrey."

"Call me Julien."

"And you can call me Luc."

Just as Luc was about to shake Julien's hand he noticed a small framed photo behind the director's desk. Julien's arm was around a handsome guy with dark hair and dark eyes. He was giving Julien an adoring look.

"Oh, that? An old flame. We've been over for some time now, but we're still friends."

Luc nodded, wondering just how friendly they were. Answering that question wasn't a priority at the moment.

14

As instructed, the two men left the metro station separately and continued to follow the directions fed into their earpieces. A third man—a security guard at La Défense—was waiting thirty feet from the Volonia Tower's main entrance. He was Southeast Asian, like them. They walked into the tower, pressing their badges against the recognition units.

The lobby was full of people. Unlike the Malaysians, the French were not yet using advanced biometric crowd-scanning systems. The country that had invented radio and movies was still living in the Middle Ages when it came to identification technology.

The two men merged with the crowd and got into an elevator, which whisked them to the fifty-second floor in less than a minute. They were the last to exit. They followed the security guard through a service door. Behind it was a stairwell leading to the last two floors, which were reserved for ventilation machinery and safety systems.

The security guard pointed to an emergency exit that was already ajar. "When you're done, take the stairs. It's a lot of floors, but you look like you're in good shape."

The men nodded. In theory, their mission today was an easy one and much more enjoyable than the one at Café les Mouettes.

The men made it to the building's windswept rooftop and found yet another door that led to a shed. Inside, there were two brand-spanking-new American M32 multishot grenade launchers, along with open boxes of high-explosive grenades. They armed themselves and went out to the parapet. The top floor of the Beau Paris Tower faced them at a distance of about three hundred meters.

The first man positioned his weapon's sight on the forty-ninth floor. The second set his line of vision on a maintenance facility just above it, on the tower rooftop.

A first grenade pulverized an expansive window. A cyclone of shattered glass shimmered in the light before raining down on the street below. Five more grenades zoomed into the now-open room.

Satisfied with his work, the first man stepped back and started putting away his equipment. The second man took his place and launched his first series of grenades, destroying the maintenance equipment on the rooftop and disabling all elevator and water systems.

15

Standing beside Pierre-André Noblecourt's naked and eviscerated body at the Paris morgue, Dr. Abel Liévin was initiating his external exam. He planned to take utmost care, as his findings would have lasting consequences—for the government, for the family, and for him as a professional. He asked Dr. Julia Paterson to join him in examining the body.

Working with Julia turned Abel on, not only because she didn't wear much under her lab coat, but also because she had observational powers as sharp as a scalpel. Julia and he were postmortem imaging experts who specialized in virtual autopsies. Using a combination of CT and MRI imaging, surface scanning, and guided biopsy and angiography, they could produce a perfect 3-D image of a body that could be archived and analyzed elsewhere. Their hands-on and virtual examinations yielded irrefutable documentation.

The two owned shares in a company that spread the gospel of virtual autopsies. They presented seminars throughout Europe and had already published a textbook. They were counting on Noblecourt's suspicious death to make their brand even more recognizable in the cold world of death investigation. It was a once-in-a-career event, one that called for a meticulous PR plan. Fortunately, Julia did not lack imagination.

Before moving on to the virtual autopsy, Abel examined the victim's neck and larynx one more time. Traces of strangulation left by the rope were clearly visible. Pierre-André Noblecourt had most certainly been hanged. There was no doubt.

Abel was furious that he hadn't been called to the crime scene. The on-duty coroner who was present when the body was removed had run to the bathroom to throw up as soon as she arrived at the institute. She was an incompetent. Luckily, staff members had immediately contacted Abel and Julia. They knew that any foul-ups could come back on them.

Abel examined Noblecourt's nose, mouth, and ears in search of any traces of chemical or anabolic products. Then he moved on and checked under the fingernails of Noblecourt's left hand.

He was lifting the other hand when Julia broke his train of thought.

"Does it seem hot in here?"

Abel looked up from the corpse. His colleague, lover, and business partner had a sweaty forehead.

"Yeah, I'm hot. Go check the lab to see if the AC's acting up. And while you're at it, find out if the blood-test results are in. I'm having doubts."

"Do you think he was drugged?"

"It's possible. What was the name of the police chief on duty that night?

"Claudine Montluzac."

"Why isn't she here?"

"No idea."

Abel leaned over the body again while Julia went into the lab. Something wasn't right. He was supposed to have pictures of the body from the crime scene and they were nowhere to be found.

In her police report, Claudine Montluzac had claimed, without proof, that Noblecourt had been hoisted five and a half feet off the floor against his will. A man of his size would have sustained more bruising, because he surely would have put up a fight. Either this Montluzac woman was a liar and trying to cover up a suicide as a murder, or the former president was drugged—maybe even hypnotized.

Abel remembered a case from a psychiatric hospital. A patient had hypnotized another resident and forced him to hang himself in the showers. As soon as they completed the imaging, he would have a heart-to-heart with this Montluzac woman. A poorly executed investigation could contaminate all eventual data. And the damage would be difficult to reverse.

He was dictating his findings into his hands-free wireless recording device when Julia returned.

"What's the problem? It's boiling in here!"

"You wouldn't believe it in there. The lab assistant's running from one hot plate to another, trying to turn them off. As soon as she turns one off, more flame up. The system's derailed. It's got a mind of its own!"

No sooner had she said this than Abel smelled the characteristic odor. A gas leak. He dropped his tools and grabbed the assistant's arm, but it was too late. The explosion sent them flying. It ripped off their lab coats and enveloped everything in an incandescent cloud. In less than a minute, the Paris morgue on the Quai de la Rapée was nothing but a flaming fire pot in the middle of Paris.

16

Victoire heard the sirens in the distance and prayed that another disaster hadn't happened. She put it out of her mind and walked through the revolving door of the Bristol, a bellhop on her heels. She descended a few steps to the lobby and headed toward the reception desk. As she walked past a mirror framed by two columns, she checked her makeup, which accentuated her Asian features. With the help of Google images, she had managed to create a pretty spot-on look.

Fortunately, she and Emma Wong were the same size. The Chinese Malaysian exuded an elegance, sophistication, and exoticism that turned the heads of Frenchmen. After a few deep yoga breaths, Victoire approached the desk.

"Good morning. So happy I finally made it."

The young man at the reception desk gave her a polite smile. "May I have your name please?"

Victoire tried to mask her anxiety. He didn't recognize her. She was supposed to be a regular here. Was her impersonation that far off? "Emma Wong. I was supposed to arrive yesterday, but had to reroute through London, with the airports here being closed."

The receptionist consulted his computer screen. "Yes, we have your reservation."

She heard a voice behind her. "Ah, Ms. Wong, what a pleasure to see you."

Victoire turned around and saw the maître d'hôtel, cinched in a gray jacket with silver buttons. He joined the receptionist and took over with the assurance of a pilot-in-command.

"Please excuse Mr. Dupré. He's new here. I'm sorry to say your usual suite overlooking the courtyard was booked, but I saved you the Murat suite. I'll show you to it."

"Thank you."

Victoire was guided to the Murat suite, which had a sitting area dedicated to the military glories of the French Empire and a horse-artillery-themed bedroom.

"The décor is a bit on the masculine side. Our interior minister likes it."

"He stays here often?"

"On occasion," the maître d'hôtel replied, glancing at the portrait of a young lieutenant grappling with a canon deep in the Russian countryside. The soldier's manly warmth filled the suite for an instant.

"Please enjoy your stay."

"Thank you."

Victoire sat down on the plush sofa situated between two battlefields and tried to make sense of the predicament she'd gotten hustled into.

As she gazed at the heroes of the Battle of Borodino, there was a knock on the door. She let the assistant concierge in. He set her luggage on the floor and handed her a package and a white envelope.

"This is the package that you sent us from Kuala Lumpur. A gentleman dropped the envelope off this morning. He was also under the impression that you'd be arriving tomorrow."

Victoire took the two objects and searched the bottom of her bag for a twenty-euro bill, which she gave to the young man.

"Thank you, ma'am. Our hair salon and fitness center have been completely renovated since last year. I was told there's an opening between seven and eight tonight—which never happens."

Victoire searched her bag for another bill while maintaining eye contact.

"The man who brought this envelope—what did he look like?" she asked, handing him the additional bill.

He slipped both bills into his pocket and leaned closer.

"I'd never seen him before. He seemed to be in a hurry."

"Is that so. Thank you."

After the young man left, Victoire walked to the window overlooking the Rue du Faubourg Saint Honoré and opened the envelope.

A phone number on the back of a postcard accompanied a message. "Call me ASAP. I'll be assuming responsibility for the French operations. Céladon."

Victoire turned the postcard over. It was an aerial view of La Défense.

The package contained two manila envelopes. She opened the bigger one first. Inside were several photos and newspaper clippings. Each had something to do with a catastrophic event. Laying them out on the bed, she saw photos and articles about a shipwreck, a railway accident, a mining fire, and a factory explosion in different parts of the world. Some lives had been lost, but not many. Victoire didn't know what to make of it.

She opened the second envelope and found the same photos that had been sent to the former president. They were all there: the chess match, the atomic clock, and the portrait of Chronosphere's CEO, Julien Lanfrey.

Victoire call Luc. "You've got to come over here."

"There's no time. I'm heading over to La Défense—that's where G. Terres has that second trading room. Turn on your TV."

Victoire switched on her television. The roof and top floor of the Beau Paris Tower were letting off a thick cloud of smoke that was drifting south. She turned up the volume.

"Fortunately, there were no fatalities," she heard a reporter say. "All the residents of the tower were able to evacuate in time. An unoccupied luxury apartment was on the top floor. The destroyed machinery on the rooftop was connected to the elevator and water-supply systems. So far, no one has claimed credit for the attack."

Victoire turned back to the bed and picked up a few of the news articles. The words spoken by the France 2 reporter were echoed in the stories: "No fatalities."

Apparently, Emma Wong was in the process of investigating a series of bizarre events that were catastrophic yet didn't claim many victims. But other than that, what did a grounded Maltese cargo ship have to do with a blown-up apartment at the top of a skyscraper?

She looked at the postcard again. It showed La Défense. What did that mean? Who was this Céladon, and what were the "French operations"?

She picked up her cell and logged into an identification app that listed phone numbers from the Les Invalides files. Fermatown had permanent access to Méricourt's powerful software.

The app immediately identified Céladon's number. It belonged to the facility management of Palatinate, a new and very powerful European credit-rating agency established to counterbalance America's dominance in this arena.

Palatinate had just opened its headquarters in Aachen, Germany, and had offices in various European capitals, including Paris, on the Rue de Penthièvre, steps away from the Élysée. Victoire couldn't find any Céladon on the board of directors. Most of them were well-known economists and analysts. Then she started going through the names of the agency's top officials, and right away one jumped out at her: Charles-Laurent Donnadieu, forty-two years old, the budget minister's former right-hand man. After leaving the government, he had taken a high-level job at an investment bank in Luxemburg. He had a suitable profile for someone directing this agency and was a pure product of the French establishment. He had to be Céladon.

Victoire found more information on the man. At the opening of the Paris office, Donnadieu had welcomed the minister of economy and finance, as well as the editors and publishers of several elite trade journals. Surrounded by his guests, the man seemed quite pleased with himself. So what would a representative from the Palatinate and a Chinese lawyer living in Malaysia be plotting together?

Victoire was both excited and intrigued. She calmed her nerves enough to take the plunge. She entered the number on her phone. "Might as well go all the way," she said to herself as she waited for a response. When someone on the other end picked up, she mustered a formal Asian tone.

"I wish to speak with Céladon…"

After three seconds of silence, a man replied, "Yes. We need to meet. I'm told you always stay at the Bristol."

"That's correct."

Victoire could feel herself slipping into Emma's skin, and Céladon seemed to be buying it. She used her advantage to dispel any doubts.

"I've never seen you in person, and I don't think you've seen me in person either."

"That's true. How are we going to do this?"

Victoire was thrilled. Céladon was an expert in the world of derivatives and sovereign debt, but he was a newbie in the world of intelligence. Still, she had to strike while the iron was hot. Her little charade could collapse at any moment.

"Meet me at the Bristol restaurant at nine thirty tonight. I'll find you. The meal's on me."

"I'll see you then."

Victoire ended the call. She was liking this Emma Wong more and more.

17

Luc weaved between the onlookers staring at the top floor of the Beau Paris Tower. The firefighters had contained the blaze, and he could see only a few wisps of smoke. He had learned about the G. Terres trading room just a few hours earlier. Now he wanted to know what kind of damage it had sustained.

When he reached the entrance, Luc calmly waited until the police officer stationed at the door turned his attention to a pedestrian, who claimed her father was stuck on one of the higher levels. While the officer called someone to check on the man, Luc slipped past him and entered the building.

Once in the lobby, he saw no signs of panic. A calm evacuation was under way, and the firefighters were already packing up their equipment. With the elevators blocked, Luc started climbing the stairs. Going up, he overheard the conversations of stragglers who were on their way down. No one understood why the terrorists had targeted the elevator and water-supply systems.

"Why not set fire to the whole tower?" he heard a woman ask.

Luc wondered the same thing. His phone rang just before he reached the fifteenth floor, and he was glad to take Victoire's call. It gave him a chance to catch his breath.

"Have they said anything on the news about the apartment on the top floor?" he asked.

"The last person to lease the space was a diamond merchant from Anvers. But he never set foot in the apartment. He died six months ago. In fact, the apartment's never been lived in."

"What does that mean?"

"I have no idea."

"This is so weird. No one died. And I heard someone say the elevators were actually in operation during the evacuation. They were running on an emergency generator. But now they're not running."

"And don't forget that the tower is home to G. Terres's second trading room."

"That's exactly why I'm here. I'm sure G. Terres was attacked in some way or another."

Luc began climbing the final floors to the G. Terres trading room. When he arrived at the glass door, he encountered a security guard with gray hair and the beginnings of a paunch. Worry was written all over the man's face.

Luc pulled out his phone and showed him the text message he had asked Victoire to send: "Ankle twisted and stuck on twenty-fifth floor."

"I'm worried about my girlfriend," Luc told the guard. "I just got this message. I have to find her."

"As far as I know, everybody's cleared out. A police detective was up here when it happened, and she was the last one to leave. I'm just on my way out too. I don't want to be around if those crazies attack the building again."

"You say a police detective was here before the attack? That's odd, isn't it?"

"How would I know? She said she was the head of white-collar crimes, and she wanted to speak with the director. Blond hair. A real looker. She got here about a half hour before all hell broke loose."

Luc couldn't believe it. Claudia Montluzac appeared to be conducting her own parallel investigation. But was she one step behind them or one step ahead?

The guard took Luc's elbow. "Now listen, we ought to get out of here."

"But I've got to check," Luc pressed. "My girlfriend's pregnant, and I'm worried that she couldn't make it down on her own."

"Okay, but let's make it quick."

The man opened the door and let Luc in. He followed the guard into the trading room, a large open-plan space with a spectacular view of La Défense and the rest of Paris.

"I don't understand how anyone could still be in here," the guard said. "I didn't lock the doors until everyone left."

"There's always someone who doesn't listen," Luc said. "I'm surprised at how normal everything looks in here. Did you get any damage?"

"No, none. The computers and other machines in the trading room kept on working. We didn't even hear anything. One of the firefighters said the terrorists were targeting the apartment on the top floor."

"Did any of the radio repeaters or other equipment on the roof belong to your floor?"

"No, none of it was ours. Like I said, we didn't have any disruptions. We were just asked to evacuate, and everything went smoothly."

As they were talking, the guard was opening one door after another and finding no one. He opened the door to the last office.

"There's no one here. Your girlfriend must have gotten out."

"That would be a relief. Thanks for your help. I'm just going to make a quick check one floor up to make sure she's not there."

18

On her way down the Boulevard Raspail, Victoire checked her cell. Roberta had sent her a video of Alexandre. He was in his bouncer, giggling away as he bobbed up and down. 'Say hi to Maman," she heard Roberta say. But instead of smiling, Victoire caught herself feeling irritated. Didn't Alexandre miss her just a little bit? According to Roberta, he had hardly even fussed. She stopped walking and chided herself. "You're being ridiculous," she muttered. "He's your little boy. He loves you and needs you." And Roberta's help was even more crucial now that her father and stepmother had taken the train back to Lyon. Victoire sighed and started walking again. She just wanted to get back to her nice life with her baby and husband.

But to do that, Fermatown needed to make money, and speaking of money, when would Méricourt be paying them? He always took too long. She planned to get her revenge that night at the Bristol restaurant by insisting that Céladon order the most expensive items on the menu.

A second cell phone in her bag started ringing just as she was turning onto the Rue Notre Dame des Champs.

"This is Claudine Montluzac."

Victoire felt a cold gust of wind on her face.

"How can I help you?"

"I'd like to put an end to this little cat-and-mouse game. I have some things I need to tell you, things that will be hard to hear. They won't make you happy."

"I'm used to that."

"Let's meet at the Mouettes bar at six thirty. Both of us will lay our cards on the table."

"I'm on my way to pick up Béatrice from school. I'll meet you there after I drop her off."

"Thank you."

Victoire stopped to collect herself and then headed toward a nearby pastry shop to get a boost of energy and call Luc.

"Guess who just called me—Claudine Montluzac," Victoire said, sitting down at a table with her *macarons*. "She's the last person I want to be meeting with right now."

"What a coincidence. Our police chief on duty and head of white-collar crimes was just at the Beau Paris Tower."

"You don't think she spotted you, do you? Is that the reason she wants to talk with me?"

"Don't worry, Victoire. There's no way she could have seen me."

"You've got to help me out here. She's going to shake me down. What was she doing at the Beau Paris Tower?"

Luc was silent for a few seconds.

"I don't know anything yet. She arrived shortly before the attack.

"Do you think she might have been the one directing the terrorists?"

"It's possible. But I've got my doubts. She is the head of white-collar crimes. It wouldn't be unreasonable for her to be checking out the G. Terres trading room."

"But moments before an attack?"

"You'll just have to make her talk, Victoire. Get her to fess up."

Victoire smiled despite herself. She could always count on Luc to lighten the mood. "You're such a jerk," she said.

"Yes. But a lovable jerk."

Victoire ended the call and ate her two confections. Satisfied, at least for the moment, she picked up her bag and left the shop.

With austere gray walls and barred windows, the Cadet's School on the Rue Notre Dame des Champs looked like an old convent. Victoire was about to enter the code when she heard her phone ring. It was Béatrice.

"Mom told me you'd be coming. Did she give you the code to get in?"

"Yes. I'm at the front entrance now."

"Come in. You have to see my school supervisor before they'll let me leave with you. You'll need to sign a paper. There've been kidnappings before."

The little girl's tone was so much like her grandmother's. How odd, coming from a child, Victoire thought. She entered the code.

The private school's large carriage entrance opened onto a wide walkway leading to a cloistered garden. Boys and girls of all ages were chatting on the grass. Others were reading on the carved stone benches. This was no typical schoolyard, with its shrieking and yelling and running. These children were quietly studying and having civil conversations. It was surreal.

Some of the students looked at her and smiled as she headed toward the supervisor's office.

A young woman in a navy-blue suit greeted her when she walked in.

"You're here to pick up Béatrice," she said. "Her mother told me you'd be coming. She must be so busy. I just can't believe the news. First Orly. Then the tower. Now I hear there's a fire at the morgue, where Béatrice's grandfather was undergoing an autopsy. When will it all end?"

"I wish I could tell you."

"Do you know if the body was removed in time?"

"I have no idea."

"I'll be right back."

Victoire had waited for only a minute when Béatrice came running in and wrapped her arms around her neck. Victoire's heart melted. When Alexandre was older, and life was sane again, she and John would try for another baby. She definitely wanted a girl. Victoire signed the required form and left with Béatrice. A harsh sun was beating down on the Rue Notre Dame des Champs.

Victoire had no intentions of telling the little girl about the fire at the morgue. That was something her family needed to do, if they said anything at all. She decided to talk about something more innocuous.

"That looks like a great school."

"It is nice, but it's not always fun."

"What grade are you in?"

"We don't have grades at Cadets."

"Really?"

"Everyone goes at their own pace in each subject."

"So a student could be behind other kids in one subject and ahead in another?"

"Yeah, that's about right. In math, I'm at the college-prep level. I'm taking engineering classes too. But in other courses I'm just a little ahead."

"You're already at college-prep level in math—and taking engineering classes?"

"I'm not the only one."

"But how old are you? Eight? Nine?"

"I'll be ten tomorrow!"

Victoire took Béatrice's hand before they crossed the Rue de Rennes and headed toward the Sèvres Babylone intersection. She couldn't believe that the nine-year-old walking beside her was already taking college-level courses.

"So you go to a school for gifted kids."

"Shh, you're not supposed to say that word. Our supervisor said we're just like other kids. I even know kids at my school who're dumber than my cousins."

"So tell me, Béatrice. Do you like any boys at your school?"

"Yes, I have friends who are boys. But not any boyfriends, if that's what you mean. I'm only nine, and Mom says I have lots of time for that."

Of course she was too young. Victoire felt stupid for asking the question.

"When you get together with your friends, what do you do?"

"Well, when it's girls, we talk about books: *Madame Bovary*, *Phantom of the Opera*, even some Camus. I have one friend who plays duets with me on the piano. When it's boys, we try to see who can identify prime numbers the fastest. It's so fun. It's like quantum physics."

"I see…"

Victoire marveled at this strange family she had stumbled upon: achievers, all of them. But they seemed to take their success and accomplishments for granted. In this family, it was expected.

Béatrice interrupted her thoughts.

"Did they find Grandpa's body at the morgue?"

"So you've heard what happened."

The little girl shrugged. "I check Twitter, just like you. You gotta keep up with the news, right?"

Victoire studied Béatrice for a moment. She didn't like this part of her job—not looking after a little girl who was pretty much forced to fend for herself at the moment, but instead, getting too intimate with the family, along with its secrets and heartbreaks. After her studies at the École Normale Supérieure on the Rue d'Ulm, Victoire had chosen intelligence because it allowed her to use her brain and appealed to her sense of patriotism. She wanted to give back to the country that had taken in her mother. But she had thought of it as an intellectual and impersonal pursuit.

She answered Béatrice. "I don't know if they found your grandfather's body."

The little girl's face turned sober.

"It was definitely no accident."

"Why do you say that?"

"Because Ninjutsu and Aikido's car got blown up too."

"But tell me. Why would they blow up the morgue and Ninjutsu and Aikido's car?"

"I don't know about the morgue. But as far as the car goes, they wanted to steal Grandpa's smartphone—no, destroy Grandpa's smartphone so no one would see what he was saying or what people were telling him."

Victoire felt a chill run all the way down her back.

"Do you think your grandpa's bodyguards had his phone when their car was blown up?"

"Obviously."

"How do you know?"

"Grandma told me. I called her before I left for school this morning."

Georgette's lie wasn't surprising, but it made Victoire nervous. As they crossed the Rue de Babylone, she glanced behind her.

"Are you afraid we're being followed?"

"I'm being careful, that's all…"

"Do you think they'll try to kidnap me? So they can have a ransom? How much do you think I'm worth?"

"A lot."

"A lot isn't a number. But I don't think they need the money. They're probably not poor."

"Who's *they*?"

"The people responsible for all the killing."

Victoire didn't like the way this conversation was going. She took another tack.

"You loved your Grandpa…"

"Yeah, he was nice. Every time he went away, he'd bring me a present. I usually asked for a panda. Not a real panda, a stuffed one. The last time, though, he didn't bring me one. It didn't matter. I was just glad whenever he came home."

Victoire saw tears running down Béatrice's cheeks, and all she wanted to do was scoop her up and whisk her off to Fermatown, where she'd protect the child and send her to a school where kids were free to run and scream. But she couldn't.

They had arrived at Titus Polycarpe's dark apartment. She entered the code.

"Another night at Uncle Titus's place."

"It's for the best."

"The real Titus was a Roman emperor. They called him 'the delight of the human race.' Are you taking me to school tomorrow?"

"Yes."

As she bent down to hug the little girl, she saw something new in Béatrice's eyes: a tinge of apprehension.

"I'll say good-bye here. I've got an important meeting to go to."

"With whom?" Béatrice asked.

"With Claudine Montluzac. I believe you've met her."

"Yes, I know her," Béatrice replied. "She does what she can with what she's got. I think she's lonely. Maybe she got her wings burned. Doesn't matter what you do in the world—you gotta be good at playing politics. Will you tell me how it goes?"

"Yes, of course I will."

Victoire handed over the girl and headed toward Café les Mouettes. As she walked, she worried. Even a bright and beloved little girl could get lost in a world where she was always getting handed over to someone else.

19

"This is where the woman was murdered." Claudine Montluzac pointed to a chalk outline on the Café les Mouettes floor.

"The two killers looked either Indian or Indonesian, according to one of our witnesses. So what do you think?" she asked, turning to Victoire. "I figure after what we've been through together, there's no need to be so formal with each other. Right?"

"Sure," Victoire replied.

Her stomach was churning at the sight of this place, where two people had been killed. A double homicide that Luc and she were partially responsible for. Her hand started to tremble, and she squeezed the glass of water that an officer had given her. She improvised an emergency breathing exercise to maintain an impassive expression. Montluzac, elegant and determined, looked at her before continuing.

"When I got here yesterday, I collected every fingerprint from all the glasses and bottles that hadn't been washed. That's standard protocol."

Victoire lifted her glass as a sign of agreement.

"So naturally, you found mine…"

"Indeed."

Victoire no longer had a choice. It would be useless to beat around the bush.

"Okay, you got me. Georgette said she found the phone in her husband's coat pocket. But you know I had it. Georgette said she didn't trust the police—you, specifically. Then she changed her mind and wanted the phone back. You were at her residence when I returned it."

"Yes, I was. An unnecessary little game."

"So I'm assuming you've examined the phone and know what was on it."

"We've found photographs of a chess match and an atomic clock. We've also found a picture of Julien Lanfrey, the head of Chronosphere. They'd been sent to the former president just before his flight to Malaysia."

"And?"

"And I don't understand any of it," Montluzac responded. "We're trying to identify the Asians who were watching the chess match, but all Chinese people look alike."

Victoire recoiled.

"I'm sorry. I didn't mean to insult you. Anyway, I know you're Cambodian, not Chinese."

"Franco-Cambodian," Victoire said. "I take after my mother more than my father, although I do have his height. It makes me look a bit Manchu. My father's family wasn't aristocratic, but one of his ancestors was a baron and fought with Lafayette against the English."

"So tell me. Why did Méricourt put you on the case?"

"Méricourt, like Georgette, doesn't trust the police. He's always worked in the world of intelligence. He wants to get at the truth right away. He's not a fan of waiting around."

"He's got a point. I don't trust the police either."

Victoire couldn't believe it. "If you don't trust your own colleagues, then what are we doing?"

"The former president's homicide is stirring up a lot of crap. I've already stepped down. I gave my boss my report this morning. An examining magistrate has been appointed. I'm returning to Nanterre to handle my white-collar cases."

"But you're still working in the shadows. Wouldn't you consider that going rogue?"

"Victoire, we're both working in the shadows. But if we don't continue this together, I doubt the justice system will find the truth. The investigating magistrates are already battling over the police unit that should be leading the investigation—antiterrorism or homicide. One of the magistrates even wants to press charges against a colleague of mine who's been working the case. There's going to be blood on the steps of the Palais de Justice. The search for truth isn't off to a good start."

"What can we do?" Victoire asked.

"Pierre-André called me from his home right before his Paris flight left for Kuala Lumpur. He was very shaken up. I remember his exact words: 'They've ruined G. Terres.'" Montluzac paused. "I'm sure you're familiar with G. Terres by now."

Victoire locked eyes with her. "What do you think he meant?"

"Pierre-André was certain that the information system in the Putrajaya trading room had been hacked in some way."

"What does Noblecourt's son-in-law think?"

"Pierre-André went to find out, but really, Serge Roussillon is a playboy. He's only interested in tennis and girls."

"Could he be mixed up in this?"

"Anything's possible," Montluzac said. "But I don't think he has the capability. Also, the Malaysians are watching him, and according to Pierre-André, the French ambassador is also watching him. I think it would be hard for him to pull off this kind of scheme."

"What about Apolline. How's she doing?"

"Let's just say she's making do."

"That woman's exhausted," Victoire said. "She seems broken."

"Apolline and Serge had a son before they had Béatrice. He died when he was just three years old—a congenital illness. It drained the couple, especially her. It's really sad, because she's a wonderful woman."

"What about Béatrice?"

"She's their second-chance child. Apolline underwent gene therapy, and Béatrice did, too, before she was even born. Very cutting-edge stuff. Anyway, she was perfectly healthy at birth and continues to be so. Actually, she's quite gifted. Pierre-André was crazy about her."

"So it wouldn't have been unusual for him to call her from Kuala Lumpur?"

"Not in the least."

"Since we're on the same team now, tell me: what exactly are you trying to do?" Victoire asked.

"I'm the head of the financial-crimes unit. For two years, I've been trying to build a case against Pascal Massicot."

"The defense minister?"

"Yes. That asshole and his friends meddle in our business all the time, especially the export-related cases. As defense minister, Massicot is Méricourt's boss. And Méricourt just hired your firm. You can see why I'm suspicious. I've got a lot of enemies, and I don't know the first thing about international relations."

"Still, you're close to some pretty powerful people."

"Fortunately, I do have some important friends. Francis Béard, who's in charge of the Directorate for Defense Protection and Security, would just love to get something on Massicot."

Victoire knew about Béard. French intelligence was a small world, and Béard and Méricourt were two top guns whose mutual admiration matched their rivalry. She nodded.

"You're aware of how things work in the government," Montluzac continued. "It's all complicated. Even though Alain Jemestre and Pierre-André have never liked Massicot either, the man has his own allies. The president gave me his blessing to go after Massicot, quietly of course, but I've been getting the feeling that I've lost some of his support."

"Why would that be?"

Claudine Montluzac took a moment to reflect.

"I don't really know. This has gotten bigger than I ever expected. Massicot's involved in a whole lot more than ordinary corruption. Just look at what's happened. I'm scared that I'll run into something that's entirely out of my realm. I was hoping you might help."

20

Luc pulled the sheets over his naked body and stared at the ceiling of Julien Lanfrey's bachelor pad on the Rue Vaneau, a mix of precision time-keeping instruments and Michelangelo-style sculptures. The two men hadn't resisted temptation for more than a half hour. They had quickly thrown themselves at each other and stumbled from the living room to the bedroom, where they grabbled without skipping any positions. Julien, with a six-pack abdomen and sculpted arms to match, had given and taken ravenously. Rarely had a man provided Luc with such pleasure.

"That was good," Luc said. "Very good."

Julien was coming out of the bathroom, wrapped in a blue star-studded kimono. He looked like a Byzantine prince. He sat down next to Luc and pushed back the sheet. Luc liked the way Julien examined him from head to toe. He was getting aroused again.

"If you handled your business the way you handle me, you'd be rolling in dough."

"If only. So how much are your Chinese friends putting on the table to buy out my company?"

"They can put down a lot. It'll all depend on the audit, of course."

"And what's your role—other than seducing the boss?"

"I'm on the front lines. I clear the field before the financiers and technocrats show up. Audit days—like the ones you'll be going through—cost a lot. Hoang Ho doesn't like wasting money."

"So you're the foot soldier who's not above sleeping with the enemy."

"I wouldn't put it that way. Let's just say I'm scouting the territory. And I like the territory."

Julien Lanfrey grinned and fell back on the bed. Then his expression turned sober. He turned to Luc.

"I'm broke. Chronosphere doesn't have enough clients, and the government isn't meeting its obligations. They're broke too."

"But according to my research, you're able to pay on your loans every month. And with the salaries you're shelling out, plus your research costs, you should've been bankrupt ages ago. So it probably doesn't look as bad on paper as you think."

"Now you're trying to sweet talk me." Julien got out of bed and walked over to a window. Luc sensed he was looking at something or someone.

"Let's say I still have some savings and a few friends who believe in Chronosphere."

"Friends from the army?"

"What makes you say that?"

"High-precision time-telling has applications in the military world, right?"

"Not directly," Julien said. "In addition to what I told you earlier—about the timekeeping devices for athletic competitions—we work for aerospace—on probes for the Americans, the Russians, and the Chinese."

"Space probes?"

"When you send a spacecraft into the solar system, the slightest timing error could have serious consequences. If you're off by a hundredth of a second on Earth, you could be off by minutes out past Neptune and by hours beyond Pluto."

"Do you also work on weapons?"

"No."

"Submarines?"

"Not exactly. We've sent clocks to government agencies, but we never know what they do with them. If you buy a watch from us, I wouldn't know how you plan to use it. Same idea. Speaking of time, I'm expecting someone. You got me so excited, I left my phone at work. I asked a staff member to bring it over."

"Is that why you've been looking out the window?"

"Yes."

Luc decided to get to the heart of the matter.

"Hoang Ho heard that your company worked with Pierre-André Noblecourt."

Julien left the window and walked back to the bed.

"Those Chinese have damned good intelligence."

"I told you. Is it true?"

Julien grabbed one of Luc's ankles.

"I never met Noblecourt, but I know he was the one who started G. Terres. The organization needed clocks to coordinate financial transactions between their two trading rooms. One's in Paris, and the other's in Putrajaya. The Paris trading room operates when the Malaysian room is closed, and vice versa. The buy and sell orders can be executed twenty-four-seven. I submitted a bid and got the contract."

"You sent them some atomic clocks?"

"Yes, sir."

Julien's hand had now traveled past Luc's calf and knee. It was inching up the inside of his thigh. Luc was getting goose bumps.

"The distance between Paris and Putrajaya is nothing, compared with the distance between Earth and Neptune," Julien said. "A simple clock is sufficient. A ten-thousandth of a second accuracy is fully acceptable in digital banking. We only use the thousand-millionth of a second in the framework of discovery research—in particle physics and atomic-explosion simulations. I'm sure that's what interested your Mr. Hoang Ho. Have you ever slept with your Chinese pal?"

"He's not exactly my type."

"What if the client's a woman? Do you sleep with her too?"

"Yes."

"You're turning me on."

Julien was about to reach a crucial part of Luc's anatomy when someone knocked on the door. Julien pulled himself out of bed.

"Don't go anywhere."

Luc stretched out his legs. This assignment definitely had its benefits. Several minutes later he saw Julien's face and sat up.

"What happened?"

"It was Mathilde. The laser room at Chronosphere caught fire. Everything was destroyed, including my phone."

21

Having visited the Hôtel Bristol hair salon on the government's dime, Victoire was adding the finishing touches to her polished look. The mirrors in the Murat suite reflected an almost-perfect image.

She left her suite and headed for the hotel restaurant, where she had reserved a table in the most secluded corner of the courtyard, one of the most coveted spots on the right bank.

The mysterious Céladon, the man who had sent the postcard of La Défense, was already there. Smiling, he stood up when he saw her. The game seemed playable. Charles-Laurent Donnadieu was the epitome of a conformist technocrat-jock who fed off the establishment's traditions.

"Hello," she said as she held out her perfectly manicured hand. "No one will bother us here."

Victoire sat down, and her dining companion took the chair across from her.

"Emma—may I call you by your first name?"

"Of course."

"I feel so honored. I don't even know where to start."

"Start with your real identity. I'm curious to know who you are."

Charles-Laurent Donnadieu slid a business card across the table. On it was a phone number, as well as his title—Palatinate Director of French Representation.

"Tell me about Palatinate, Charles-Laurent. I hear it's doing well."

"It's a wonderful cover. It's opening every door for me. When Palatinate was created to counterbalance the Big Three credit-rating agencies—especially in the realm of rare earths—all the ministers wanted to talk to us. They were disgusted at how the Americans had triggered Europe's sovereign-debt crisis. The ministers showed us everything. They were desperate to turn around their downgrades."

"Did you meet with Pascal Massicot, France's defense minister?"

"No, I didn't meet with him personally. But I interviewed a cabinet chief I knew from my time with the Budget Ministry. He opened the Defense Ministry's books for me. I didn't find anything of particular note, which hardly surprised me. I informed our mutual friends, who were greatly appreciative."

"You didn't see anything of note in regard to the submarine case I'm working on?"

"No, Emma. I'm aware of all the rumors swirling around that sale. The books were clean, for all intents and purposes, but that doesn't mean anything. And I haven't even mentioned Ludivine Massicot, the defense minister's wife."

"Oh?"

"We have a paper trail for her—literally. Ludivine had Kabul pay her 150 thousand euros for a bogus report on the education system in Afghanistan."

Victoire—alias Emma—shook her head as she distractedly looked over the menu. Who were these mutual friends uniting Emma Wong with Charles-Laurent Donnadieu? Broaching the subject wouldn't be easy.

"Ludivine Massicot's so-called report was fifteen pages lifted straight off a document on the UNESCO website. What a scam. Your friends from Kuala Lumpur were right to be distrustful of France. No one's holding the reins in Paris."

"Believe me—those of us in the Malaysian legal world are quite upset, as well," Victoire replied. "Working with France is very difficult. We're always at the mercy of their scandals."

"The Orly disaster has triggered a shift in power. Pascal Massicot's friends in Kuala Lumpur are slipping dangerously. You, Emma, are the one who's going to tell him that we're cutting him off—until we know what's behind all these incidents. You've shown up at a good time. Massicot is scared of you. Our mutual friends want you to give him a slap on the wrist while waiting for the cards to be reshuffled."

Victoire was starting to realize how vital Emma Wong was in the interplay between France and Malaysia. The idea of giving a defense minister a slap on the wrist amused her as much as it worried her. Would she be up to the task?

"Massicot won't like this."

"If he reacts poorly, tell him the director-general of UNESCO is poised to expose his wife. And that could lead to an even more embarrassing exposure, one that could send her to prison on corruption charges. That'll put him in his place. Tomorrow at Fort Mont Valérien, Massicot will be placing wreaths on the graves of soldiers who've been brought back from West Africa. Use that to your advantage, Emma."

"Believe it or not, I discovered the postcard that you left at the concierge desk just as the top floor of the tower was being decimated. Are you a sorcerer, Charles-Laurent? Or perhaps you just have incredible intuition."

"Don't worry, Emma, I didn't know about any of it. The attack took me by surprise. It's also putting the spotlight on some slipups, which our mutual friends intend to quash. The attack on the morgue, for instance. Our friends are very upset that someone's lashing out at a former French president—even *after* his death. It's disgusting. They suspect Massicot played an indirect role in Noblecourt's elimination. They're trying to figure it out."

"Your fellow Frenchmen are insufferable. I feel for you, Charles-Laurent." Victoire took a bite of her flaky *saumon en croûte*.

The time had come to show one of her cards. She needed to find out more about these mutual friends. Victoire remembered her conversation with Apolline and made herself an easy target.

"Some advanced cyberattack code was stolen from them, right?"

"Yes."

"Who stole it?" Victoire asked, praying to the god of shadow warfare.

"Massicot's Malaysian friends. To show off, evidently."

Victoire settled for an enigmatic nod. It would be hard to admit that she didn't know these Malaysian friends. She decided to venture into territory that wasn't as thorny.

"Why did you send me that postcard with the tower on it? And less than twenty-four hours before the assault on the top floor?"

"Because we're going to buy that top floor."

"Why?"

"Office space for the regulatory administrators and staff who oversee rare-earth trading. Our mutual friends are obligated to apply Article 9 of G. Terres's founding treaty, which they signed."

"But there's already an internal auditing department, which seems to be working. It's not finding anything, which serves our purposes."

"Yes, but the treaty anticipated that this new and more comprehensive regulatory function would be needed. It's not enough to enact rules. You have to enforce them too, unfortunately. Particularly these days, with people up in arms about flash crashes, erratic trading, spoofing, quote stuffing, front running, and all the other dangers inherent in high-frequency trading. Investors rattle easily, and the ripple effects impact economies worldwide. In any case, we need to be seen setting up the regulatory body. And that's where we'll be needing your advice, Emma."

"What kind of advice, Charles-Laurent?"

"Advice on how to establish an oversight function that won't see anything."

Victoire took a deep breath and gave herself time to think as she picked at her vegetables in a dish worth a hundred euros. Emma Wong's role in all of this was revealing itself, and it appeared to be vitally important.

"Charles-Laurent, if you want a group of regulators who won't interfere with anything, hire Nobel laureates in economic sciences and former finance ministers from G.Terres member states. They'll be thrilled to have a *pied-à-terre* in Paris. Drown them in Champagne, and bombard them with interviews with fawning reporters. Give them tablets and force-feed them financial facts all day long. Then ask them to write reports. Make the reports look important, but also make sure they're inconsequential. That'll keep your regulators out of your hair."

"What about their investigations?"

"Hire long-time cops from a criminal investigation unit and stay away from intelligence officers. Your people should be legitimate investigators, but they shouldn't have much imagination. Then flank them with judges who are also from G.Terres member states. Make your investigators go to lectures on money laundering and conferences on financial misconduct—the more boring the better. Honor a few members of your team, but never the others. Before you know it, the spurned investigators will be investigating the ones who've been honored. They'll turn on each other and forget what they were hired to do. They'll be too busy fighting each other. You'll sleep like a baby, believe me."

Victoire read a look of astonishment on Donnadieu's face. He raised his third glass of Romanée-Conti to Emma's health.

"I was told you were our ace strategist. I hope you're being remunerated as well as you should be."

"Don't worry. Our friends always keep their word."

"I know."

"Now, how about we talk a bit about you, Charles-Laurent. What have you been up to since graduating from *École nationale d'administration?*"

22

It was ten thirty. On any other night, John, Victoire, and he would be having a glass of wine or a cup of tea and discussing Alexandre's bath time or Caresse's need of a good grooming. But tonight Fermatown was completely deserted, and Luc was feeling alone in the world. He was grateful when the screen on his cell phone lit up, and he saw that it was a message from Victoire. "Get the names of Emma Wong and Charles-Laurent Donnadieu's mutual friends."

Okay, he would do that—as soon as he caught up on the news and checked on the tracking coins. There weren't any developments on the tower or the morgue. He snapped his fingers, and a geographic visual on the touchwall showed the location of the coin he had dropped in the catacombs. Nobody had picked it up. Luc focused on another coin that John had slipped into the pocket of the French ambassador's chauffeur in Kuala Lumpur. It wasn't likely that he was as smart as Claudine Montluzac.

The ambassador's driver wasn't far from the Chinese embassy.

"Well, well," Luc said. The driver was probably helping the Chinese by spying on his boss. Overseas Chinese were known for their strong ties with the triads—transnational crime rings—as well as official agencies like the ministry of state security. Emma Wong, a Malaysian of Chinese origins, could have been working for the ministry of state security too. Sure, she supported good causes in Malaysia, but who knew where her real loyalties lay?

Luc was about to respond to Victoire's text when the touchscreen wall signaled two pit stops made by the Malaysian coin.

An hour before reporting to the Chinese embassy, Grapefruit's driver had spent a long time at No. 376 Jalan Tun Razak, near the Royal Selangor Golf Club, a hot spot for Asian movie stars and various government officials.

"Would ya look at that?"

The address corresponded with the American embassy's.

"Why not the Americans too?"

Then the touchscreen wall displayed the location of the other halt: the Indian embassy.

Luc launched his analysis software, which examined information from every intelligence source possible, using key words entered in threes and making connections.

It listed the two submarines and Emma Wong's role in defending the whistleblowing Indian submarine captain. The software also brought up the Indian missile attack on the president's plane. Was it possible that Emma was working on India's behalf?

Luc texted Victoire, who was still dining with the shady guy at the Bristol: "Their mutual friends could be the Chinese, the Americans, or the Indians. Hang in there."

TUESDAY

1

Barely awake as he lay in bed, John was now aware of the latest developments in Paris. Instead of providing answers, the reports from Luc and Victoire raised even more questions. Dutreil wasn't answering his cell phone.

John got out of bed and dressed quickly. The ambassador's driver was crossing the dewy yard just as he was buckling his belt. The man offered his services, but John declined. He wanted to walk. He exited the embassy grounds and turned in the direction of the Chinese embassy, a successful mix of Chinese and Malaysian architecture.

Discreetly installed cameras at the building's corners were surveying the sidewalks. John did a loop in search of clues. No suspicious windows, no parked cars, no street vendors indicating the presence—even a subtle one—of Malaysian counteespionage. It was hard to draw any conclusions. Surveillance techniques had evolved so quickly.

Disappointed, John hailed a taxi. Barely inside, he heard the ringtone designated for calls from Méricourt. Paris hadn't forgotten him.

"John, I just got a call from Mortemar de Buzenval. Dutreil's nowhere to be found. He's not at his office or at his apartment at the embassy. Do you have any ideas?"

"I haven't seen him today." John thought it best not to say anything about the man's sudden disappearance the previous night. At least not yet.

"Please find him. I don't want his computer falling into the wrong hands."

"Don't worry. The embassy is well protected."

"When I say the wrong hands, I'm talking about Buzenval."

"I'll see what I can do."

"Thanks, John. Victoire's doing an excellent job."

"She's taking too many risks, if you ask me. I'm not happy. You know we've got a baby now. We need to be around for the next twenty years or so, especially Victoire."

"I get it, John. You're mad that I dragged her into all of this."

"I don't want to tell you twice."

John hung up. Kuala Lumpur's cityscape was whizzing by, but he paid no attention. He focused on the idea of going to see Emma Wong's father.

John paid his fare and got out of the cab. Although his knowledge of the area was limited, he didn't think he had been followed. The Wongs' house was built in the Baba Bling style of Malaysia's Chinese community. The boxy shape reminded him of Fermatown—but this was posher and more colorful. The home's pastel hues made it look like a confection surrounded by tropical trees and scarlet bushes.

An employee in a black skirt and white apron greeted him on the front steps. She bowed, pressing her palms together.

"Mr. Wong is expecting you."

"I'll follow your lead."

They entered a foyer with fine wood flooring, red columns, and beams on the ceiling. Through an expanse of windows at the back of the house, John could see a pool with lush vegetation all around it. He followed the young woman through the foyer and into a dimly lit room. An old man in a black jacket was sitting behind a desk.

"Have a seat, Mr. Spencer Larivière. I'm sorry to be meeting you like this, but my family is very upset. I believe you've come straight from Paris. Is that correct?"

"Yes, sir."

"Well, perhaps you'll be able to explain what this means."

John sat down in a red-lacquered chair and watched his host turn on a tablet.

"Listen."

John sat attentively and waited for the worst. He recognized Luc's voice. "No, we can't give you any confirmation. We still haven't identified all the passengers. We have three survivors who are unconscious. Does Emma have any distinguishing features or specific physical attributes that could help us?"

Feeling guilty, John listened to the entire conversation before trying to respond.

"We called the Val-de-Grâce hospital," Wong said. "No one could confirm the existence of this nurse. This is unacceptable."

"Yes, it is."

"Is it possible that Emma's still alive?"

"I'm trying my hardest to find out."

"You know, she was originally planning to leave later in the week, but she bumped up her trip at the last minute. I don't know why."

"At this point, I have no new information. We're wondering if your daughter was a target in that plane disaster. Someone tried to kill me during my flight over the Indian coast. There could be a connection. That's why I asked to see you."

"You are most welcome in this house."

"Your daughter met the former French president during his last trip to Kuala Lumpur. Do you know why?"

"Emma and Mrs. Noblecourt have worked together on human-rights issues. She was close to the former president, as well. It wouldn't be all that unusual for her to meet with Mr. Noblecourt."

"She was representing a submarine captain's family. It's believed that he was blackmailing high-ranking officials in connection with the purchase of two submarines and was killed by corrupt police before he could blow the whistle. How much do you think she knew about the kickbacks those officials allegedly received?"

"I would think she was quite well informed. She's always done her homework."

"In your opinion, is it possible that the plane was destroyed because of that?"

The elderly man shook his head. The soft babbling of a fountain that John couldn't see filled the room.

"Everyone here knows that our defense minister, Syafiq bin Rodney, along with his friends and family members, made money off that contract. That's the way it's done in Malaysia's ministry of defense and just about everywhere else in the government."

"But your country signed all the international anticorruption conventions."

"For show, nothing more. Here, we make sure everyone gets what's owed them. We respect family and property above everything else. There's rarely a problem, except when France is involved. And then it all gets complicated and sticky."

John listened silently. The man needed to unburden himself.

"My daughter is well educated and has integrity. She's defending the honor of an unjustly accused marine officer. She would never get involved in a legal affair that's the least bit tainted."

"So then why would someone try to kill her?"

"Because she discovered something shocking about G. Terres. That's what she discussed with Mr. Noblecourt when he came last week."

"Can you be more specific?"

"No, I don't know any more than that."

"Right before the former president arrived, your daughter sent him a series of documents." John took out the photos of Julien Lanfrey and Chronosphere's atomic clock. He placed them on the coffee table. "Do these mean anything to you?"

The father looked long and hard at the photos and turned on a lamp to examine every detail. He shook his head.

"No."

John pulled out the photos of the chess match.

"Do you recognize any of the people behind the chess players?"

Emma's father pulled out a magnifying glass from a drawer in his desk and scrutinized the faces.

"I don't recognize these people, but I recognize the room. These photos were taken at the Shangra-Li casino in Putrajaya. My company does work for them. The casino hosts chess and poker tournaments. It's run by a man named Ange Cipriani. It attracts players from all over Southeast Asia."

John pointed to the two men whose faces appeared clearly beside boards thirty-seven, forty, and forty-one of the chess match.

"Do you recognize them?"

"I'm sorry, but I've never seen these people."

"How might your daughter have gotten these photos?"

"Either from the Malaysian Chess Federation or from the casino management."

"Do you know anyone with the chess federation?"

"No, I'm afraid I don't."

John took out a card and scribbled a phone number on it. He held it out to the father just as he was dimming the lights, most likely to hide his tears.

"One more question, Mr. Wong. Did Emma know Benoît Dutreil, the French embassy's cultural attaché?"

"I can't answer that question, either. Emma has always told me only so much. She's independent and secretive—has been ever since she was a little girl."

"If you hear from your daughter, please tell her to call me. And if she's gone, help me find her killers. Anything you remember might be important in our investigation."

Wong snapped his fingers, and the housemaid appeared. It was time to leave.

No sooner was he in the cab taking him back to the embassy than he got a call. It was Emma's father.

"I wasn't very hospitable," Wong said.

"You weren't ungracious at all, sir. It was my fault for disturbing you at such a difficult time."

"Thank you for your understanding. I've just questioned Fang Yi, one of Emma's lawyer friends. She's given me a surprising piece of information about a skyscraper in Paris."

"I'm listening."

"Emma wanted to know the height of the Beau Paris Tower in La Défense, the business district."

"Thank you."

"That's not all. Emma didn't want to know just how many floors the building has. She wanted the exact height in meters and centimeters."

"Why?"

"I don't know."

2

John's taxi exited the Putrajaya Highway and started heading down a more picturesque road. An enchanting Asia emerged from the fog. Pine forests blanketed the hillsides. Along the flatlands, intense greens separated fields of dusty ocher. John could see clusters of brightly colored houses. The taxi turned onto a road that descended through a skillfully maintained forest. After a few switchbacks, they came out at a circular intersection.

The driver pointed out a white mosque with a pink minaret.

"Kampung Kling Mosque. UNESCO has classified it as a world heritage monument."

"It's beautiful," John lied with enthusiasm.

The taxi continued twenty meters, passed through an archway, and stopped in front of a police barrier. John didn't need to spend much time explaining who he was before the two men in black-and-silver summer uniforms waved them through.

The home of Amir bin Muhaimin, Malaysia's minister of home affairs, was situated on an expanse of grass so vivid, it seemed unreal. The mansion was a hodgepodge of yellow and blue octagonal structures with terraces and towers. The residence was well worth the trip and made an extraordinary impression.

A butler appeared between the jets of water spraying the lawn. He greeted John with a bow.

"His Excellency is waiting for you in the chandelier room."

John followed the man into the home. After crossing the foyer, they entered an interior garden with a glass roof. In it was a huge variety of plants. John admired a row of orchids that would have made any master gardener green with envy.

"This way."

The man opened a door and stepped aside to usher John into the room. John stopped in the doorway, mesmerized by the crystal and blue porcelain chandelier. The monstrous object dominated the space. Crushed by its massiveness, the room's couches and chairs were mere accessories.

"That's the reason I bought the house. This one-of-a-kind piece was created in the eighteenth century in France for an Indian maharaja."

Amir bin Muhaimin was looking at his chandelier with great affection. John wondered if he loved his wife that much.

"It does make a statement, doesn't it," John said. Right away, he regretted not saying something more complimentary.

The minister of home affairs ignored it. "Good to see you again, Mr. Spencer Larivière. Please, have a seat."

The minister sat down on a sofa and motioned to a chair across from him. His eyes gleamed with craftiness and impatience. "I'm told you visited the Wong's residence."

"Yes, we're aware that Emma Wong was on the plane. She had borrowed the ambassador's seat."

Bin Muhaimin stared at him, silent.

"Do you know if she survived?" he finally said.

"No, not at the moment."

John read the same look in Bin Muhaimin's eyes that he had seen in Dutreil's.

"Do you know what she intended to do in Paris?" Bin Muhaimin asked.

"I believe she was investigating the submarine sale."

The minister sighed. "I wasn't in favor of that deal," he said.

"People are talking about kickbacks allegedly made to French and Malaysian politicians."

"That's how things are done here. But it sounds like the French are shocked by the practice. You want to know exactly who got money, how much, and in what form, right?"

"That's correct, Your Excellency."

"I'd love to have this information, as well. To be honest, I was counting on Emma to find out. Now I'm counting on you."

"You may have more faith in me than you should."

"Don't be so modest, Mr. Spencer Larivière. When you travel on the plane reserved for the president of France, you must have certain *connections*, as you say in Paris. I love that city—what neighborhood do you live in?"

"Daguerre Village in Montparnasse."

"You're lucky."

"It's not so bad here either."

"Malaysia is a tapestry of ethnicities and religions that have more or less gotten along for centuries. It's not a great nation, as France was once."

John ignored the minister's reference to the past and got back to the subject at hand.

"You say you were against the submarine purchase?"

"It was my colleague, Defense Minister Syafiq bin Rodney, who masterminded that deal."

"Syafiq bin Rodney is famous in France for his crackdown on piracy in the Strait of Malacca," John said. "He's a celebrity. He even came to Paris to counsel our marines in their fight against Somalian pirates."

Bin Muhaimin smiled weakly. The light from the chandelier, along with the sunlight coming through the windows, eliminated all shadows in the room. John could see the man clearly. He looked fatigued.

Bin Muhaimin was silent for a moment. Finally, he pulled himself up in his chair and leaned in.

"My dear John, if I may call you by your first name."

"Be my guest, Excellency."

"You are very French. Don't be so impressed by the affectations of a Malaysian politician. Bin Rodney is no more an eradicator of piracy than I'm an Anglican bishop. The Americans with their satellites and commandos were the ones who suppressed piracy in the straight—with the tacit cooperation of the Chinese and the Indians. Nothing is done in this region without discreet agreement between the three big nations. At least not for the time being."

The minister of home affairs continued his spiel.

"Of course, Bin Rodney had to make himself look good. Every now and then, he'd sink a boat or free some hostages in front of the cameras. But it was all for show. And with Prabat Sankar's agreement. The head pirate reinvented himself in the real estate business, and Bin Rodney never lost track of him."

John was almost taken aback. Bin Muhaimin had no compunction about accusing his country's defense minister of colluding with those he was in charge of fighting.

"Am I to believe that Bin Rodney negotiated with the pirates?"

"That was his bread and butter. The Americans took away his livelihood. Raw materials—and rare-earth metals in particular—pass by our coasts and were an easy target, until the countries of this region and the United States decided to stop the piracy by preemptively killing a certain number of pirates and their families. Prabat Sankar quickly realized the game was over. If you chop up those thugs' wives and children, piracy comes to a halt. The Indian Ocean isn't a place where Westerners waste any time worrying about human rights."

John, with all his experience, was feeling overwhelmed. He had grown increasingly cynical over the years, but what governments and power-hungry individuals were capable of doing still shocked him.

"So am I to assume that your defense minister, Syafiq bin Rodney, shared what he made from the sale of those submarines with Prabat Sankar?"

"That's not exactly front-page news. Everyone knows it. It may be unethical for you, but no one gives a shit here. They think it's normal. The question isn't whether French and Malaysian politicians got their palms greased and greased other palms, in turn. The real question is: Why did America and China let my country buy those two submarines?"

"I don't understand."

"The bigger powers have always called the shots when it comes to Malaysia's naval and air forces. Why didn't any of them stop the sale?"

"I don't know."

"I don't know either."

"But you're minister of home affairs…"

"I don't deal in international relations like Syafiq bin Rodney, who gets all that camera time at important political summits. I was hoping you could fill me in."

Before John could respond, the butler burst into the room and rushed over to his boss. He leaned down and whispered in the minister's ear.

Startled, Amir bin Muhaimin thanked him and turned to John.

"Your ambassador is dead. They've just found his body, and they think he was murdered. I'm sure you'll want to leave at once. Would you permit me to accompany you?"

"Of course," John answered, already on his feet.

Grapefruit had left a bad taste in somebody's mouth.

3

Through the limo's tinted windows, John took in all the police vehicles and officers in black uniforms. The minister's car crossed the police barricade and stopped in front of the embassy residence. Right away, John spotted the ambassador's personal secretary, whom he'd seen when he met the diplomat. The man looked defeated.

A police officer greeted John and the minister and led them across the lawn to the pool. Nicolas Mortemar de Buzenval's body was floating in a sea of blood. His torso was full of huge welts, and his face was smashed to a pulp. His murderer had made a heyday of it. John turned away from the spectators crowded around the pool and walked over to the secretary.

"Why didn't you call me?"

"I didn't have your number. Where's Dutreil?"

"I don't know. You find him, dammit!"

John returned to the minister of home affairs. A handful of people were huddled around him.

"Some of my staff members have made it over here, and they've gotten more information from the police," Bin Muhaimin told John. "The investigators think the killer used a blunt object: a pipe or the handle of a pickax. The ambassador and I were supposed to deliver a speech on the war against terrorism at a conference a couple of weeks from now."

"I didn't know anything about that."

John looked back at the ambassador's battered body. Why hadn't Dutreil told him? He approached the secretary a second time.

"Take me to the apartment that Dutreil stays in—and let's be discreet about it."

The man looked at him, expressionless.

"I'm sure you have access to the pass code," John said, his tone terse.

The secretary took out his smartphone and headed toward the main building while looking up the pass codes for the private apartments. John followed him into the building and up a set of stairs. Arriving at Dutreil's apartment, the man fumbled with the code. His hands were shaking. Finally, the door opened. They entered and turned on the lights.

"What the hell!" John shouted inspite of himself when he laid eyes on the walls.

They were covered with photos of Emma Wong, from her childhood in Malaysia's Baba Bling universe to her celebrity as an attorney. Also on the walls were newspaper and magazine articles detailing Emma's cases. Most were about her campaign to end sex slavery and her work in the wrongful death case. The worker bee from the intelligence agency had succumbed to the charms of Southeast Asia's beautiful and sharp-as-a-tack lawyer.

"Is this the first time you've been here?" John asked.

The secretary nodded.

"What about the ambassador? Did he ever come here?"

"I don't think so. They never even spoke very much. I would have facilitated any meetings."

"You mean they didn't get along?"

"They hated each other."

John walked over to a window and looked down at the courtyard and pool. The minister was now talking with the police. Ambulances had arrived, and paramedics were pulling out a gurney.

"No one heard anything?"

"It happened during a fireworks show near the embassy. It was loud as hell."

"Fireworks in the middle of the day?"

"A conservative Islamist group won a case in the High Court. The ruling came in this morning."

"What case was that?"

"They were opposing an effort by the Roman Catholic Church to use the name of Allah in their newspaper."

"I thought this was a tolerant country."

The secretary joined John at the window.

"It was the minister of home affairs himself who prohibited Christian publications from using the name."

"Really? I didn't know he was that conservative."

"He's more of an opportunist. He can tell which way the wind's blowing. He also knows where the money is."

"Was that noisy celebration expected?"

"Everyone was aware that the High Court would rule in the Islamists' favor."

"At that exact time?"

"I don't know."

"You should go now. I have to call the Élysée," John said, patting the secretary's back. "Keep the police at bay for a minute while I examine the apartment."

Once alone, he grabbed a pair of socks from a drawer. He slipped them over his hands and began a methodical search of the apartment. Finding nothing, he returned to Dutreil's desk to grab his laptop and flash drives. But just as he was scooping them up, he noticed a stationery pad. John could make out the impression of handwriting on the top page. Dutreil had written a note and torn it off. John didn't have time to decipher the impression. He took the pad, too. Back on the ground floor, he hurried to the presidential suite, making sure he wasn't seen. He deposited the computer, flash drives, and pad on his bed and left the suite just as quickly. He retraced his steps and emerged from Dutreil's building just as Bin Muhaimin was coming to see him.

"My good friend, I have to leave you now. The police are doing their work. My sincerest condolences to your country. Your ambassador was admired by many Malaysians. I hope you'll keep me informed."

"Of course, Your Excellency."

John took advantage of the commotion to slip back to the presidential suite. He'd been obsessing over a troubling thought. He closed the French doors and shut the blinds. Once he was absolutely sure that he couldn't be spotted from the outside, he opened his closet door and compared its contents with the photo he had taken. As he suspected, the baseball bat was gone.

"Jesus Christ!"

John hardly had time to react. A text message had just popped up on his cell phone. "I'm waiting for you at the Royal Selangor Club." It was from Serge Roussillon. He collected Dutreil's things in a backpack and headed out.

4

Victoire planted herself in front of her suite's plasma TV. All the stations had interrupted their regular schedules for a news bulletin.

Dr. Abel Liévin, the medical examiner who performed the autopsy on former President Pierre-André Noblecourt, is in critical condition in the burn unit at Saint Louis Hospital. But we've obtained a copy of his autopsy notes from his secretary, who retrieved them from Dr. Liévin's cloud storage. Although she faces a reprimand for releasing the notes, she said the pubic is entitled to his findings.

Police and family members have claimed that one or more intruders entered the apartment through a window in the former president's study and murdered him. According to Dr. Liévin's notes, however, the former president committed suicide.

The medical examiner concluded that Mr. Noblecourt hanged himself with no help from anyone else. His body bore no traces of a struggle, and postmortem tests yielded no evidence of drugs in his system.

Dr. Liévin is the creator of a virtual imaging system that is revolutionizing forensic medicine.

Victoire called Luc.

"Did you hear about the autopsy report?"

"It's a farce. I showed you the second source of heat. The thermal camera can't make these things up. There was someone else in the attic when Noblecourt was hanged."

"Everything just keeps getting thornier."

"If it weren't, you wouldn't be living it up at the Bristol."

"Did you figure out who Emma's mutual friends are?"

"She's got as many reasons to work for the Chinese as she does for India or the United States. I dug up a postgrad stint at Columbia University, which could mean something," Luc answered.

"I'm sending a message to John to let him know that the cyberattack at Orly could be connected to one of those countries, but we don't think any of them knowingly targeted France. There was a slip-up. Do you agree?"

"Yes," Luc replied.

"What do you think about the Beau Paris Tower's height?" Victoire asked.

"I have absolutely no idea. I don't see why the exact height—down to the centimeter—would interest Emma."

"What about the ambassador?" Victoire asked.

"John sent me the photos. I'm thinking some kind of sex crime gone wrong. Emma Wong's familiar with sex crimes. We know that."

"What isn't that woman familiar with?"

"What about the guy from the credit-rating agency?"

"Charles-Laurent isn't as handsome or smart as you. He's kind of nerdy. I don't especially like him. He's figured out how finance and politics work, and he and Emma have the same friends. The clock's ticking. I gotta go."

Once seated in the back of a cab, Victoire called Roberta to get an update on Alexandre. Assured that he was just as fine as ever, she focused on her next meeting. The weather was heavy and humid. The Ganges River couldn't be any muggier than this, she thought. India was coming up quite often in this case—too often.

5

Victoire paid the fare and got out of the cab. She pushed open the door to Titus Polycarpe's building after entering the code. The marble surfaces and mailboxes gleamed in the sunlight coming through the windows. Before she reached the first step, Victoire saw Béatrice sliding down the handrail. The child straightened up and leaped to the floor with cat-like agility.

"You look different!"

"I got my hair done," Victoire replied.

"Did you do it for your investigation?"

"Yes."

Béatrice took Victoire's hand and walked out to the sidewalk with her.

"Did you listen to the radio this morning?"

"Yes. It sounds like Grandpa hanged himself all on his own. That's what the medical examiner said."

"What do you think about that?"

"I don't understand any of it anymore," Béatrice replied. "I'm positive someone killed him somehow or another. He had no reason to commit suicide."

"Before your grandfather flew home from Kuala Lumpur, when you were talking to him on the phone, what exactly did he say?"

"He said he had a real-life pirate story to tell me."

"Did he sound worried?"

"No."

"Did you tell your mother or grandmother?"

Béatrice shook her head and looked away.

"In Kuala Lumpur, your grandpa met with your dad."

"No he didn't!"

"Well, the ambassador said he did."

Béatrice tightened her grip on Victoire's hand and pulled her into an entrance to the Bon Marché. She led Victoire to a corner of the store, removed her backpack, and took out a school notebook. Victoire watched as the little girl covered the upper part of her face with the notebook and smiled.

Victoire recoiled. It couldn't be... That smile.

Then Béatrice covered her mouth with the notebook.

"You know who I look like now, don't you? Serge Roussillon is just my mom's husband. My real dad is Alain Jemestre, the president of France. If you're still wondering why you're here, you have part of the answer. Hardly anyone knows this, which is proof that my father trusts you. Or that he doesn't have a lot of trustworthy people around him."

"On Sunday I thought you reminded me of someone, but I couldn't put my finger on it," Victoire said, still blown away. "Why did your grandfather meet with your stepfather in Kuala Lumpur?"

"Probably to talk about G. Terres. Where his fake job is."

"Is it possible that he does some real work for them?"

Béatrice didn't answer and looked at her watch.

"We'd better get going. I don't want to be late."

As they made their way to the Cadet's School, Victoire reflected on the absurdity of the situation.

"Did your grandfather ever mention two submarines that France sold to Malaysia? The sale has been causing some problems. And as for G. Terres, it's possible that everyone working there isn't nice, like your stepfather."

"No, I don't know anything about the submarines, but as for my stepfather, yes, he's nice enough, even if my grandmother thinks he's lazy."

"I'm wondering if your grandpa knew something—if he learned something horrible while he was in Kuala Lumpur. Something that could have led to his suicide—or his staged suicide."

Béatrice stopped on the sidewalk about a meter from her school. Once again, she looked up at Victoire.

"Grandpa saw or heard something bad, something that involved the pirates. And he died because of it. Suicide or not, the result's the same."

"Your stepfather may have heard something bad too."

"I'd be surprised."

"Why's that?"

"Because he isn't the kind of person who hears about bad things. Will you come pick me up tonight?"

"Yes."

Victoire watched Béatrice join her friends in front of the school. The child fascinated her. She glanced at the road and noticed two undercover cops standing by a car. The president was scared for his daughter. He probably had reason to be.

6

John crossed the impeccable lawn of the Royal Selangor Club. The club's mock Tudor architecture, reminiscent of sixteenth-century England, seemed out of place in Kuala Lumpur. But John was getting accustomed to such visual surprises.

"I have an appointment with Serge Roussillon."

"This way."

John followed a lovely woman in a wrap dress as she led him to an alcove, where a few men sat silently, their eyes transfixed on their cell phones and tablets. The French ambassador's murder had made the international news, and John was sure they were following the developments.

A man in his forties stood up to greet him. Serge Roussillon seemed concerned and slightly confused.

"I'm sorry for making you come here, but I figured it would be more discreet. Considering the circumstances…"

"No, this was a good idea."

John studied the man, a reputed playboy. He had the sculpted face of a male model, and John could tell that his bronze skin, blue eyes, perfect white teeth, and full head of blond hair attracted the ladies. John followed him to a veranda.

"Apolline told me you'd be coming. She said you were sent here by the Élysée."

"Yes," John answered tersely.

"I wanted to go back to Paris after the Orly disaster and my father-in-law's death, but I was asked to stay here in case you needed anything. And now Mortemar's been murdered. I don't know what to think anymore. What can I do for you?"

"What did you and your father-in-law discuss when he was here last week?"

"He told me how things were going with Apolline and Béatrice."

"Did you discuss anything else?"

"He asked me about G. Terres, and I told him everything was fine."

"You're in charge of G. Terres operations in Malaysia?"

"Yes."

"Can you take me to their premises?"

"Right away?"

"Well, as you said, considering the circumstances…"

Roussillon twitched and glanced around.

"Okay. Follow me. We'll go in my SUV."

John followed Serge to the parking lot. Climbing into the luxury vehicle, he noticed a pair of lace panties on the floor and a tube of male lubricant in one of the cup holders.

"Sorry about the mess."

"Don't worry about it."

Serge started the car and turned on the AC.

"Did you and your father-in-law discuss anything else?"

"We only met for an hour."

"That was a short meeting, considering how far he had come to see you."

"He wasn't a sentimental person."

"Did he meet with anyone else?"

"He saw the ambassador and Emma Wong."

John played dumb. "Who's Emma Wong?"

"She's a very influential Malaysian lawyer. My in-laws ran into her at the embassy on several occasions."

Serge passed a long line of trucks and a few seconds later took the exit ramp to a highway where a sign specified the number of kilometers to Putrajaya. John asked a follow-up question.

"Don't you think it's strange that shortly after your father-in-law got together with the ambassador and Emma Wong, all three met with disasters?"

"Of course, I think that says a lot."

"And you have no idea of a motive that could explain what happened to these three people—not to mention everyone else who died at Orly?"

"I thought it might be connected to G. Terres, but how would I know?" Serge answered.

"What kind of relationship did you have with the ambassador?"

"An excellent one. For all intents and purposes, he was my boss, as I am the French representative for G. Terres. From an administrative standpoint, I depended on him. And personally, I thought he was a friendly guy. I'm crushed by what happened. According to the news reports, the killer pounded him to a pulp."

John kept his suspicions to himself. The photos he had found in Dutreil's apartment left no room for doubt. The man was in love with Emma Wong. More than that, the worker-bee spy was obsessed with her—the woman to whom he owed all his information. By offering her the seat on Flight 912, the ambassador had given Dutreil's love and informant the kiss of death. Dutreil, in turn, had murdered the ambassador.

The French agent in Kuala Lumpur certainly had his reasons. And John was the one who had unintentionally revealed the crucial piece of information to Dutreil. How could he have seen it coming? The deeper he got, the more central a role Emma Wong appeared to play. Which world power was the lovely Chinese woman working for? This woman who had enchanted Dutreil could have seduced Noblecourt, as well.

"What was the nature of your father-in-law's relationship with Emma Wong?"

"It's not what you think."

"I'm not thinking anything in particular."

"Emma was well connected in Southeast Asia's political circles. When Pierre-André was still president, she met him and Georgette, and I believe they got on well. Georgette is still campaigning against sex slavery, especially when it involves children."

"Before going back to Paris, your father-in-law called Béatrice."

"He called her on a regular basis."

"He mentioned a story about pirates. Does that sound familiar?"

Serge shook his head. "I wouldn't know anything about that."

"Did your father-in-law have enemies?"

"In politics, you always have more enemies than friends. But did he have any enemies who would go as far as murdering him? No, he didn't have enemies like that."

"Your father-in-law wasn't actually on Flight 912. Do you think he knew it was going to be attacked?"

Serge didn't say anything for a few seconds and then shot a quick glance at his passenger.

"He would have warned the police or told Mortemar. I find it hard to believe that he'd keep that kind of information to himself. It wasn't like him. Definitely not."

Serge seemed sincere. John fell back on a more reasonable theory.

"Maybe he didn't want to fly in the same plane as Emma Wong?"

"That's ridiculous. He knew her too well."

"Yes, but Emma Wong was also interested in the kickback scandal involving the submarine sale."

"My father-in-law would have loved talking with her on the flight home. I'm sure he wasn't the one opposed to her investigation. In fact, I'm convinced he would have helped her—unlike what some people want everyone to believe."

"Some politicians in Paris made money on that scheme."

"Think whatever you want, but my father-in-law was always against corruption. Kickbacks are illegal, and offenders have been receiving harsher and harsher sentences. *That's* where the scandal lies."

"What do you mean?"

Roussillon passed a slow-moving car.

"You've got to ask the right questions. Who benefits in the war against corruption? There will always be officials on the take, relatives of government officials, business people, and celebrities looking to hide money or skirt the system. Crack down and who takes over? Organized crime. Now that's a real venture-capital business. Don't go thinking that today's underground is run by Al Pacino lookalikes. Who's in charge now? Brains from the Ivy League schools and the elite universities in China and India. They're looking for high yields in the short term, and they're risk takers. They're willing to do whatever it takes, including muscling out the competition, breaking the law, you name it… That's today's organized crime. They've got the corrupt government officials in their pockets, and they know how to work the system under the radar. They are the first ones to demand sanctions against corruption, because it raises the price of their services."

Serge seemed to know what he was talking about. He was so absorbed in what he was saying, he didn't see the car bearing down on them at full speed. John grabbed for the steering wheel, but Serge managed to veer onto the shoulder just in time. The other car whizzed past them, its horn blaring. Without missing a beat, Serge continued.

"Crooks can be such a clever bunch. Say you're a government official in Paris, and you make sure a certain contractor gets an important job. Don't forget—commissions are perfectly legal. But you figure you deserve more than the commission. Three months later, one of the countries where the contractor does business asks for a silly fifty-page report on the irrigation of desert regions, for which you charge thirty thousand, seventy thousand, maybe even more than a hundred million euros, all of it tax-free."

"But not cash you want out in the open?"

"That's right. And you can't trust lawyers and tax havens anymore, so you go to the mob. It's all connected."

"So you know all about this, but you've never been part of it?"

"I can say with a clear conscience that I'm not on the take. I don't have enough influence. I'm here only because of my father-in-law and my wife. You have to know how to stay in your field of expertise. My talents are in the area of that skimpy little thing on the floor over there."

John nodded.

"Clearly, you've got people in mind when you talk about corruption. Do you have any names?"

"Of course."

"Who?"

"You're not afraid of trouble, are you? I thought that the moment I saw you walk into the club."

"So who are they?"

"Pascal Massicot, for one. He's a sleazebag."

"France's defense minister?"

"Yes. His wife too. She squeezed money from the Afghan government."

"Seriously?"

"Pierre-André told me the whole story. He also said some people were surprised that he never got on the gravy train after he left office. With my mother-in-law's work fighting sex slavery, they could have made a fucking bundle. The legal system never would have caught them. They're chasing Ferraris on bicycles. And it doesn't matter which party's in power. They manage to keep their jobs."

"How can you be so sure about your father-in-law?"

"There are politicians who aren't corrupt—Pierre-André was one of them."

"So was Mortemar Buzenval, our late ambassador, on the take?"

"I don't have any proof."

"But you have suspicions."

Serge swerved past a truck loaded with Chinese workers.

"I think he was too big an idiot. He got his job because he slept with the secretary-general of the Ministry of Foreign Affairs. All the chancelleries in Asia knew about it."

They were getting close to Putrajaya, and Serge got off the highway. Construction sites were giving way to elegant buildings. John could make out fancy homes with pools shimmering beneath pastel-colored lights.

"Now can I ask *you* a question?"

"Go ahead."

"Do you know who Claudine Montluzac is?"

"I've heard of her. Why do you ask?"

"Because a month ago, she called me on behalf of my father-in-law."

"Why?"

"She wanted to know about G. Terres."

"You're going have to repeat your whole spiel," John answered, laughing.

"I'm used to it—I'm kind of a tourist guide here."

7

The cab arrived at Fort Mont-Valérien. Victoire paid the driver and got out. The fortress, which overlooked Paris, had been built in 1841. It had defended the city during the Franco-Prussian war, withstanding several months of artillery bombardment. During the Nazi occupation, it was used as a prison and place of execution. These days it served as a national memorial. It was here that the dead were honored, and their survivors remembered them.

Victoire introduced herself to the gendarme at the bottom of the steps. "The *cour d'honneur*," he said, directing her to the three-sided courtyard. "The minister has just begun his speech."

"Thanks."

It was drizzling, and the stone steps were slippery. When Victoire reached the top, a female gendarme greeted her and took her to the area reserved for families of fallen soldiers.

Standing behind a podium, Pascal Massicot was giving a speech. The politician's straightforward way of speaking always seduced his audience. He came off as competent, honest, and serious. Massicot had worked hard to perfect his presentation, both on and offstage. He had reached his pinnacle of success, thanks to a sincere-looking exterior and an ability to wheel and deal behind the scenes. His looks certainly helped.

Victoire looked at a father standing next to her who was clearly trying to hold back his tears. She diverted her gaze to her feet.

"No, you did not die for nothing," Massicot said, looking at nine coffins covered with French flags. They held the bodies of young soldiers who had died in West Africa. "You've brought honor to your country. Your sacrifice is not in vain. Freedom embraces you, as we embrace you. Your children and parents can be proud. Thanks to you, we are a greater nation, a better nation."

Massicot left his platform to the sounds of a funeral march. The weather was changing from summer to winter in the course of a single day, and now the drizzle was a wet snow.

One by one, the minister greeted the members of each family. Every now and then, Victoire spotted a look in her direction. During her dinner at the Bristol, she hadn't been in a position to crack the true nature of Emma Wong and Massicot's relationship.

Victoire was anxiously watching the minister's progress. Maybe most French people thought all Asians looked alike, but she was taking a huge risk. Everything would blow up in her face if Massicot found out that she wasn't Emma. She shivered.

The closer she got to the moment of truth, the more Victoire felt her guts twist in a knot. The rope knotted around Noblecourt's neck flashed in her mind. At last, the minister addressed the father standing beside her, who wanted to know how his son had died.

Perhaps Massicot wasn't the monster that Claudia Montluzac had made him out to be. After promising the father that he would find out, the minister turned to Victoire, who had managed to muster an air of authority.

"You look even younger than you did last year."

Victoire cracked a half-smile in the spirit of the character she was impersonating.

"I have some things to tell you, Mr. Massicot."

"Since you're not calling me by my first name, I'm guessing this is bad news."

Victoire glanced furtively around the courtyard, indicating that it wasn't an opportune place. "I'd rather speak elsewhere."

"Can I suggest my car?"

"Yes, that would be preferable."

Victoire walked with Massicot to his government car. The minister told his cabinet chief to take a taxi and motioned Victoire into the backseat. He slipped in beside her.

"Take us to Le Cottage in Marly-le-Roi," Massicot instructed his driver.

The car pulled out of the parking area and started cruising past the old stone walls. The gray ramparts bore down on Victoire, adding to her feeling of heaviness.

"I do this a lot, but it still gets to me every time."

"You said what they needed to hear."

"Your French has also improved, my friend. So, what's this bad news you've come to tell me?"

Victoire nodded at the driver, who was within earshot. Massicot smiled.

"David has been my driver for thirty years. He's an extension of me. Lucie, my assistant, has been with me for twenty-two years. You see, Emma, there are two types of politicians: those who have their own driver and assistant and those who put up with the ones assigned to them. Politicians in the second category have shorter careers. You can speak with peace of mind."

Victoire nodded. She could only hope that her voice wouldn't shake.

"Our mutual friends have instructed me to tell you that the wire transfers are suspended until everything is under control again."

"I was expecting that. It's not surprising, given what happened at Orly."

"Our friends are investigating the incident."

"Who's on their radar?"

"Everyone."

"Don't tell me they suspect France!"

Victoire went silent and looked Massicot in the eye. He fidgeted in his seat.

"We weren't the ones who destroyed that plane. We didn't blow up the morgue or the top of that tower. I myself have been trying to figure out why those attacks occurred."

"Me too."

"Listen, Emma, you are very familiar with our government. You know we wouldn't do these horrible things—in our own country, no less! As soon as Méricourt finds out who's behind these horrible attacks, I'll let you know, using complete discretion, of course."

"Thank you, Pascal."

"There's something I don't understand, Emma."

"What is that?"

"When our Malaysian intermediary, Musa Kherrican, was in charge of the financial transactions, everything went smoothly. Everyone was paid right on schedule. It may have been a bit unstructured, but at least we had someone who had a sense of honor. I'll add that he was also highly cultured."

"I give you that."

"Now he's been replaced with a totally impersonal system. You don't even know who you're talking to anymore."

Victoire thought quickly and took a calculated risk.

"Yet you and your friends have no reason to complain. You've been taken care of."

"Understand me. I'm not complaining. The suitcases were dangerous and a big hassle. The same goes for the people carrying them. But I miss my talks with Musa at Plaza Athénée and the Bristol. We could discuss politics and international relations. It's not just about the money. You've got to keep the human element. At the end of the day, the new system isn't very efficient. Look at what just happened at Orly. And with Noblecourt. It was his fault. What a waste."

The look in Massicot's eyes had turned bitter when he said Noblecourt's name. Things were getting delicate. Victoire was holding a grenade whose pin she was removing ever so cautiously.

"The truth is, Noblecourt was a victim."

The expression on Massicot's face went from bitter to incredulous.

"I think you're being very soft."

"Well, he was the one who gave the Chinese and the Americans the idea of sharing rare earths. He was the one who wanted to replace the traders with technology, both here and in Malaysia."

"No, Emma, I thought you were better informed. It was our Chinese and American friends who wanted to get rid of the traders. Noblecourt didn't do anything. He was told what to do. I'm in the position to know. He and Georgette had no reason to complain. I imagine you'll be cutting her off, as well, until order is reestablished."

Victoire turned toward the window. She needed to think, retreat, and use her ability to impose silence—until she could figure out what to say.

"You're not obligated to respond. But you're perfectly aware that Georgette has a son-in-law in Malaysia who's in charge of the system and a daughter at the Élysée who works in rare-earth elements. I'd love to hear a lecture from them on ethics, but I'm no idiot. They think they're entitled to more than anyone else. Just ask your friends."

"My job is also taking care of you, Pascal."

"Well, with the Noblecourts, it's not just Georgette and her daughter and son-in-law. There's Titus too."

"Titus?"

"Yes, Titus Polycarpe. A cunning man. You should pay him a visit."

"I'm responsible for reexamining everything from square one," Victoire said.

"And that's why I'm having you meet with someone. This'll blow you away. You'll see the Noblecourt family's true nature."

"I'm on the edge of my seat."

8

Luc zoomed in again on the source of heat captured by the thermal camera in Noblecourt's office. The medical examiner hadn't found any signs of a struggle. But the truth remained: the former president wasn't alone in that attic. Did Georgette help her husband hang himself? What horrible reason could she have had for doing that?

Why make the world believe it was murder? What was the point? And Georgette couldn't have been the second person. It didn't add up. The person had come in and gone out through the top-floor window. Considering her age and physical condition, Georgette would have just used the door.

Frustrated, Luc asked the touchscreen wall to display the documents Victoire had obtained on Noblecourt's personal computer. Analysis of his bank accounts showed a fortune of more than eight million euros. More precisely, the couple's assets amounted to 8,235,126 euros, not counting their home, a family inheritance that was worth millions, considering its coveted central location in Paris.

The financial investigation application provided by Méricourt had reexamined the couple's stocks, bonds, and derivatives. Pierre-André and Georgette had been frugal and staid and had gotten their financial advice from investment professionals with serious game but a lack of imagination.

Nothing indicated fraud on the part of the companies in the couple's holdings. There was no trace of insider trading, the discovery of which could have explained the suicide of the family's patriarch or even his murder. Either the Noblecourts were shadow banking geniuses, or what Luc saw was what they had.

Luc decided to switch gears. Digging through the database of the Bonneval architecture firm in Boulogne-Billancourt just outside the city, his search engine was able to find the measurements of the Beau Paris Tower. It was 270.26 meters from the ground floor to the top. Starting at the building's foundation, it was 290.59 meters in height.

"So what?" Luc asked out loud.

Luc didn't know what to make of it. What did those two figures mean? What was Emma Wong trying to understand? The most recent news reports on the tower attack hadn't revealed anything Luc didn't already know. The uninhabited top floor had been blown up. And a portion of the building's water-supply system had been damaged. What else was there?

If Emma Wong's so-called friends were planning to set up shop on the top floor, why would the attackers go after it when it was deserted? Of all the catastrophes raising havoc in Paris since Flight 912, this one was the most mystifying. But it was also the least deadly. Still, Luc was positive that the exact height of the tower was somehow related to the attack.

"They destroyed something. They erased some clue. I've got to go check it out."

9

John stroked the fine leather armrest. His chair was one of thirty-two evenly spaced around a massive table in the G. Terres boardroom. Each belonged to a representative of a G. Terres member nation. Beyond a bulletproof picture window, John could see a man-made lake in the shape of a crescent. It even had a beach. On the lawns of the houses all around the lake, landscape lighting showcased lush flowerbeds.

John looked up. The ceiling of this top-floor meeting room was glass. He gazed at the moon and the stars and then looked around the room again. He marveled at the space. It could put anyone in a good mood.

Serge emerged from the kitchen and walked over to the table with two dinner trays. He put the trays down and pulled out the chair next to John.

"This is where the organization's executive-council meetings take place three times a year. I sit in one of those chairs over there—against that curved wall. This chair belonged to the French ambassador."

"Tell me about him."

"He was always on good behavior when he was here. He'd show off for the interns. UN leaders in Paris always prepared everything thoroughly, so he didn't have anything to do with that. I wanted to show you the boardroom so you could understand the context in which my father-in-law was murdered. Please, eat. Your dinner's still hot."

John didn't need to be told twice. He picked up his porcelain spoon and started scooping up the pork in his spicy *bak-kut-teh* soup.

"We have a full-time Malaysian chef on staff," Serge said. "She does quite a job for us. I didn't know a thing about Malaysian cuisine when I came here. But I'm a convert now. Enough of that. Let me fill you in. Pierre-André was the one who pitched the idea of G.Terres at a G20 summit. Since you've been sent to Malaysia, I'm assuming you know what rare earths are."

John nodded as he spooned up his soup. He hadn't eaten all day, and he was starving.

Serge continued. "What you might not know is that rare earths aren't really so rare. Thirty-two nations have them, and all those nations are represented here."

"I see."

"Only China had the foresight to develop and implement a long-term strategy. They did this way back in the nineteen eighties. At one time they controlled more than ninety percent of the supply used in renewable energy, advanced electronics, and defense. But they shot themselves in the foot by imposing strict export controls. When prices rose to nearly thirty times their previous levels, other countries either got in the game or upped their game, and prices dropped. Smuggling operations and illegal mines in China didn't help. When they loosened some of their export restrictions, the bubble burst, hurting producers everywhere. Unfortunately, the companies hurt the worst were the ones in the West, the United States, for example."

"Okay, so it's the old law of supply and demand," John said. "Supply goes up, and prices go down. Isn't that a good thing?"

"You would think, and usually that's the case. But we're dealing with precious commodities—remember, the reserves are finite—and nations that often work at cross purposes. Some alternatives to rare earths have been developed, but my father-in-law recognized the need for cooperation and a unified, strictly aboveboard way of dealing with these elements, which are essential to the future of the entire world. He came up with his idea at the same time that he was relaunching his European economic intelligence program, which he hoped would ease unemployment and encourage innovation."

"I remember that."

"It was the opportune time to ensure that rare earths would no longer be an object of wild speculation or huge fluctuations. The Chinese, having experienced their own downturn, realized it was in their best interest to cooperate. That's how G. Terres was created."

John finished his soup and went after the *ayam masak kicap*, a chicken dish with soya. Serge swept his arm around the room.

"G. Terres members are the ones producing—and sometimes transforming—rare earths. Some nations, like France, engage in both production and processing. Our country has large deposits in the Pacific."

"I'm aware of that."

"The idea is to have all the countries come together here, so they can trade information, as well as the rare earths themselves, on an equal footing and with complete transparency. It's the first attempt to establish global governance of a major—and crucial—commodity. The organization sets all the rules, and every member nation has a say."

John nodded, wiping his mouth with a napkin.

"We'll visit the trading room, which is in another building. Traders accredited by the organization use the high-speed algorithmic platform to scan multiple exchanges and markets for emerging trends and execute rare-earth orders in the blink of an eye. But this is no ordinary investment bank or hedge fund. G. Terres adheres to specific international regulations. The idea is to let competition play out while avoiding speculation and wild fluctuations in prices. The use of derivatives and other sophisticated financial toys is prohibited. Soon, any trader—or group of traders—from anywhere in the world who's caught in the exploitation of rare-earth elements will face criminal charges. They'll go before a high court headquartered at La Défense, and it will have the power to fine and sentence anyone found guilty of insider trading in the rare-earths industry. The maximum penalty will be twenty years in a member-country prison selected at random. There will be no right of appeal."

"So what happens in the meantime, while you're waiting for the court's headquarters to open?"

"G. Terres has an internal audit system to evaluate any transaction's authenticity. It's a foolproof computerized system that can analyze billions of pieces of data every microsecond."

"It actually works?"

"Yes, it works wonderfully. We already have a case that will go to trial."

"What's the case?"

"A South African mining company concealed its discovery of a large deposit of monazite near Cape Town. Insider trading related to this monazite was discovered in a G. Terres audit. Now the company's CEO and board members could be fined more than a hundred million euros. We're just waiting for the court's headquarters to open so the case can be heard."

"I'm assuming that those headquarters are slated to be at the top of the Beau Paris Tower," John said. "That space was just blown up."

"Probably an intimidation tactic."

"Whose intimidation tactic?" John asked as he moved on to his deep-fried bananas with caramel sauce.

"It could be the South Africans. They're capable of anything. They've got connections all over and have been tight with the Indians ever since apartheid ended."

"So we have the last missing piece."

10

Sitting next to the defense minister, Victoire admired the famous Marly horse statues and the royal pool at Domaine National de Marly-le-Roi. Pascal Massicot's car climbed a hill overlooking the park and pulled onto the Grande Rue. The frigid rain was coming down much harder now. The driver parked and got out of the car. Armed with an umbrella, he opened Victoire's door. She thanked him and stepped onto the pavement. At the top of Le Cottage's front steps, the cheery-faced restaurant owner offered an enthusiastic welcome.

"I've reserved the pink room for you," she said. "There's already a gentleman waiting."

Victoire entered the cozy space. It was a real oasis of friendliness and charm. Nothing like the cold and impersonal alcoves of the ministries. Massicot made the introductions.

"Emma, this is Thierry Vander. He's a strategic advisor based in Lausanne, Switzerland. Thierry has been working with me for twenty-two years."

"Twenty-three, Mr. Minister."

"We can skip the small talk. It's just us here. Emma is the person our friends have put in charge of auditing the distribution of commissions and other contract-related income. She's been tasked with cutting off our revenue stream while we're waiting to find out what happened."

Victoire gave Thierry Vander a once-over. He had the physique of someone who worked out regularly—outside and year-round, from the looks of him. He gave Victoire a polite bow, and all three sat down. Picking up their menus, Massicot recommended a Scandinavian-style brunch.

"I was telling Emma how Noblecourt's crew was so deeply entrenched in the practice of divvying up the commissions. I'm actually wondering if Pierre-André was somehow involved in the Orly attack."

"What makes you say that?" Victoire asked.

"I'm sure he wasn't all that thrilled about you coming to Paris."

"How could he have known?"

"The ambassador could have told him. Luckily, you took another flight. You must have sensed something. You're a very smart woman, Emma. Most likely, Noblecourt was just waiting for you to be turned into black dust."

As a deathly silence fell over the table, Massicot put his napkin on his lap and poured himself some tea.

Finally, the Swiss strategist asked a question. "If Noblecourt was their accomplice, why would they have hanged him? It doesn't make sense."

"That's just it, Thierry. He committed suicide."

"But why?" Victoire asked.

Massicot turned to Thierry. The Swiss man pushed his plate aside and put his arms on the table. He locked eyes with Victoire.

"Noblecourt married into a banking family. His brother-in-law, Titus, was a banker, the same as his father-in-law. Banking is a genetically transmitted disease. Money and politics, a classic pair. It's so much more fun here than back home. Between us, Swiss political scandals are a bore. Good thing we've got France. Right, Mr. Minister?"

"Stop digressing, and get back to the facts."

"When Noblecourt formed G. Terres and brought France in, he didn't forget his little family. Titus Polycarpe helped finalize the financial-data system for La Défense and Putrajaya."

"Wouldn't a banker be responsible for that kind of thing?"

"It's not exactly what you think, Emma."

"I'm all ears," Victoire replied. It wasn't a lie.

"Titus is an old-school banker. He can't tell the difference between a computer and a flatiron. But he's an orchestrator. Titus knew very well that he'd have to make everything look a hundred percent safe and ethical. Remember, G. Terres was the first of a kind—an entirely transparent international organization using high-frequency trading with oversight. His model had to be flawless."

"Indeed, I remember," Victoire said with a nod.

"Titus found a French company that could develop a system for monitoring all G. Terres transactions. This system would use large-volume buy and sell orders to identify insider trading."

Victoire remembered Chronosphere and Julien Lanfrey. Their ties to the Noblecourt family were still unclear.

"The insider trading, which your penny-pinching friends divulged to us, sweet Emma, was meant to be evaded by a system developed by the Noblecourts themselves. Their hypocrisy is mind-boggling! A high-tech company that makes atomic clocks is at the heart of Noblecourt's system. It's called Chronosphere."

Victoire turned to Massicot. "Please explain how Chronosphere was able to help the Noblecourts. Yes, it was the internal-audit company that Titus picked himself, but wouldn't the system have detected any abnormal activity benefiting the Noblecourts, the same way it detects any other insider trading? You're perfectly aware that we've been keeping an eye on things. How does the Chronosphere system work?"

"Why are you asking me? I don't know anything about that," Massicot answered.

"But you're France's minister of defense. You have access to this kind of information." Victoire caught herself. She was losing her assumed persona. She paused and made another stab. "The French government has a stake in monitoring Chronosphere. Wouldn't your department be doing that?"

"Yes, in theory my department would. But that's where things get complicated."

"Please, enlighten me. I've come here from Kuala Lumpur to clean up operations in France."

Massicot took another sip of his tea.

"Chronosphere did do work for the defense department—in other words, for my ministry."

"Then it should be easy for you to find out how they were able to secretly assist the Noblecourts."

"Chronosphere had a contract with the Directorate for Defense Protection and Security, the military counterintelligence and counterterrorism sector of my ministry."

"Okay…"

Victoire could tell by the chagrined look on the minister's face that the situation wasn't so simple.

"So what's the problem?"

"General Francis Béard is in charge of that sector. He's an honest guy. More important, he's a stickler for the rules."

"There's one of those in every organization."

"It gets worse. Béard is friends with Claudine Montluzac. If he finds out I'm interested in Chronosphere, he'll tell her, and it'll probably go straight up to Méricourt and perhaps even to Presidend Jemestre. I'm stuck. I don't trust any of the bureaucrats in my ministry. They'd all love to pin a scandal on me, because I've put so many budget restrictions in place. I've cut spending like a beast."

"Who's Claudine Montluzac?"

"She's a police higher-up who nitpicks my every move."

"Why would a police detective be interested in what you're doing?"

"She works for white-collar crimes. But she's also been investigating the former president's death. And I think she may be working for a foreign country."

"Which one?"

"Thierry's looking into that."

Victoire turned to the strategist.

"I have a few ideas…"

11

A s they finished up their meal, John asked, "So, I've got a question. Have you ever heard of a company called Chronosphere? It's based in Paris and specializes in high-precision clocks."

"Yes. They developed our auditing and network surveillance system. The founder is Julien something or other. I've forgotten his last name. It was with their help that we found out what the South African mining company was up to. We can be a little less formal with each other at this point, right?"

"Sure."

"The boss is a cool guy. He came here with a pianist named Mathilde. She played at the tennis club in Selangor. She also performed at the opening ceremonies of a chess tournament at the Shangra-Li casino. She was amazing."

"A chess tournament, you say?"

"Yes, they have lots of them in Putrajaya."

John took out his cell phone and showed Serge the photos of the chess match with the clearly visible Asian gentlemen in midconversation.

"Have you ever seen these people before?"

Serge leaned in to take a look.

"Never."

"No worries."

"So why don't we head over to the trading room I was telling you about," Serge suggested.

He led John out of the building and into another one. They walked through the lobby, where a few cleaning women looked like they were finishing their work. The women gathered up their buckets and mops without making eye contact with John or Serge. The two men continued on to a glass door. An armed guard was in front of it. He greeted Serge, glanced at the badge John was wearing, and stepped aside.

John and Serge entered the trading room. It was oval in shape, with a balcony. In the center was a heavy glass table surrounded by fifty or so chairs. At each place there was an array of computer screens and telephones to facilitate the trading of rare earths all around the globe.

"This is the system envisioned by my father-in-law and approved of by the other member countries. Every transaction is centralized and regulated. The process is totally transparent. Check out the balcony."

John looked up.

"When it's running from six in the morning to six at night, visitors can watch everything from the balcony, as long as they're quiet."

Serge showed John a stock-market board with rare-earth listings.

"The price of every strategic mineral is displayed here in real time. Everyone can see what's happening and find out which companies are selling and which are buying. All rare-earth sellers and investors are obligated to pass through here. At six p.m., when the Putrajaya trading room closes for the day, the one at La Défense in Paris takes the baton. Over there, it's ten in the morning, and the traders work until ten at night. With this system, we're in business twenty-four-seven."

"Do your traders get security clearances?"

"Of course. They're thoroughly vetted before they're hired."

"And there's no black market in rare-earth commodities?"

"It's next to impossible to stop all black-market activities. But what you see here is as close as you'll get. The members of G. Terres are committed to keeping all trading confined to this room and the one in Paris."

"So what about the black-market stuff that does get by you?"

"As I've said, our system makes that very difficult. Our system analyzes every transfer in real time in order to detect any attempted insider trading, abusive speculation, money laundering, or embezzlement in rare-earth sales and purchases."

"In other words, organized crime would have a hard time worming its way into the rare-earths industry."

"It would be very difficult, but again, not impossible."

"How could it happen?"

"Someone who isn't legit could buy all or part of a company that mines or processes rare-earth minerals. But even that person—or business—would have to comply with G. Terres regulations or risk being found out and prosecuted in that court I was telling you about."

"Considering the hundreds of people who died in the Orly disaster, your father-in-law's death, the slaying of his two bodyguards, and now the ambassador's murder, it's quite possible that somebody wants to meddle with what you're doing here. You don't have any ideas?"

"My father-in-law met with some people, but I don't know who or where. I'm sure he discovered something—with Emma Wong's help—that he wasn't supposed to know about."

"He didn't tell you anything?"

"My father-in-law didn't trust me in that way. You'd have to ask my wife. She's the one who oversees G. Terres operations from the Élysée."

"We've already met with her. She doesn't know any more than you do."

"We'll give her another call. Do you want to stay at my country cottage?"

12

Luc watched Julien in admiration as he tried to boost the morale of his employees, who were huddled in Chronosphere's sooty courtyard. Although there was no way any work could get done, he had asked his engineers and office assistants to come in, as he wanted to meet with them.

Luc's eyes were stinging, and his chest felt heavy. He could tell, though, that the heavy hearts all around him were much harder to bear.

"I don't want any of you to worry," Julien said. "We're insured. There's nothing in the laser room that can't be replaced.

We didn't lose anything major. We'll start putting everything back together right away."

Luc could see that the receptionist was teary.

"Mathilde, that goes double for you," Julien said. "I don't want you to fret."

"It's not that, Julien…"

"What is it then?" he asked.

"I thought you were still in there."

"Fortunately, I was with this gentleman," he said, looking over at Luc.

"Are you going to sell to the Chinese?" one of the workers asked.

"No—not for the time being. The Chinese—and anyone else who's interested in us—will just have to wait."

Luc stared at the forlorn employees, their arms dangling helplessly at their sides. No doubt about it: this was a setback for Chronosphere—another hurdle added to a whole obstacle course. But Julien was right. If he sold now, he'd get pennies on the dollar, even if it was the company's ideas that any buyer would want.

"We have to get on our feet," Julien said. "We've made a name for ourselves all the way to China and India. We'll turn a profit eventually. And until we sell—if ever—we're safe from predators, because we're in a strategic sector."

Luc was impressed. Julien was laying out a reassuring future for his workers.

He cleared his throat and continued. "You've all been wonderful. Now go home. I'll be keeping in touch with all of you, and with any luck we'll be back in business in no time."

The chief of the Paris Fire Brigade was waiting off to the side. After everyone had filed out, he led Julien and Luc through Chronosphere's smoky premises to the laser room, ground zero. The door, which the firefighters had been forced to break open, had partially melted.

"The fire started here and then spread to the rest of the plant," the chief told Julien. "It was extremely hot. Look—everything's melted."

With tissues over their noses, Luc and Julien examined the extent of the damage. The walls and ceiling were black with soot. The equipment used to turn out Chronosphere's high-precision clocks was twisted from the heat. The tables and workbenches were charred masses on the floor. Everything had a rank smell.

"Did you find my cell phone?" Julien asked.

The chief handed him the device.

"Here you go," he said. "We found it in the middle of the room."

Luc looked at the black lump. Why had Julien even bothered to ask for it?

"What caused the fire?" Julien asked.

"So far, we haven't found any evidence of explosives or detonating devices, but we've just begun our investigation. You must be a Defense Ministry contractor, because they've already contacted us."

Luc was looking at Julien's defeated expression. The head of Chronosphere had immediately realized the probable connection between his phone and the fire. Someone was hell-bent on destroying Chronosphere—or its founder, going as far as trying to incinerate him in this crematory. Luc went back over the details of the fire at the morgue.

"You said the door was closed?" Luc asked the chief.

"Yes, it was melting when we arrived. We had to use an ax to get it open."

"It can be locked from a remote location," Julien said.

"Good thing no one was in here," the chief said.

"Exactly."

Julien exchanged a few more words with the chief and said good-bye. Then he turned to Luc and suggested that they go to a Breton crêpe restaurant on the Rue du Montparnasse.

"I'm guessing you could use something to eat," Luc told Julien. Luc also had a hoard of questions screaming in his head for attention. But he waited until they got to the restaurant before quizzing him.

"You told your employees that you're protected from any hostile takeover, especially a Chinese takeover."

"Yes, Chronosphere works with a research center that simulates nuclear testing for the Atomic Energy and Alternative Energies Commission. It's considered a strategic sector. We've done work that the French government doesn't want the Chinese to get their hands on. I'm surprised that Hoang Ho didn't explain this to you."

Luc felt embarrassed.

"They don't let me in on everything. I'm just an intermediary."

"You can tell them that I'm not selling Chronosphere, but I'm very interested in doing a joint venture with the Chinese. They'd provide the money and own forty-nine percent of the joint-venture partnership. We'd do the research and own fifty-one percent."

"I think I'd have a hard time selling that," Luc said. "The Chinese don't typically like being minority shareholders."

"Well, I don't need to know now. I've got other things to take care of."

Luc gave Julien's shoulder a consoling squeeze before asking the crucial question: "Why would someone want to kill you in your laboratory?"

Julien sighed. "I'm trying to figure that out."

"I'm sure you have some idea. Or at least you'll try to find one. Hoang Ho is well connected in Paris. If you give us the go-ahead, we can help you."

"This case is very French-specific. I don't think the Chinese would know how to go about it."

"You're wrong about that. The founder's son teaches courses in French politico-administrative decision making at the University of Shanghai. Every Asian executive and diplomat who aspires to a high-level position in France takes those classes. And quite a few French ministers teach at the university after they've left the government. Also, French firms arrange conferences in China to explain how the government works and how the French do business. You'd be surprised at how well the Chinese can navigate the corridors of French business and government—ethically and responsibly."

"Ethical. Responsible. That's bullshit."

"Not at all. There's even a course at Shanghai University called French Operational Ethics."

"Maybe I should take it," Julien said. "Some days I don't have the vaguest idea of how this country's run."

"We still need to know the answer," Luc said, looking him in the eye.

"The answer to what?"

"Who wanted you dead?"

"Look, Luc, I know you mean well, and I appreciate your concern. I really do. But I can't tell you. I need to check on a couple of things. Those French operational ethics, or whatever the University of Shanghai calls it, are fucked up."

"Okay, but my offer stands. We can help you. Plus, it would make me happy."

"We should get going. And put that check back down. I've got it."

"But I'm not the one whose business just got burned to a crisp," Luc protested.

"Paying will make me feel good—like I'm really not broke."

Julien waved to the waiter.

"I have a question for you now, Luc."

"Shoot."

"Back there in my apartment, did I make *you* happy?"

"Julien, you made time stand still."

"You've got a corny sense of humor."

"Yeah."

13

Settled in comfortably at Serge Roussillon's country house, John was searching Benoît Dutreil's computer. Despite his repeated calls, John hadn't reached Dutreil. His colleague had disappeared without a trace, most likely after murdering Grapefruit with a baseball bat.

In the intelligence world, a star-crossed love could go violently awry. Mortemar should have been more careful and bitten his tongue. John too—because, in truth, he had been the unwitting force behind this violent chain of events. Saying too much always led to trouble.

A meticulous government worker, Dutreil had kept copies of all notes sent to Méricourt via the ambassador. It was usually just gossip couched in administrative jargon. But the most recent months of the French spy's activities had definitely become more interesting. The intel was of a higher quality and was more relevant. John could see Emma Wong's hand in all of this. The lovely lawyer had been serving Dutreil secrets on a silver platter, which he had immediately transferred to Paris.

Dutreil had given Emma Wong a nickname: Butterfly. Running across it a second time, John had a sudden realization. He straightened up in his bed, his brain in high gear. Serge's country house was called Butterfly Horizon. Was it possible that Emma Wong had captured not only the ambassador, his spy, and the former presidential couple in her net, but also Noblecourt's son-in-law?

John stood up and paced the room, and then he slowly opened the door and quietly walked down the hallway to the living room. Landscape lighting softly illuminated every piece of furniture. In the dining room, he paused in front of a photo of Apolline, Béatrice, and Serge. An ordinary family at an ordinary beach. Feeling reassured, he went into the kitchen to get a glass of water and returned to his bedroom.

He finished skimming through Dutreil's notes on the laptop. Then he pulled out the pad of stationery, which he had also brought along, and took it to the desk, where he found a number two lead pencil. John grinned. Every once in awhile, a twenty-first century spy had to rely on a trick learned in childhood. He lightly shaded the top sheet of paper to discern the indented impression of the writing. When he was done, he turned on the desk light and held the pad under it. With considerable effort he could make out the message. It was a letter that Dutreil had written to Hubert de Méricourt.

Mr. Director,

I'm sending this letter through the post to your personal address, as I no longer trust Mr. Nicolas Mortemar de Buzenval and won't even take a chance with a diplomatic pouch or our encrypted lines. I don't know how far the corruption goes.

This is the first time in my career that I've felt forced to use these means. You will quickly understand why. I know from a very reliable source that Mr. Buzenval has received kickbacks connected to the sale of two submarines to Malaysia. I will explain how in person. But it gets much more serious than that.

I have discovered a powerful and centralized system of political corruption in Southeast Asia. This system is of major strategic importance to nations concerned about the influence of India, the United States, and China in this region.

Mr. Buzenval is working with at least one party in this system, and he claims to have been authorized by a high-ranking French official.

I have also discovered an even more troubling situation. Malaysia's defense minister, Syafiq bin Rodney, has usurped an American information-pirating program. This instrument of cyber warfare allows any enemy to control industrial and military computer systems from a distance. The theft occurred two years ago, during an intentional breaching of the cruise ship Sovereign of the Sea *in the Strait of Malacca. I've learned from a reliable source that the Pentagon discovered this only a few months ago and is conducting an investigation.*

Given that Bin Rodney and our ambassador are close, I preferred to use pen and paper. I'll await further instruction.

Sincerely,

Colonel Benoît Dutreil,
Officer of the Legion of Honor

Chastising himself for underestimating the man, John folded the paper and put it in a pocket. Beneath the cultural attaché's worker-bee act was a brilliant analyst. Whether influenced by Emma Wong or not, he had dissected the situation beautifully. Through his source, he may have even reached a deeper level in his investigation—just as the foundational rules of his profession stressed.

John tried contacting Dutreil again. No luck. He needed to know if the man had sent the letter. Had Méricourt withheld information from him? Was he a puppet in a show he did not comprehend?

WEDNESDAY

1

John showered, threw on a bathrobe, and went out to the patio. Serge's lawn, maintained as diligently as a golf course, sloped gently toward a misty area filled with palms and exotic trees. To his right, a stone path curved around a lush bed of roses before ending at a bean-shaped pool. Nearby, three migratory cranes strolled across the grass. John heard a bell and looked in the other direction. Just beyond a fence, two cows were grazing. Serge hadn't been kidding when he called this his country home.

He tightened the belt of his bathrobe and walked out on the grass to get a better view of the house. In the early-morning sunshine, it looked like a strange blend of Le Corbusier and kitschy pagoda. The cow mooed, and John turned around. A man was emerging from the misty area. John squinted. It was none other than Benoît Dutreil.

Relieved to see Dutreil again, John hurried his way. "Everyone's been looking for you," he said when he finally reached him.

Dutreil, sweaty and unshaven, was looking nervously around the patio. "Is Serge home?"

"Why did you run off? Méricourt is worried to death. Were *you* the one who killed Grapefruit?"

"No, it wasn't me!"

"It's strange, but I thought of you instantly. When I told you that Emma died on the plane, your reaction was so extreme.

And then Grapefruit was murdered, most likely with a baseball bat that just happened to disappear from my closet."

"Anybody could have taken that bat out of your closet. That said, I could have killed that piece of shit, and I wouldn't have needed a bat. I'd have done it with my own two hands. And enjoyed it. But as I said, it wasn't me."

"Who then?"

"No idea. Emma was surprisingly well informed. She was a freelancer who used her business connections and ties to the Chinese diaspora to full advantage in providing analysis and advice to those willing to pay for it. I'm sure a woman like Emma had no trouble making friends. I'm guessing you searched my room, and by now you know about my letter to Méricourt."

"Yes. Did you send it?"

"Right before you arrived. I'm guessing Méricourt hasn't gotten it yet."

"Jesus. Is there an arrest warrant against you?"

"I don't know."

"I'll ask Amir bin Muhaimin for an update." John took out his phone and sent the minister a text.

"Do you think you'll get an answer?"

"I hope so. Listen, I'm hungry. Let's see what we can find for breakfast. You look like you could use something to eat too."

No sooner had he said this than a servant appeared with a tray filled with coffee, juices, and tartines. As they sat down, John was wondering how to steer the conversation back to Emma Wong, Dutreil's apparent mistress and Noblecourt's confidante. He didn't have to wait long.

"I went back to Emma's place last night," Dutreil said as he poured himself a glass of juice. "I found some documents from her legal cases." John watched as Dutreil gulped half the juice. "Emma was a wonderful woman. She's the one who secured a meeting with Singapore's minister of home affairs for Noblecourt. It was from there that he flew back to Paris without passing through Kuala Lumpur. Otherwise, they would have taken the same flight. And both of them would have died at Orly."

"That's crazy."

"It was Emma who sent Noblecourt those photos. She never told me. I didn't know she was that close to him."

John realized that Dutreil must think Emma was secretly working directly with the Élysée.

"She wanted to protect you," John offered. "That's why she didn't say anything."

"She could have told me."

"She didn't trust the French embassy. And she didn't want to put you in an awkward position by disclosing what the ambassador was doing. She knew to keep quiet. Right until the moment that—for reasons I don't quite understand—she broke the silence and told you everything. That's when you wrote to Méricourt. You did the right thing."

Dutreil looked up from his juice. His eyes were teary.

"Emma didn't want to ruin your relationship. Her silence was proof of her love." John had found the right words, but he felt like a terrible actor and hypocrite.

"At least *you* get me," Dutreil responded, his voice cracking.

John looked down, thinking Dutreil was as sentimental as he was.

Dutreil warily glanced around the patio and then leaned toward John. "I don't trust Serge," he whispered. "He's always snooping at the embassy. I found out that Emma was interested in him not too long ago. We have to be careful."

He looked to his right and straightened in his chair. John turned in the same direction and saw Serge heading toward them. His host was cinching a bathrobe identical to the one he was wearing.

"Benoît! It's good to see you. All I need is the green light from the Élysée, and I'll be on my way back to France. But meanwhile, what about the embassy? What happened with Grapefruit?"

"I was telling John that I'm not the one who killed him."

"That's reassuring. Well, make yourself at home, Benoît. Take a shower after you eat. Whatever you'd like."

2

Victoire couldn't take her eyes off Alexandre, who was fast asleep. It had been too long since she had seen him. She wanted to pick him up and kiss him all over.

"He's such a beautiful little boy. Hardly cries at all and so alert." Roberta had walked up behind her. "Don't worry. Rainbow Warrior and I are taking good care of him."

Victoire felt the dog brush against her leg.

"Roberta, I don't know what I'd do without you. If things don't settle down soon I'll have to hire a nanny."

"For now, Alexandre stays here, in my home. Now go see Luc. I'm assuming John's doing well, wherever he is."

"Everything's okay for now."

Victoire left Roberta's apartment and walked over to Fermatown. Caresse was there to greet her.

"Poor kitty! Luc forgot all about you, didn't he? I bet he didn't even feed you this morning."

She went upstairs, checking the kitchen first. It was as clean as a science lab. Her father and stepmother had gone over the place before leaving. Not a single trace of the baptism celebration.

Victoire suddenly felt an excruciating loneliness. She hadn't been able to say good-bye to her father and stepmother, either. Victoire wanted her baby and husband back home, where they belonged. But it was no use feeling sorry for herself. They had to finish this job. She opened a can of tuna for Caresse and headed toward the main room with the touchscreen wall. There, she found Luc staring at an ocean liner stranded on a beach lined with palm trees. Rescue vehicles and boats surrounded the ship.

"I see you're up at the crack of dawn—or at least the crack of dawn for you. What's that you're looking at?"

"It's two-year-old footage of the rescue of a thousand passengers and crew members on an American ship, the *Sovereign of the Sea*. Pirates seized the ocean liner in the Strait of Malacca and threatened to sink it if the United States didn't fork over a ransom. But they lost control of the ship, which wound up on this beach. John asked me to look into it."

"I don't remember the incident," Victoire said.

"John thinks the United States used a cyberweapon to take over the ship, forcing it to wash up on the beach and, in the process, saving the passengers and crew. Two senators were on that ship, which explains why the White House made the decision. The pirates, of course, abandoned ship when they lost control."

"Then what?"

"To carry out this maneuver, the US marines had to let the Malaysians in on the secret. Soldiers from Syafiq bin Rodney's clan could have gotten their hands on the American software."

"What does that mean?"

"It means that they could have used this advanced technology to hack into strategic French systems, causing the attack at Orly, as well as the one on John's plane. I've gotta go. I have a meeting in Vanves."

Victoire took Luc's spot at the touchscreen and requested photos of Syafiq bin Rodney. Instantly, the search engine gave her a series of images showing the defense minister alongside Malaysian, American, and French dignitaries, as well as other notable people. She recognized Pascal Massicot in one photo and Emma Wong in a few others. It was difficult to read the enigmatic expression on the French official's face.

Victoire checked herself in a full-length mirror to make sure the resemblance was still there. After examining her hair and features, she turned this way and that and realized that their carriage and posture were the same. Her strategy was working, and Victoire was beginning to feel connected to this woman who had died at Orly.

The way Emma was looking at the other people in the photos was also rich in information. She didn't seem to be especially taken with anyone—with the exception of one person: a jovial-looking character sporting several Legion of Honor badges. She appeared to be amused—almost admiring.

"Let's see who this guy is."

Musa Kherrican, a Malaysian citizen of Pakistani origins. According to secret US State Department archives made public by WikiLeaks, Kherrican was a key figure in the distribution of commissions and kickbacks between Southeast Asia, Washington, and Western Europe. The man, whom the State Department had nicknamed Jerrican, also appeared to be connecting nonprofit organizations and governmental agencies around the world with people who could supply strategic position papers and counsel. French Defense Minister Pascal Massicot's wife, Ludivine, had written at least one of those papers.

There was even a photo of Kherrican, aka Jerrican, in the company of France's defense and interior ministers. It had been taken at the Bristol.

"What a small world."

She had the photos of the Asians attending the chess tournament rescanned in the identification program. No results. All the faces were unknowns.

Frustrated, she delved further into the life of Musa Kherrican. He had addresses in Washington, Geneva, and Temerloh—a town near Putrajaya. It was a dream home, according to an article published a year earlier in *Architectural Digest*. Victoire flipped through the pages and stopped when one photo in particular caught her eye. Along the wall of one of the rooms was a glass case filled with silver bonsai trees. They were identical to the ones she had seen in Titus's apartment. Jerrican had told the *Architectural Digest* writer that in the sixteenth century of the Common Era, the sultans of the Strait of Malacca often sent works of art to Chinese emperors and Indian maharajas as a sign of friendship and loyalty.

"*Nihil sub sole novum,*" Victoire said in Latin. Nothing new under the sun.

3

Luc parked his car in the visitors lot and headed toward the entrance to the fort, where he showed a soldier his ID.

"I have a meeting with General Francis Béard."

"Yes, we're aware of that. Please sign the register, and go on in. I'll let the director's secretary know you're here."

The secretary, a woman who looked no more than twenty-five, showed up almost instantly. She looked Luc up and down. Luc smiled. Was it because the general didn't get many early-morning visitors or because the young woman liked what she saw?

"Lovely morning, isn't it?" she said, leading the way to the man's office.

"Yes, and very warm already."

Luc and the secretary reached the glass doors of a modern two-story building in the center of the nineteenth-century military complex. Fort Vanves was part of an old ring of fortifications that protected the capital at a time when battlefields were far from virtual.

"It's on the first floor."

"I know," Luc lied.

The sway of the secretary's hips and the curve of her legs below her pencil skirt were definitely energizing his step. How would he have known that a woman in uniform would turn him on? For his meeting with the head of the counterespionage unit, Luc had put on a crisp Zegna seersucker blazer. He felt confident and professional. Most likely, it was a turn-on for the secretary.

"Your visitor is here, sir."

"Thank you."

The secretary turned around and sashayed out of the room, with Luc getting one last look before greeting Francis Béard, commander of the Defense Ministry's Directorate for Defense Protection and Security. His bearing couldn't have been more different from the secretary's. Luc submitted to the general's crushing handshake.

"I met John during training at Saint-Cyr," the general said. "We crossed paths again at the ministry, when I did my time as chief of staff. It was a deplorable position with nonstop paperwork and unproductive meetings. How is John?"

"He's doing well and sends his regards."

"I bet you're happy to be working with him. You met in Méricourt's unit at Les Invalides, right?"

"Yes."

"Tell John that the ministry's minions are shipping me off to retirement next November. If there's a position for me at Fermatown, I'm in."

"Of course, General." Once again, Luc was lying. Fermatown was just fine with its three associates. No one else was needed.

"Let's have a seat over there," Béard said, motioning to a table. "We'll be more comfortable."

The two went over to the table, and Luc immediately noticed a file whose cover displayed the name Chronosphere.

"I believe you're interested in this company?"

"Correct."

"Chronosphere manufactures very high-tech products. It has had contracts with the defense ministry and the Atomic Energy and Alternative Energies Commission. The company undergoes regular audits for its security clearances. I'm prepared to answer certain questions that you may have."

"Thank you, sir. We have several questions. First, let me ask this: Does Chronosphere work in the maritime arena—or more specifically—with submarines?"

"I know what you're referring to, and I can answer with absolute certainty that Julien Lanfrey has never set foot on a military submarine—and certainly not the Malaysian subs that your firm's interested in."

"What kind of work do they perform for the government?"

"Chronosphere has supplied high-precision clocks to the defense ministry. They're used in simulated nuclear tests. This is a strategic sector that France does its utmost to protect. For that reason, we provide the company with safety and security advice."

"Yet, with all that counsel, the laser room caught fire yesterday. Do you know what happened?"

"We've received a preliminary report from the fire brigade. As you can guess, it's extremely suspicious, but we don't know exactly what happened."

Francis Béard leaned back in his chair and placed both hands on the table. The general had most likely deduced that someone had targeted Julien.

"We initially believed it was a cyberattack, as was most likely the case with the fire at the morgue, the Air France disaster, and probably the missile strike against the plane John was in. But the laser room had no computer terminals. There were no devices that could have been sabotaged or hacked from the outside."

"You're forgetting about Julien's smartphone."

The general gave Luc an enigmatic smile that hinted at an intimate knowledge of the situation. Luc felt himself go red, like a middle schooler embarrassed by a wrong answer.

"A smartphone alone couldn't have caused the fire. Theoretically, it could have served as a conduit or a remote control for a robot or a machine. But there were no such mechanisms in that room. We were very familiar with the laser room. Its safety was a stipulation of the government's contracts with the company."

"But the phone could be instrumental in a murder attempt. Isn't that true?"

"Yes, that's true.

"We have reason to believe that someone tried to kill Julien after his location was pinpointed—via his smartphone—in the laser room."

The general took a moment before responding.

"I think that's what he wants you to believe."

Luc took a deep breath to keep himself from getting red in the face again. He had fallen in the sack with Julien. Had he fallen for a line too?

"Why would he lie to me?"

"To make you believe someone wanted him dead," Béard replied.

"Why would he do that?"

"To hide the real reason for the fire. He used the terror attacks at Orly and the morgue to serve his own purposes."

"What's your theory?"

"Six months ago, Chronosphere alerted us to the theft of an atomic clock. Under the terms of our contracts with them, they were required to report it."

"So how does that relate to the fire?"

"The firefighters found the remnants of an atomic clock in the laser room."

"So you think the atomic clock was not, in fact, stolen, and Julien purposely destroyed the laser room as a cover-up?"

"Atomic clocks retain every experience and connection they've ever been exposed to. They remember the time splicing inherent in a hydrogen-bomb detonation, the development of a nano-surgery laser, the speed at which a chemical solution settles, and who knows what else."

"In other words, an atomic clock would remember something that, as you said, Chronosphere might want to hide," Luc replied.

"That's what I'm thinking, but I don't have proof."

From his briefcase, Luc took out the atomic clock photo that Emma Wong had sent to Noblecourt. Béard looked at the picture and jotted down the number sequence on the clock.

"Please excuse me for a moment," the general said, taking the piece of paper back to his desk.

Luc waited while Béard consulted his computer. A few minutes later he returned to the table.

"This is the clock that was reported stolen. I'm guessing—and it's really more than a guess—that it was witness to something strange and possibly even compromising that Julien Lanfrey wanted to erase."

"I have another question, sir."

"Go ahead."

"Chronosphere's finances are in bad shape. The company owes money all over the place. I'm wondering how they've managed to stay afloat."

"We're aware of that, but I don't have the resources to scrutinize the balance sheets of all the companies that do work for us. My staff is shrinking like the Arctic glaciers. And the defense minister has been adamant about cutting my budget. Pascal Massicot is trying to destroy counterespionage, and I'd love to know why."

"You must have some idea."

"John was smart to hire you. I'm not discouraging you from investigating Massicot, but for the time being I can't say any more."

"Thank you, sir."

"I hope I've helped you."

"Yes, you've helped quite a bit."

"There's something else. I shouldn't be telling you, but John's a good friend, and your team needs to know."

"What is it, sir?"

"Julien Lanfrey has bid on a top-secret contract with the Pentagon. He should have told us, but he didn't."

4

John was staring impatiently over Dutreil's shoulder at the line of cars snaking slowly toward the bridge on Federal Route 87. Serge's SUV had been stuck at the top of a hill for half an hour. What was going on?

John was tempted to order Dutreil to just veer onto the berm and speed past all the other cars. They had an appointment to keep, and didn't working for the French embassy have some perks? But he knew the proper spy wouldn't go for it. Besides, for all they knew, Dutreil was wanted for murder by now, and drawing attention to themselves was the last thing they should do. A few seconds later two motorcycle officers sped up to the front of the line and started asking drivers for their registration.

"It's just like France. Instead of getting to the bottom of the problem, they screw around at the top."

Dutreil turned to John in the backseat.

"What now?"

"We definitely shouldn't make a run for it. They've spotted us. It's no accident they're here."

The two cops made their way to Serge's vehicle and asked for the registration. As Serge pulled it out, one of the officers gave John and Dutreil a once-over. John figured this was it. The cops would be asking for IDs and arresting Dutreil. But nothing of the sort happened. The cops thanked Serge and moved along.

Ten minutes later, the SUV had progressed a couple of car lengths, thanks to the vehicles that had turned around and sped back the other way. John could now see the reason for the traffic jam. Two major demonstrations were taking place on the bridge. The opposing groups didn't seem inclined to call it a day, and John cursed under his breath. Speeding ahead on the berm wouldn't have gotten them very far anyway. Serge looked at his watch, and then turned to him.

"I'm gonna see what's going on. I don't get it. This never happens here. It feels suspicious."

"Let us know if there's anything we can do," John said.

"You should both stay here. I won't be long."

John waited until Serge was out of earshot and tapped Dutreil on the shoulder. "You wanted to tell me something earlier."

"Not here."

Dutreil pointed to the roof of the SUV and the dashboard to indicate the potential presence of cameras and microphones. "Let's get out."

John was all for stretching his legs. The two men stepped out of the vehicle and started walking up a hill. Some children were playing under a palm tree. The landscape in this part of Malaysia was filled with the trees, as palm oil was one of the country's major exports.

They continued walking and came across a blue, yellow, and red building where teenagers were playing ping pong. John always enjoyed watching the game. He liked its precision. But at the moment, he was more interested in what Dutreil had to say. They headed toward a small outlook where they could see the road descending toward the bridge. They could make out Serge, who was halfway to his destination.

"Let's hear it."

"I sent the pictures of the chess match to the Singapore office."

"And?"

"The Chinese men watching the chess match are simply players from Singapore. They're as innocent as lambs."

"You said earlier that Emma didn't trust Serge. Now that he's down there, you can tell me why."

"She had become very interested in Chronosphere and Julien Lanfrey. She said she had proof that Serge knew what business Julien was doing."

"What kind of business?"

"She said it was something amazing—and that was the word she used. It defied imagination. But she had to go to Paris to measure something."

"Measure what?"

"No idea. She just said that the Noblecourt family was cashing in on a few clever centimeters."

"What could that possibly mean?"

"I don't know, but she seemed shocked. Blown away, actually. And for Emma Wong, that's saying a lot."

John thought immediately of the Beau Paris Tower measurements that Emma wanted with centimeter precision.

He was about to share this with Dutreil when a text message popped up on his smartphone. It was from Amir bin Muhaimin, minister of home affairs. "John, I have some bad news."

Immediately, his phone rang.

"Your Excellency," John said.

"The police found your fingerprints all over the baseball bat. Some elements are pushing for your arrest. I'm working on holding the investigators off. I know you didn't do it."

"Does that mean you know who did?" John asked. Bin Muhaimin clicked off without answering.

"Bad news?" Dutreil asked.

"Just some bullshit," John replied as he tried to digest the news.

Before he could say anything else, he heard an uproar below them. Drivers caught in the traffic jam were honking their horns and yelling.

"What's going on?" Dutreil said.

They rushed toward the overlook. A large tanker truck was careening along the side of the road, bypassing the long line of motionless cars. It was exactly what he had wanted to do just a little while ago. The giant truck scraped the sides of the stopped vehicles as it plowed toward the bridge. John could make out Serge down below, in the middle of negotiations with the protesters. When John glanced back at the truck it had veered and was now speeding up the hill—in their direction!

"He's here for us," John yelled. "Move!"

John grabbed Dutreil, dragged him to the side, and started running as fast as possible. John shouted at the teenagers to do the same, but they couldn't hear him. He knew exactly what to expect. The truck exploded just as they reached the building with the ping-pong tables. John felt like he was back on the Afghan mountain the day his helicopter crashed. The earth shook under his feet. He threw himself on the ground and felt the flames swoosh behind him, destroying everything in its path. Overhead, the palm trees were burning like torches.

In loud rhythmic bursts, the cars below them exploded, one after another.

John checked on Dutreil, who was lying next to him.

"You all right?"

The man was moaning. John was about to get up and help Dutreil to his feet when he saw the smoking steel plate stuck in his chest. It was pointing at the sky.

"John… It's important…"

John leaned in, and the man whispered in his ear.

With that, Colonel Benoît died a combat hero's death.

John reached into Dutreil's vest pocket, removed a lighter-sized object, and then checked himself for any injuries and found nothing but a lump on his head. He stood up and trotted to the outlook. He saw two goons climbing up the hill.

John turned back to the lifeless expressions on the faces of the ping-pong players and the incinerated remains in the decimated cars.

"I'm getting tired of this bullshit." With that, he sprinted off behind the closest building and slipped into a network of back alleys. It was going to be a long, rough jog.

All this to meet Musa Kherrican, aka Jerrican. He'd take care of the goons later, if he had a chance.

5

Luc enlarged the images of the men playing chess and called Victoire over. She was tidying up the space they called the confessional. It was where they met with Fermatown clients.

"Look," he told her.

"I've practically got them memorized. They're getting us nowhere."

"Don't pay attention to the spectators, Victoire. Just focus on the chess match. We've been way off base from the beginning. Emma Wong wasn't showing Noblecourt the spectators. She was showing him the chess game. *That's* the interesting part. Shocking, even."

"I'm more of a Go fan myself," Victoire replied with a shrug. "Chess is brutal. The game has you killing your enemy's king.

In Go, no one dies. You take in your opponent and conquer them by giving them the illusion of independence—which is clearly what Emma was doing with all these guys."

"Stop making things as complicated as a Chinese finger trap, and look at the significance of what you sent Méricourt."

"You do know that Emma's the one who sent the chess match pics, don't you?"

"I'd never confuse the two of you. You're way more beautiful. Seriously, you look hot today. I'll have to enjoy it while I can. John's on the other side of the planet and can't kill me for lusting after you."

"Okay, quit it," Victoire groaned. "Get back to your point."

Luc walked over to the chessboard sequence and pointed to the part of the touchscreen that showed each move.

"This is the end of the match. The only pieces left standing on the sixty-four squares are a black rook, a white rook, and a few pawns. The moves made by the rooks in the first three boards make sense, but when we get to the fourth one, the black rook can't make it to that square without getting killed by the white pawn."

"If you say so."

"Once we get to the fourth photo, the game becomes ridiculous. The black rook here should have been taken by the white pawn. And yet the pawn does nothing. It lets him pass. The black rook makes thirty-seven consecutive moves without the whites reacting at all. Then the white rook makes four moves that are just as crazy."

"What does this mean?"

"It means the two players are communicating in code," Luc replied triumphantly.

"Explain."

"In chess, each square corresponds to a letter between A and H and a number between one and eight. In the fourth image of the chessboard, the white rook is on D3—which, by itself, means nothing. But if we assume that the rook—"

"Okay, Luc, you lost me at eight," Victoire said, holding up her hand. "Just cut to the chase."

"I know. You already told me—you're not a fan of chess. Long story short, you follow all the moves on the board, and you get the exact height of the Beau Paris Tower, believe it or not. And if you continue studying the moves, you get a measure of time. I'm not positive, but I think it's a thousand-millionth of a second."

"What? That's crazy!"

"I'll say."

"But how does this fit into the attack on the tower?" Victoire asked.

"I don't know why the exact height of the tower would be of interest to the people who attacked the building."

"There must be something else," Victoire said. "Maybe something so obvious, we haven't seen it."

"Let's go with what we know. There's a clear connection between the exact height of the tower and the calculations that an atomic clock can make. Someone was wondering how long it would take for something to travel the distance between the top and the bottom of the building."

"Or the distance between the bottom and the top, which would be the same."

"This is starting to give me a headache," Luc said. "Why not have Emma pay Julien a visit? Might as well ask the second-slicer himself what this means. What do you think of that idea?"

"It's risky. He may have met with Emma in Kuala Lumpur."

"You've been pulling it off so far. Plus you've got a secret weapon, which he won't be expecting."

"What's that?"

"Julien bid on a Pentagon contract without telling the French Defense Ministry people. What if our Emma—and that means you—is working for the United States, which is perfect-ly possible. See what I'm getting at?"

"A double agent. Or should it be triple? I'm losing track."

"Our Emma Wong was a mystery woman, wasn't she? But I'd say you're on the Wong track."

Victoire cracked a smile. "You've got a corny sense of humor. Did I ever tell you?"

"No, but somebody else did."

6

John thanked the kind Malaysian man who had picked him up after the tanker explosion and gotten him to the town of Temerloh. It had taken a while to get going, because enough debris had to be cleared from the road to allow vehicles to pass. John needed the time to collect himself anyway. Serge had disappeared in the chaos, and John had been left to fend for himself with ripped clothes and a lump on his head. After getting the ride, he had walked the last few miles to Musa Kherrican's home.

Kherrican came to greet John with his servants, a Sikh in a turban and two Indian women in saris. The man was small, quick, and bubbling with clever intellect.

"Amir bin Muhaimin has great respect for you. Make yourself at home in this humble space. Once you feel recovered, it would be an honor to sit down with you and address every one of your concerns."

John expressed his gratitude and followed the two women into a room with both a whirlpool bath and a hammam. Undressed, pampered, and soothed like a baby, he was now on a massage board, his body being worked every which way. Standing off to the side was the Sikh, holding a robe as grand as any the Prince of Wales had ever owned.

John stared at himself in the mirror and decided he looked pretty stylish in the suit that Musa Kherrican had lent him.

"Now you look human," he told himself.

John admired the décor and appreciated the delicate serenity of the place. Kherrican had not only a sense of hospitality, but also good taste. The dining room where a light meal awaited them was a typical Malaysian mix. This country had mastered the art of architectural blending. Luckily, good taste often trumped the kitschy mistakes.

"Have a seat, good friend."

John pulled out a Louis XVI armchair at the mahogany table and sat down. He peered up at the ceiling, which was breathtakingly beautiful.

"It's a replica of the Sistine Chapel. My mother was Catholic."

"It's amazing."

"I attended a Jesuit school in India that was run by the French. It shaped my mind and my judgment."

Kherrican spoke perfect French. The somewhat portly man with steely eyes routinely handled dirty money, but he had a unique elegance. John took note of the height of his host's chair, clearly designed to compensate for his size.

"The great theological debates of the French Renaissance have always captivated me. You have no idea how much I owe your wonderful culture. Your people taught me how to think."

"Thanks."

"But you didn't come to Malaysia to listen to me lecture."

"Well, kind of…"

Kherrican went silent as the first course was placed in front of them. He picked up the conversation again when the servant left the room.

"I heard you went to see Emma Wong's father."

John gave a brief summary of his visit to the home of the Baba Bling in Kuala Lumpur.

"I believe you know Emma."

"Who doesn't know her?" Kherrican said. "Your former president knew her, of course. How tragic."

"Who did Emma work for?"

"My good friend Emma did the same kind of work for intelligence that I do in my business. She was an intermediary and, in a way, a psychic. Let's say she had a preference for Uncle Sam."

"Had you seen her recently?"

"Yes, Emma wanted to know why Syafiq bin Rodney had squeezed me out of the submarine deal. It seemed strange to her. I'm usually the one who manages the commissions and other payouts. I distribute them here and in Paris, Washington, and Beijing. They go to high-ranking officials and those a tier or two below them. You can't forget about the latter group. The politicians who are always in the spotlight aren't necessarily the ones who get things done. We need the bureaucrats. They influence their superiors and see to it that everything works the way it should. You can tell who some of them are by just going to dinner at a fancy restaurant, like Le Bristol."

Kherrican smiled. "Le Bristol. I've had many memorable dinners there."

After a pause, he continued. "Despite what some people think, I've always done this job honorably. You can't do it any other way. I love France. Whenever a contract is signed thanks to me, it means many jobs are secured in France or elsewhere in Europe. I make sure the politicians are behaving properly. The transparency that people want to impose on us means guaranteed unemployment and poverty for French workers."

"So you're a humanist."

"Yes. And it's because I started at the bottom, with nothing. My first job was in London. I was an assistant translator for a minor importer. Eventually I was placed in the service of the great Tallas Al Mani. When his son was killed on an icy road between Deauville and Trouville, Tallas took me under his wing and taught me the art of doing business in weapons and raw materials, his two specialties. I have always behaved honorably. My word is sacred, and no one has reason to complain about my services. Not in Europe, the United States, or Asia. And God knows how difficult the Chinese and Japanese can be."

"Why did bin Rodney squeeze you out?

Kherrican wiped his mouth with an embroidered napkin before responding.

"That son of a bitch told me that Malaysia was planning to sign the OECD Anti-Bribery Convention. You know—the one that criminalizes bribery of public officials in international business transactions. The Americans were forcing that convention on the rest of the world. And the French bought into it. Your country jumped into the trap feet first."

"And then what?"

"Bin Rodney stayed quiet for a bit. I didn't know anything about his little arrangements with the pirates. Finally, I gave him a list of my competitors in Southeast Asia and asked him which intermediary had replaced me."

"Your competitors?"

"Yes, young Chinese guys, graduates of the best business schools in Shanghai. Little rude racist smart-asses with no talent or manners. These boys are pampered drama queens. A real pain. And an embarrassment to the old Chinese traditions."

"One of them replaced you in the submarine deal?"

"Bin Rodney pathetically admitted that he had been forced to modernize the way he was doing things. No more suitcases full of money or Swiss and Guernsey bank accounts."

"Who replaced you?"

"I was replaced by G. Terres itself!"

"That's funny. According to what I've heard, they're a straight-from-the-shoulder operation."

"Yes, that's the craziest part. The whole trading-room system is spotless. I paid millions of dollars to find out how it works. Everything happens ahead of time."

"What do you mean?"

Musa Kherrican sipped his water and wiped his mouth again.

"There are people in the G. Terres trading rooms in Paris and Putrajaya who do my job now."

"How does that work?"

"Malaysia buys two French subs. It's important to know that this kind of contract requires years of negotiations. Administrations change with the political tides, which goes back to my point about the importance of bureaucrats. They ensure continuity and grease the cogs. Generally, everything works the way it should."

"How does it actually go down?"

"A French minister and his friends want their piece of the pie, which is normal. Instead of getting suitcases full of money, they meet with someone from the trading room at La Défense. The trader directs them to a fiduciary or a law firm based in Switzerland or India. This agent buys shares of a company that mines or processes a rare-earth element. It's done on the trader's behalf, using money borrowed from a Chinese or Indonesian bank. Six months later, something happens that spikes the company's value. Bin Rodney can even orchestrate that 'something' using stolen cyberwarfare systems. Of course, Bin Rodney charges more for that. The lawyer or financial agent sells the shares. And the minister and his friends reel in the jackpot. No one can prove it was insider trading."

"But it *was* insider trading."

"Absolutely. But try proving it. A shutdown at a Chilean factory or a flood in a Chinese mine, combined with news of a power outage in Canada, can dramatically boost an Indonesian rare-earth producer's stock prices. In the past, stock speculators could see a direct correlation between an event and the price of a certain company's shares. Here's a rough example: people taking a certain acid-reflux medication suddenly start dying, and the pharmaceutical company's stock falls. A results in B. But now factors that seem unrelated can dramatically affect the price of a company's shares."

"Tell me more."

"The trading room is always reacting in real time to what's going on in the world, whether it's social, political, or financial. High-tech finance algorithms interpret the data and automatize a sale or buy. It's mostly machines that are raising and lowering the price, down to an infinitesimal fraction of second. And all the while, the information is there for anyone to see. Nothing is hidden.

"Still, those seemingly unrelated events coalesce to raise a company's stock price."

"Exactly. But even expert analysts can't put these things together. Something insignificant that happened six months ago combines with two things that happened in different parts of the world three months ago. Something else happened a few minutes ago, and now a certain rare earth is far more valuable than it was yesterday, and you've got shares in a company that are worth four times what you paid for them. I'm simplifying, of course. What I'm saying is this: billions of pieces of information are going through the system in a mathematically logical, normal, and transparent way, and they're dramatically influencing rare-earth prices—and thus the value of the companies that mine and process them."

"But anyone who wants to play this system would have to be in the know."

"Yes, you couldn't be more correct in that regard. Someone who wants to play the system needs to work with the algorithms."

"But the calculation method is public."

"Absolutely. Everyone has access to it. In the past, audits and inspections could get to the bottom of a stock-market manipulation. The investigators could go over everything to make sure all the calculations were based on real circumstances and good information. But now they'd have to go through billions of pieces of information to find the three or four factors that initiated a butterfly effect. And even if they did find those three or four things, what proof would they have that the tanker accident was avoidable?"

John could see that Kherrican was getting angrier the more he talked. His face was red, and his eyes were blazing. With a shaky hand Jerrican picked up the big pitcher and refilled his water glass. John had a few more questions.

"How can you be certain that three or four unrelated events will combine months later to spike a company's stock price? Even if you know the calculation method, it all seems so random."

"Bravo, John Spencer Larivière. Your government was wise to send you here. That is, indeed, the real question. How can we be sure that the three or four little random events will lead to an abrupt shift in stock prices six months later?"

"And you know the answer?"

"I only have the question, which isn't a bad start."

"Who does have the answer?"

"A company called Chronosphere."

John was ecstatic. All the pieces were starting to come together. He could almost see the big picture.

"This French company was pivotal in creating the calculation method. Emma wanted to find out exactly how involved they are in this new system of distributing kickbacks."

"How did she expect to get that information out of them?"

"She has a powerful lever. Chronosphere has bid on a Pentagon contract. Before they even consider Chronosphere, Pentagon officials want to know what role the French played in the new system."

"What ties does she have with the United States?"

"Malaysia was under British occupation for a long time, and relations between the Chinese here and the English-speaking world have always been strong. The Baba Bling are well-connected in Washington."

"What's Ange Cipriani's role?"

"That's your fellow countryman who's in charge of dealing with French politicians who come to Kuala for advice."

"Why at the casino?"

"Because the casino belongs to that piece-of-garbage Bin Rodney and the former pirates he was supposed to be fighting against. But I believe they crossed a line. Amir bin Muhaimin and our American friends are going to reestablish order. If you want to understand what happened, I suggest that you go see Cipriani while he's still alive."

John and his host had finished eating. John wiped his mouth, placed his napkin on the table, and stood up.

"Please excuse me for being so abrupt, but I need to get going," he said. "Thank you for the suit and your hospitality.

"My driver can get you to the casino before midnight. It's not too far from my home."

"You've been a most gracious host."

"We'll talk again one day at Le Bristol. You'll do me the honor of enjoying a meal with me. I'll introduce you to some very interesting French people. You'll be surprised."

"I don't doubt that for minute."

John left Temerloh in Kherrican's Rolls Royce. Not long after leaving his residence, John noticed a police car trailing them.

"Are we being followed?"

Kherrican's driver checked his rearview mirror and shrugged. John's phone began vibrating in the pocket of his new suit.

7

Victoire sat down in the chair that Julien Lanfrey had indicated.

"Don't tell me you've traveled all the way from Kuala Lumpur just for Chronosphere."

"Our American friends want to check on several things you've handled before letting you work with them."

"What things?"

"I'm going to be very direct. What was your role in the development of the G. Terres information system? How exactly did you contribute?"

"I've already addressed that in my phone conversation with the Pentagon."

"I know, but your answers were very superficial and full of IT jargon. I want the truth. It's your call."

"I've already told the truth!"

"You're being deceitful by omission, Mr. Lanfrey. Lying won't get you the Pentagon contract you're so eager to land. You neglected to tell me, for instance, that the Chinese firm Hoang Ho has recently expressed an interest in your company."

Julien Lanfrey's face turned pale. Victoire noticed that his lower lip was quivering. Her first arrow had hit the target.

"How did you know that?"

"Surely you knew that anyone bidding on a Pentagon contract would be thoroughly vetted."

"Not *this* quickly. That's insane. So you're working for the United States? I always thought you were a Chinese agent."

"Let's not get off track. Tell me the truth."

Julien Lanfrey paused and straightened in his chair.

"My company is bankrupt."

"We'll take care of that later. Are you ready to talk openly with me?"

"Yes."

"Then let's go somewhere else to talk."

Victoire stood up and led Julien out of the building and onto the Rue du Montparnasse. Then they walked to the main boulevard.

"Let's hear it, Julien."

"I did simulated trials for G. Terres's internal auditing. The trials were related to certain economic events and their influence on G. Terres interests."

"What events?"

"Strikes, industrial accidents, power outages, train derailings, shipwrecks, but also patent submissions and sales and purchases of laboratories throughout the world."

"So what exactly did your simulated trials do?"

"They projected the price of stocks and derivatives for rare-earth mining and processing companies based on a variety of factors."

"What for?"

"To deter manipulations."

"How does it work?"

"I adapted calculations that Chronosphere uses for simulating nuclear explosions and predicting weather patterns. I made them applicable to the financial sector. I devised a calculation method that lets you factor in any nonfinancial information. Then I integrated it into high-frequency trading algorithms. From there, you can simulate the effects of an infinite number of events, from inconsequential to earth-shaking and deter-mine the impact on stock prices."

"So this method is your baby. It's secret."

"You know that's not true!"

From the look on his face, Victoire could tell that she had slipped up. She was on thin ice. She took a breath and re-grouped. He hadn't found her out yet. She was okay.

"My calculation method is no secret," Julien said. "Everything can be downloaded from our website. Anyone can see the al-gorithms. G. Terres is very transparent. The Shangra-Li team never needed to use illicit means to infiltrate the trading-room information system. It's not the system they pirated, but the events that the system depends on. They were never anywhere near the La Défense or Putrajaya trading rooms."

"When you say 'they,' who do you have in mind?"

Victoire once again felt Julien Lanfrey's judging eyes. One more slip-up, and Emma Wong's sudden naiveté would betray her. She needed to dispel his suspicions and be quick about it.

"Julien, I'm asking you these questions because they're the same ones that our friends at the Pentagon will be asking you. And they'll be asking them in this same order. I want to be sure of your answers. I also have to report back to my people."

"I understand."

As they walked toward the Montparnasse train station, Victoire began to regain her composure and feel more natural in her Pentagon-spy character. She was actually becoming the beautiful Baba Bling from Kuala Lumpur who was helping the US government understand the strategic and private in-terrelations of the countries of Southeast Asia and the Pacific Ocean. She just had one more thing to nail down.

"By 'they,' I mean the Shangra-Li gang," Julien said.

"What gang?"

"The one led by Defense Minister Syafiq bin Rodney and the reformed pirate Prabat Raman Sankar. I've never done business with them or even met them."

"Who is your contact at Shangra-Li?"

"Ange Cipriani. He's the director of casino games."

"Does Cipriani do computer engineering?"

"Ange is an illiterate shepherd from Corsica," Julien said. "His gaming house in Paris was shut down by gambling enforcement. At Shangra-Li his job is meeting with authorized government people from around the globe and ensuring that legitimate transactions are converted to kickbacks and other under-the-table payouts."

"Where do these arrangements take place?"

"At the casino, around the gambling table. Remember, it's owned by a group controlled by Prabat Raman Sankar. The pirate even has his office there."

"Why a casino?" Victoire asked. "Nothing's private in a place like that."

"That's why it's ideal. Everything is seen and heard—taped and recorded. With this kind of business, the spoken word is sacred. No one can say that they agreed on fifteen percent and then later say it was any more or less. Chiefs of staff and lawyers for politicians come to Putrajaya from all over the world to negotiate these arrangements, totally outside the purview of G. Terres. And besides, everyone knows that casinos have highly advanced and secure computer systems, so no one can track their usage back to the source. It's ideal for a pirate."

"I've never set foot in the casino."

"You don't approve of gambling? I didn't think you were a Muslim, Emma."

"No, I'm not a Muslim, and I don't have anything in particular against gambling. I just hate Putrajaya. How can we get closer to the key figures?"

"If we really want to investigate them, we can't just analyze their transactions, based on sales and purchases. That'll get us nowhere. There's about a one in a billon chance of finding connections between events that are more or less random. We need to look at individuals. If I've got a suspect's name, I can ask the trading room databases to tell me what Mr. So-and-So bought."

"Mr. Massicot, for instance?"

"I already ran Massicot's name," Julien said, looking at his smartphone—a new one, evidently. "On January 3 at two hours, thirty-two minutes, eight seconds, and five thousand-millionths of a second, the man bought eighteen thousand shares of a company in Vancouver. On March 16, the company's value increased fivefold, following unexpected economic, industrial, or financial events."

"So? I'm not getting this."

"So, I devised a hyper-sophisticated tool to deter manipulations. It's capable of factoring in a myriad of factors that ultimately affect the price of a company's stock. But these factors themselves can be manipulated, and if you don't know what—or who—you're looking for, you'll never see what's going on. There's just too much information, believe it or not. No single investigative body is capable of overseeing a system as complex as this. That's the problem with the whole idea. And in the end, it's not my problem."

Now Victoire was comprehending how the G. Terres trading rooms were completely transparent, but the regulatory body would be totally impotent. It was brilliant. There was no way to reproach the system, as there was no way—due to the abundance of available information—to oversee it. Noblecourt's vision—an aboveboard system—was, in fact, an illusion.

"Speaking of sophisticated tools, can you tell me how the exact height of the Beau Paris Tower is connected to the splicing of time into thousand-millionths of a second?"

Julien Lanfrey stared at Victoire.

"Look, Emma. I think you should ask Noblecourt's brother-in-law, Titus Polycarpe, about that."

"Why?"

"Because I can't answer for him."

"Can you see if he'll meet with one of my partners?"

"Yes. You've worn me down. So you work for the Pentagon. I should have known."

"That's why you don't want to tell me about the tower's height?"

"That's part of it. It's also that there are some things I'd rather not talk about. Not everything's for sale, Emma. You should tell that to your American friends."

8

"John Spencer Larivière."

"Yes, Your Excellency."

"I have cleared up all suspicion that you were involved in the ambassador's death. In exchange, I have an urgent question to ask. I'll throw in some information that may be of interest to France."

"Go ahead."

"Who is Titus Polycarpe?"

"He's the brother of Georgette Polycarpe, Pierre-André Noblecourt's wife."

"Syafiq bin Rodney has been exchanging messages with Titus Polycarpe for years. Do you know why?"

"I have no idea."

"Bin Rodney is in serious danger. I fear he'll be the victim of a terrorist attack within the next hour. I'm doing everything I can to avert a disaster. Look into this, please, and get back to me as soon as you can."

Amir bin Muhaimin was using John to leave an audible trail of his good intentions. At the same time, he was informing John of Syafiq bin Rodney's imminent demise. Bin Rodney had used a cyberweapon stolen from the United States. He had used it for unknown reasons against France and Malaysia, because most of those who had died at Orly were Malaysian. Two good reasons to disappear, with Washington's blessing. And the Pentagon certainly hadn't appreciated the loss of Emma Wong.

"I'll look into it, Your Excellency. Would it be pushing it to ask what Mr. Noblecourt was doing in Singapore right before boarding the plane to Paris?"

"I'll call you back."

"Thanks."

A few minutes later, John got out of the Rolls Royce. The police officers continued to follow his every move. Maybe they hadn't gotten the memo.

He headed toward the Shangra-Li casino while trying to sort through all the information he had gathered. To sum up, a centralized underground operation that played the rare-earth market was headquartered at the Shangra-Li casino. It was run by the Malaysian defense minister and his pirate buddies, who were more than willing to orchestrate cyberattacks to achieve their financial ends. It seemed that a number of French politicians were on the take, including, perhaps, the Noblecourt family. Still, John didn't understand exactly what motivated the recent violence. He needed more information.

Then an idea—inspired by the file on Ange Cipriani that Luc had just sent—came to him. He was passing some shops in an arched passageway. He opened the door of a men's accessories shop and approached one of the two saleswomen.

"I would like to buy these rings."

"All six?"

"Yes."

John held out his hands, as big as a lumberjack's, and spread his fingers. The saleswoman slipped the signet rings on the fingers of both his hands.

"Thanks."

After paying for his bling, John left the store and headed toward one of the trees lining the sidewalk. As soon as he reached it, he started punching the trunk with both fists. A couple walking his way quickly sidestepped him. John knew they thought he was a lunatic, but his hands hurt too much to care.

John headed toward the casino. Topped with a gigantic neon sign, it was something of a Buddhist temple with green and white minarets. How odd and yet so fitting, John thought. A gaudy business wrapped in ceremonial garb. Though his hands still hurt like hell, he couldn't help smiling. God and big business had come together.

Inside the place, John walked over to the front desk. Workers in pink and black uniforms were checking clients' IDs while musclemen in blazers stood off to the side—just in case.

"I'm here to see Mr. Cipriani," John told one of the workers. "Tell him I'm from the French embassy in Kuala Lumpur."

The young Malaysian man smiled and pressed a button beside his computer. Less than a minute later, Ange Cipriani materialized. He was short and as skinny as a rake. He wore a scowl that looked permanent.

"I'd like to speak with you."

"Of course."

John followed the gambling director across a large slot-machine room crowded with Asians and Caucasians, their eyes glued to the flashy screens. The commotion made any conversation impossible. They passed some cashiers and then walked through a door that led to a private hallway. After taking an elevator, they made their way to an office the size of a tennis court. Its picture window offered a view of a gambling room as spectacular as the Grand Palais.

"It's amazing."

"It's the most beautiful casino room in all of Southeast Asia, but I'm guessing you're not here to play roulette."

"Not exactly."

Before being invited to do so, John sat down in one of the armchairs in the large sitting area. Ange Cipriani sat down too, keeping a distrustful eye on his visitor while occasionally glancing at the financial news on a wall-mounted television.

No G. Terres stock alerts were popping up. Yet John was sure of the impending assassination attempt on the defense minister. Bin Muhaimin hadn't made the effort to call him for nothing. The message intended for France was clear. The silent partner behind the Flight 912 massacre would pay. Malaysia was on the brink of rendering justice for its victims—using its own methods.

"I heard the minister of home affairs greeted you at the airport."

"That's right," John replied, crossing his arms. "The Orly disaster was a trauma for both Malaysia and France. And Bin Muhaimin had a lot of respect for our former president."

"I've just learned that the French ambassador's body was found in his swimming pool," Cipriani said, clearly distressed. "He'd been beaten to death. That kind of thing isn't done here. That's what Amir bin Muhaimin just said on TV."

"If the minister said it, then it must be true."

"Do we know who did it?"

"We're investigating."

John slowly uncrossed his arms and noticed Ange's eyes locked on his raw and swollen fingers. The gambling director flinched like a frightened animal. In the space of a minute, he had become a quivering little creature.

"We're in the process of reevaluating who's in charge," John said. "Buzenval was no longer reliable. We'll be revisiting the matter—with renewed harmony, as you say here."

"Buzenval did nothing but comply with Syafiq bin Rodney's orders," Cipriani replied, shifting in his chair.

John nodded as he glanced at the screen behind his host's head. The news flash was finally appearing.

"Sidelining Grapefruit was only the beginning. Take a look behind you. Now that's sweet harmony."

Ange Cipriani turned around and raised the volume. On the screen, flames were shooting from a car. A reporter provided the context. "The attack occurred as Syafiq bin Rodney was leaving the Defense Ministry in his car."

The gambling director was now nothing more than a gelatinous blob in a hotel jacket. John got ready to drive his performance home.

"Our friend Amir bin Muhaimin will now be responsible for international transactions. On the French side, I'll be filling in until the new ambassador's named. I have to conduct an audit. Show me the operations that concern France."

Ange Cipriani glanced once again at John's hands and walked over to his desk. He powered up his computer and turned the screen toward John as he began typing.

"Does this connect to the whole system?" John asked.

"Of course. It's all integrated."

A list of names and numbers began scrolling up the screen. "It's all there, down to the cent."

John scanned the list of people who had made dirty money on the system: politicians, high-ranking bureaucrats, artists, and shady journalists, among others.

"Each payout was fair and based on a prior agreement. This isn't the case for every country."

"I see. Show me the foreign accounts."

"I don't have access to them."

"But you must have some idea."

"The Western countries represent only a fifth of the operations. The Chinese, the Japanese, and the Koreans account for half of the revenue. The power has shifted to the East."

John knew it was time to introduce his chess match. He pulled the photos out of his pocket and showed Cipriani the boards.

"I've learned that this match took place in one of your casino's private gaming rooms."

Cipriani leaned in to look at the images.

"That's highly possible. We often organize international chess tournaments. Syafiq bin Rodney is very passionate about them."

"Who are the two players competing in this match?"

"I'll try to find out who they are, but that may take some time. Would you like to have something to eat while you wait?"

"I'd love to."

"Let's meet back at the Lady Blue in an hour. I'll open my private lounge for you. You'll see. The food is unforgettable."

As they left the room, John pulled out the lighter-sized object he'd retrieved from Dutreil and set it on Cipriani's desk, just inches from the computer.

9

Luc locked his motorcycle to the fence that surrounded the square between the Bon Marché and the Lutetia Hotel. He crossed the street and checked out his reflection in the pharmacy window. His hip high-roller trader look wasn't a bit mussed. He pressed the button corresponding to Titus Polycarpe's apartment and waited.

"Who is it?"

"Luc Racine. I've come on behalf of Julien Lanfrey and Emma Wong."

"I'll buzz you in. Fourth floor."

Luc preferred to take the stairs. In these times of cyberterrorism, he was losing his confidence in machinery. Even the crummy elevator in Titus Polycarpe's building could be hiding a sneaky trap.

Once on the fourth floor, he found the banker waiting for him in a dressing gown and a pair of dated sunglasses.

"You don't use elevators?"

"Just trying to get my ten thousand steps in."

"You look healthy enough. You certainly don't need to lose any weight."

"They say walking's the best form of exercise."

"That's what I hear. Please come in."

Luc stepped into the dimly lit apartment, which Victoire had described to him. Titus led him into the living room.

"So what's the emergency? Julien called me in a huff. He said I had to meet with you ASAP. You work for Emma Wong, correct?"

"Do you know her?"

"I saw her in Malaysia. Julien tells me she can open doors for him in the United States."

"Nothing's been done yet. There are some shady spots in Chronosphere's file."

"I'm happy to answer all of your questions. Make yourself comfortable."

Luc slipped onto the white leather couch and immediately spotted the chessboard by a window facing the Sèvres-Babylone intersection. The pieces were in starting position. A computer rested on a table not more than two feet from the board, and a chair with a plush cushion was next to it. Luc felt his blood getting hotter and his neurons firing faster. He was getting closer to their goal, but he sensed danger.

Titus Polycarpe removed his sunglasses and apologized.

"I have to be in dim lighting. Bad eyes. I'm sorry, but I can't handle bright light."

"I understand."

What Luc really understood was that the man sitting across from him was putting on an act. Was he actually incapable of being in front of a computer screen? Luc intended to find out.

"What can I do for you, young man?"

"Is it true that you are Chronosphere's banker?"

"Yes."

"According to both the Pentagon and Miss Wong, Chronosphere's finances aren't in great shape. The company should have gone under a long time ago. It's only managed to stay afloat because of lines of credit from Martin and Polycarpe Bank."

"That's right, young man. It's no secret. All you need is access to the statements, debt records, and valuations from the Bank of France to know Chronosphere's situation. In France, foreign investors have the right to see everything."

"Our American friends have what they need," Luc said. "They just have one question."

"And what is that?"

"Why are you helping Chronosphere? Your bank's board of directors, and ultimately your shareholders, could seriously question why you're bent on underwriting a failing operation."

"My dear boy, a banker is always in the wrong. Either he offers support and is accused of throwing his bank's profits out the window, or he doesn't offer support and is blamed for obstructing his country's economic growth. To answer your question, I decided to help Julien because the French government wasn't upholding its responsibility."

"How's that?"

"When Chronosphere worked on simulated trials for the Defense Ministry, it wasn't paid enough, and even then, it was paid late. That's why Julien bid on the Pentagon contract. He needed the money."

"He bid on the contract without telling the French government."

"For a long time, Julien wanted to close his operations in Paris and open a facility with some of his engineers in the United States. A company is nothing more than the sum of its intellectual parts. Julien was sick of all the constraints in France. I'm not surprised that he wanted to leave. I even tried to persuade my brother-in-law to help Julien when he was still president. But politicians have only so much power. I helped Julien as much as I could. Now I'm retired. My health isn't what it used to be. I live in the shadows."

Luc nodded as he kept an eye on the computer screen and chessboard. Bin Muhaimin had told John that Syafiq bin Rodney was in frequent contact with Titus Polycarpe. How could he lift the rock to find the insects hiding under it? He was so close.

"Chronosphere even worked on the trading-room systems in Paris and Putrajaya."

"That's true. My brother-in-law and I supported Chronosphere's participation, although we were very discreet. And in the end, Chronosphere got that project because of its capabilities."

Luc couldn't take any more of this. He pointed to the computer. "I'm guessing you heard about the latest developments in Malaysia."

"What? You think I get my information on that thing? I never use it. Hurts my eyes. I make do with the radio. I listen to BFM and France Inter. Both stations give me more than enough information."

Either Titus was being sincere, or he was an incredible actor. Luc couldn't determine the truth. He was feeling totally thrown off. He decided to focus on the chessboard.

"At any rate, it's clear that you love chess. That set you have is beautiful."

"I haven't played in a long time, young man. That chessboard is mostly decorative. But getting back to the point, if Julien moves to the United States, I'll try to help him. You can tell Emma Wong. You should know, however, that Martin and Polycarpe is no longer in a strong enough position to finance his operation. Our participation would be symbolic. I even wonder, considering my brother-in-law's death, if this participation would hurt Julien's image. You should talk to my sister about that."

"I could do that."

"I could discuss it with her myself, for that matter. Georgette comes over every week, sometimes more than that. We've stayed close. Politics, on the other hand, never interested me."

"Oh, so your sister visits you often," Luc said. "That must be nice."

"Yes, it is. Sometimes she'll spend the better part of a day here, making sure my apartment's being tended and my medications are in order. And if I'm napping, she uses my computer to do her banking and catch up with her friends."

"She uses your computer a lot?" Luc pictured Georgette at her brother's computer, sending messages to Syafiq bin Rodney.

He decided to make a bold move.

"I know that Emma Wong adored your brother-in-law."

"The feeling was mutual. I wouldn't say as much for Georgette."

"Do you know much about the work that Julien did on the Beau Paris Tower?"

"Can't say that I do. I just know that G. Terres wants to establish an investigations department and a high court that would hear financial cases."

"Why would the tower's height down to the centimeter be of interest to Chronosphere?"

"I really don't know."

Titus Polycarpe seemed genuinely surprised, and Luc gave it a rest.

He emerged from the meeting with a fresh hunch. Back on the Rue de Babylone, he took out his phone and sent John a text: "Georgette Noblecourt's the one who's been contacting Bin Rodney."

10

As soon as John thanked Luc, he felt his second cell phone vibrate in his pocket. It was a Chinese phone that Amir bin Muhaimin had given him before he left his home. The minister's voice sounded grave.

"Is that you, John?"

"Your Excellency, my deepest condolences on the loss of your colleague."

John would have loved seeing Bin Muhaimin's face.

"It's a tragedy. These terrorists aren't backing down at all. You know I tried my best to keep this from happening."

"I know, Your Excellency. You did everything you could. I do have a partial yet interesting response to your question."

"Let's hear it."

"I have reason to believe that Bin Rodney wasn't in communication with Titus Polycarpe, but with his sister, Georgette, instead."

The minister of home affairs went silent.

"What exactly could those two people have been talking about?" he finally asked. "I'd known Bin Rodney ever since he quit school when he was twelve. There's no way he could have held a conversation in a foreign language. Speaking coherently in his native tongue was a huge accomplishment. I met Georgette once at your ambassador's residence. She's not the kind of woman who'd bother with a brute like Bin Rodney. There's something off with your Paris investigation."

"I'd really like to believe that."

"But I know why Pierre-André Noblecourt went to Singapore at Emma Wong's insistence."

"Why, Your Excellency?"

"Your former president went to see Singapore's minister of home affairs, who has just assured me of his complete cooperation in the investigation of Bin Rodney's death."

John was drooling with anticipation.

"Your former president asked for the intel Singapore had on his brother-in-law, Titus. He then got on a plane from Singapore and arrived in Paris three hours before the Air France flight."

"What was that information?"

"A few years ago, Titus was arrested in Singapore for engaging in sexual activities with minors. One of your politicians was with him."

"I'm only somewhat surprised by that."

"Titus asked his sister to step in and fix things. I'm sure you're aware that pedophilia isn't taken lightly in Singapore."

"Yes, I know. Singapore's no-tolerance policy has been all over the news."

"Georgette Noblecourt asked Bin Rodney to use his influence in the region to help her. Of course he had ins with government officials in Singapore. I don't know how much it cost to have the charges against Titus dropped and keep the whole thing quiet. But I think someone was blackmailing Titus. I've got to go now. Good luck."

John ended the call and looked up at the monumental bronze Buddha guarding the entrance to the Lady Blue. A smiling hostess in a silk mini-dress welcomed him and led him to a private lounge.

"Mr. Cipriani reserved the Madame de Montespan."

"What an honor."

John's eyes followed the curvy piece of eye candy up the steps to the Montespan. True, he was a father and the husband of a beautiful woman, but what harm was there in looking? He had to anyway, because she was right in front of him. Cipriani, smiling like a domesticated shark, appeared at the top of the steps.

"You've got quite an empire, Cipriani."

"I'm just a lowly employee. Please, have a seat."

The Corsican was adapting to local jargon. A bottle of Champagne—a respected Lanson vintage—was propped in a bucket next to the table.

"Are we toasting something special?"

"Your coming here will boost investors' confidence—after all those tragic deaths. I have a welcome gift for you."

"I'm listening," John said as he unfolded his napkin.

"There's going to be a strike at a Nigerian mine that will seriously disrupt the uranium market. If you buy shares in Trepose International, which stores and packages uranium, you'll make a fortune. You have no idea how stirred-up the market is at the moment."

"I'm afraid I don't have the finances right now to be buying shares in any company."

"You can win big here playing roulette. What's your favorite number?"

"Twenty-two."

"It's been at least ten hours since twenty-two was called at one of my tables. I'm shocked."

"If that's all it takes, I'm ready to test my luck. Have you identified the two chess players?"

"You're in for a real surprise. You might even fall out of your chair."

"I'm holding on tight."

From his pocket, the casino director took out photos of a chess game. John could see that it was a similar match—if not the same one—but the players had been photographed from a much better vantage point.

"The boy's name is Jamal bin Syafiq. He's eleven and the cherished son of Syafiq bin Rodney, the man your pals just sent to paradise. Bin Rodney was a good Muslim. That was the only thing he had in common with our friend Bin Muhaimin. His son, who's seen here, is a prodigy. Bin Rodney had him with his favorite wife. She teaches math in Cyberjaya, Putrajaya's rival city. The father was a meathead, but the well-respected mother could be a mathematics professor at any elite school in Paris."

"What about the girl?"

John thought the child looked like a Raphael angel keeping tabs on the mortals. Something in her eyes resonated.

"That's President Alain Jemestre's daughter. Her name's Béatrice."

"She's got his eyes and his smile. And his expression too. It's uncanny."

"She goes by her stepfather's name, Roussillon. I've met him. He came here with his family during the tournament. Béatrice and Jamal became friends in Malaysia, and they got closer in Paris, when he took a French course at her school. They're both chess and computer geniuses."

John clutched the table. The daughter and granddaughter of two French presidents had become central to this whole affair.

"Incredible, isn't it?"

"I didn't see the Noblecourts on the list that you showed me earlier."

John awaited Cipriani's response with apprehension. The fact that half of the government was composed of cynical profiteers hardly surprised him. But the possibility that the first family itself could be part of it was sending him for a loop.

Cipriani waited for the comely server to finish refilling their flutes before responding.

"For a long time, I've been trying to figure out how they did it. To this day, neither the Noblecourts nor the Jemestres have shown up in any of the gambling rooms. I've never met any of their front men or intermediaries. It always seemed strange to me, but after you got here, I realized what was going on. They're using Béatrice!"

"But she's just a little girl." John feigned disbelief as he connected the dots between the chess match, Chronosphere, Titus Polycarpe's computer, and Jamal, Syafiq bin Rodney's son. John could imagine Béatrice in the dark apartment on the Rue de Babylone, sitting in front of Titus's computer. Noblecourt's granddaughter was communicating with her friend Jamal and making shadow transactions via a faraway casino where a new kind of underground trading was taking place, run by a new kind of mafia. John still didn't understand how unrelated events could be correlated to stock variations so the crew could make money, but it had something to do with the tower. Béatrice had indicated the exact height of the Beau Paris Tower, the same tower whose roof and top floor had been blown up for reasons still unknown. In any case with Jamal's help, she had been making money.

"What's wrong?"

"I'm thinking," John replied.

"Jamal and Béatrice are extremely gifted children who were participating in an international tournament. The photographs from the chess match were, indeed, taken here at this casino by my employees."

"But how did Jamal and Béatrice become players in this whole investment scheme?"

"That's exactly what we need to figure out. I know there's a way of spotting suspicious purchases once the stakes go above fifty euros. But Jamal's and Béatrice's names have never come up. There must be something else… I'm only beginning to understand."

John, on the other hand, was only getting more confused.

He stood up, bringing this meeting to an end. Cipriano signaled for someone to show him out. Before leaving, John turned around and surveyed the gambling room. He pulled out his phone, tapped a text message, and hit send. As he walked out, the glittering lights seemed to flicker for an instant.

THURSDAY

1

Luc parked his motorcycle on the sidewalk while quickly checking out the nearby pedestrians and parked cars. Before ringing the doorbell, he consulted a map of the neighborhood on his phone one last time. The previous night he had begun to make sense of everything. Fermatown's investigative app had mapped out the key locations. A genius move, which Luc himself had thought of.

All they had to do was study the geography. Together, the Noblecourts' residence, Titus's apartment on the Rue de Babylone, Julien's place on the Rue Vaneau, and the little wooden toolshed in Labouré Square provided a rational explanation. Victoire, as sharp as ever, had picked up on the wet-paint sign on a door dried by the wind and heat.

Luc smiled as he pictured the look he would soon see on Julien's face. He pressed the button on the speakerphone.

"It's me."

"Come on up."

Julien, wearing a white shirt and a worried look, opened the door. The pleasant aroma of toast was wafting from the kitchen—the exact spot from which the topography app had traced a virtual line. This clever line explained the series of dramatic events that had put Paris in mourning. Luc decided to go in for the kill.

"Listen, Julien, I'm worried. Hoang Ho knows that you were involved in rare-earth speculation."

"That's not true. I just developed the surveillance system that detects suspicious purchases and sales in down to split-second real time."

"You didn't tell me you had ties to Titus Polycarpe."

"Titus is my banker." Julien Lanfrey looked at Luc like a child caught in a lie. "That's my only connection with him."

"What about your US connections?"

Julien turned pale and started to tremble.

"Don't lie to me," Luc pressed. "You bid on a Pentagon contract."

"How did you know? The bidding wasn't made public."

"It *wasn't* made public, Julien. But the elders of Hoang Ho have their sources, even in the Pentagon."

"Hold on. You're freaking me out now. I need a drink."

Luc followed Julien into the kitchen. The founder of Chronosphere was unnerved and could slip up at any second. Julien poured himself some water and sat down at the table, while Luc walked over to a window. He could see the little toolshed. It didn't take him long to spot the binoculars on top of Julien's fridge. The very binoculars allowing him to detect the presence or absence of the wet-paint sign that Victoire had seen each time she walked through the park. Everything was coming into clear view, like a rainbow after a storm. From his kitchen, Julien Lanfrey was able to spot the signals sent by Béatrice, the former president's granddaughter. Using this system, they could communicate any need to meet without using phones that could so easily be tapped by law-enforcement officials or be reviewed under France's local-usage-details regulations.

"Explain how Hoang Ho knew I submitted a bid for a Pentagon contract."

"The how isn't important. The contract isn't even important. Hoang Ho knows that the Americans are going to start pressuring you as soon as your company sets up shop in the United States. Military agents have been watching you for quite some time."

"What do you mean by that?"

"One of their agents will be getting in touch with you."

"Why?"

"Like I said, they want to pressure you. The US military wants you to help them with certain nuclear and climate initiatives. They have plans for a weather weapon in connection with El Niño in the Pacific. They know you've worked on it."

"They can't pressure me into doing anything I don't want to do."

"Think again. They're not above using blackmail. You'll find out when that agent gets in touch with you."

Julien went even whiter and took off his glasses.

"Who?"

"A woman. I wanted to warn you first."

"What woman?"

"Emma Wong. She's a lawyer from Kuala Lumpur. She's going to come see you and ask for information. She'll say she's checking you out because you've bid on a Pentagon contract. She'll ask you about the auditing system that you developed. It'll be a pretext to hook you and force you to hand over your climate and nuclear system—for free."

Slumped in his chair, Julien was an emotionally rattled teenager. Luc sank his scalpel deep, exactly where it needed to go.

"Emma Wong will show up at your home with an American agent, a Frenchman working for the new Palatinate credit-rating agency. I've come to warn you on behalf of Mr. Ho. Do you want to see what Emma Wong looks like?"

Julien grunted as Luc brought up a photo of the madeover Victoire on his cell phone.

"She's a Baba Bling. For generations, her family's been working for the Brits, and now she's working for the Americans."

Julien was speechless. He studied the photo for a long moment and then looked back at Luc.

"You say she's going to blackmail me?"

"Not right away. First she's going to seduce you—intellectually and in other ways if things go well. She's a spy. And one hell of a woman."

"I need to know about the blackmail."

"Once she's in your apartment, she'll try to get you into the kitchen."

Luc took the binoculars off the top of the refrigerator. Then he walked to the window, opened it, and put the binoculars to his eyes. He looked at the toolshed in Labouré Square and then at the adjacent bench. He nodded.

"She'll do that, and then she'll turn around and ask how often you check the shed to see if Béatrice has put up the wet-paint sign. You'll give her a stunned look, as though you don't know what she's talking about."

"Then what?"

"She'll explain how Béatrice and you have been accomplices for some time now. Further, she'll threaten to implicate you in the explosion of the Beau Paris Tower, a crime that could land you in prison for many years, my friend. But she'll say all this very nicely, because she's an artist, a woman with life experience. You know what I mean."

With wide eyes, Julien looked once again at Emma Wong's photo.

Right on time, Luc registered a soft clicking sound coming from the entrance way.

"She'll explain what you already know. Titus Polycarpe has been supporting your company for reasons that have nothing to do with patriotism. You've been using Titus's weakness for children to bleed his bank. And little Béatrice has been doing the same thing, for her own reasons. True or false?"

"True…"

"At that moment, Emma Wong will threaten to expose you as an extortionist."

"What do I have to do?"

"China doesn't want the Pentagon to get its hands on your work. It stays in France. We're going to protect you from Emma

Wong, but first you've got to tell us everything. It's in your best interest. It won't be long before she contacts you."

"She's already been here."

"No!"

Swept up in his performance, Luc seized the opportunity.

"What was at the top of the Beau Paris Tower?"

"A computer for recording transactions in G. Terres's Paris-based trading room. An atomic clock was also up there for a while."

"The one you destroyed in the laser room in order to eliminate any trace of your connection to the computer on the roof of the tower?"

"Yes."

"And to be clear: you're talking about the transactions that converted the kickbacks into legitimate deals?"

"Yes."

"And why an atomic clock?"

Before Julien could answer, Victoire stepped into the kitchen. "It was Béatrice's idea, wasn't it?"

Julien swung his head around and jumped out of his chair. "What the—"

"Explain the clock, Julien," Luc said, hardly containing his predatory instinct. Victoire, aka Emma Wong, took position opposite Luc.

The prey tensed and scanned the room, but there was no way out. Luc and Victoire each took a step closer. Defeated, Julien slumped back into his chair with a sigh.

"You know Einstein's theory of relativity?"

"Vaguely."

"Basically, Einstein said that time and space aren't as constant as you'd think. Time can run slower or faster, depending on how fast you're traveling and how high you are. With really precise atomic clocks, you can measure the difference. We've found that time runs more quickly at the top of a skyscraper than it runs on the ground because of earth's gravitational pull. Mind you, we're talking about billionths of a second."

Luc was feeling giddy at these revelations.

Julien continued. "The distance between the top of the tower and the ground is 270.26 meters. Information received at the top of the tower arrives ten billionths of a second sooner than what we call real time."

Now Luc understood what he had grasped the night before.

Victoire leaned in. "So you're saying that since the internal auditing system examines suspicious data starting at one hour and one second on the dot, by adjusting the time of a transaction a tiny little bit, crooks can slip through the cracks of the auditing system."

"Exactly. The criminal transaction is artificially sent back in time by ten-billionths of a second, meaning it can escape the surveillance system's memory."

"That's amazing," Luc said, his eyes full of admiration.

"You're such a geek," Victoire said smiling at Luc before. focusing on Julien. "That was Béatrice, right?"

"I would have never thought of it on my own. Scientifically, it's crazy. Applying Einstein's theory to volume trading on a stock exchange. A spectacular notion. Don't you think?"

"Definitely," Luc said.

"And it was a ten-year-old kid who suggested it." It was Victoire's turn to be admirative.

"But what if one day the audit program is asked to spit out all the transactions before or after the hour of purchase?" Luc asked.

Julien was smiling, apparently unaware of the compromising position he had gotten himself into. Luc, meanwhile, was trying to find a flaw in the system concocted by Béatrice and her little boyfriend, Jamal bin Rodney.

"The system will show you billions of transactions that are very difficult to examine…"

"… But eventually we'll find the transactions that Béatrice made."

"Actually, no. All of Béatrice and Jamal's transactions have been automatically fixed at 49.9999 euros, and the internal auditing system only examines market orders above fifty euros."

"They're small-timers!"

"Yes. They're kids, Luc. Béatrice and Jamal are like little squirrels. They save one euro here, two euros there. Béatrice tells me she's worried about the future. Remember, she's got an IQ that's much higher than her parents and her grandparents."

"Where does the money go?"

"It goes into an offshore bank account in Guernesey that Mathilde opened."

"Chronosphere's receptionist?"

"Mathilde is also Béatrice's piano teacher. She gives her lessons in her apartment, which is one floor below mine. What's going to happen now?"

2

Wearing her pink backpack, Béatrice rushed out to the sidewalk. She was beaming. Victoire walked up to meet her.

"So, you're the one who's taking me in? That's gotta be weird for you."

"How did you know?"

"Jamal was taken into custody after his father was assassinated, but he paid off a guard and was able to get in touch with me."

Victoire said nothing, but stepped back and gave Béatrice a concerned but stern look.

"I'm guilty of underhanded trading, okay. But the rest didn't really involve me, although I knew what was going on. The Americans wanted their stolen software back, and they figured they could kill two birds with one stone and uncover the whole kickback scenario by allowing France to sell the two submarines to Malaysia and tracking down the pirates. Emma was a good agent."

"And what happened after that?"

"When Emma got further in her investigation for the United States, she discovered Jamal and me. She found the chess match and the atomic clock, and she realized what we were doing. Emma told Grandpa and got on a plane to Paris. When Grandpa came back from Singapore and was waiting for her, he saw the plane burst into flames. He realized it was an attack."

"Who killed all those people?"

"Jamal had panicked. He told his father, the defense minister, that Emma had discovered our little business. Syafiq bin Rodney panicked too. When the ambassador told him that Emma was on that plane, he asked his Shangra-Li gang to use the weapon they had stolen from the US Navy. They wanted to keep Emma and Grandpa from meeting with my father."

"Your father?"

"The president."

Victoire nodded and looked intently at the little girl as she kept telling her story. It was as if she were reading a fairy tale.

"Who killed your Grandpa?"

"No one. He committed suicide. Grandpa founded G. Terres and had faith in its integrity. But then he discovered that his system wasn't foolproof, despite all its sophisticated technology. It could be corrupted. He discovered that his brother-in-law was being blackmailed into financing Chronosphere, and his grand-daughter was siphoning money from it. He realized that the Pentagon—with Emma Wong's help—would use G. Terres for its own political agenda. Knowing all that, he was still willing to meet with my father. But then he found out that Grandma was making money on the shady G. Terres transactions too—back-stabbing him, in effect. And the plane exploded. He couldn't take it. All those people, including Emma, would have been alive if it weren't for him. He was depressed and humiliated. I guess I understood."

"So you helped him?"

"Yes." Béatrice bit her lip.

"And you covered up his suicide so it would look like an assassination?"

"I wanted to protect his legacy. He was a great president, and I loved him. After he did it, I grabbed the stepladder and tossed it out the window, along with one of his shoes to throw the police off. Then I made my way down the wall and hid the stepladder and shoe in the toolshed."

"You went down that wall all by yourself? All that way?"

"Shimmying down the wall was easy. Remember Grandpa's two bodyguards, Ninjutsu and Aikido? They'd been teaching me how to do things like that, although we weren't telling Grandma."

"You're the one who warned Jamal about the morgue?"

"Yes."

"Why did you want to destroy your grandfather's body?"

"So that the medical examiner wouldn't find out it was a suicide. That could have tipped the police off to what really happened. So what are you going to do with me now?"

"I'm taking you to Roissy airport. You'll get on a plane with your mother. You're both going to visit your father in Putrajaya."

"You know he's not my father. My real dad is a wonderful man. I guess that's why I get to go free. I know for sure he'll get elected for another term. I'll be close to twenty when he leaves the Élysée Palace. And maybe when I decide to run for office he'll still be young enough to help me."

"Oh, so you want to hold office someday?"

"Yes, you could call politics the family business."

ONE MONTH LATER

John, Victoire, and Luc were reviewing cases in the confessional. "You'd think Méricourt could speed up payment a little, don't you? And maybe even bump it up, considering the excessive risk of the assignment and all," Victoire said, closing the accounting app on her tablet.

"He'll pay, eventually," John said.

Luc threw John an exasperated look. "Let's not do this again, John. You're a father now. Méricourt is nothing but trouble."

"Come on, guys, all's well that—"

"Ends. Full stop," Victoire said.

"I will give John that—it did end well." Luc's face had softened as he cast admiring eyes on his boss. "That stunt with the remote control code-wiping virus was way cool. Those Americans! There was nothing in the report, obviously, but go on, give us the details."

"When Dutreil heard Emma had died on the plane, he rushed off to her place. He probably also contacted her US handler. In any case, just before he died, he told me about the device. I had to get close to a computer in the casino that was integrated with the system. Then, I sent a code from my cell phone as I left, and *voilà*. I'm not sure how it actually works, but I gather it sent a worm-like virus that sought out the American cyberweapon code and destroyed it. Emma's whole assignment had been to find the seat of the pirate's operations and disable the code. Of course, she uncovered a lot more along the way."

"I'm still irked that almost everyone got off with a slap on the wrist," Victoire said.

"What are you saying? Bin Muhaimin cleaned up in a fairly radical way. First the ambassador—although that may have been the Chinese or even the Americans—and then Bin Rodney. A few days later the casino collapsed. The media went on and on about faulty construction. I don't know what happened to Jamal, but I fear it's not good."

"You're right there, but here, what happened? Massicot resigned. But I'm betting after a sabbatical he'll be back in the game, and maybe even run for office. Georgette and Titus were asked to refrain from all public appearances, and that's all. Nobody wants to tarnish the former president's family. And the kid gets sent away. How will she ever know the difference between right and wrong?"

"You're forgetting Julien. He was the scapegoat," Luc said.

"Is that some sadness I see in your eyes?" John asked. "Was he that good?"

Luc blushed and was saved by the doorbell.

John headed downstairs and greeted Alain Jemestre and Apolline Roussillon.

"Mr. President, this is such an honor."

"We're the ones who should be thanking you for inviting us."

"How is Béatrice doing?"

"She's in Switzerland—in Carouge, not far from Geneva. She's at a school for gifted children. It's a rigorous establishment. She's really into illustration these days. We might wind up with an artist."

John took his guests upstairs and introduced them to Victoire and Luc.

"What a pleasure it is to meet you in person," Jemestre said, shaking Victoire's hand.

John turned to his wife. "The president tells me that Béatrice is doing well."

"Yes, she is," Apolline said. "She's seeing a therapist, who's helping her deal with her remorse in regard to her grandfather's suicide. Shortly after she arrived in Geneva, she realized that she should have tried to stop him. But we're so relieved that she didn't have anything to do with the other tragedies. Everything was done from the Putrajaya casino by Syafiq bin Rodney's gang of former pirates from the Strait of Malacca."

"Béatrice has a good heart," Victoire said. "She loves both of you very much. I suppose all she wanted to do was make a little nest egg for herself in case the world took a crazy turn. As if the world weren't crazy already."

Alain Jemestre's eyes looked moist. For her part, Apolline, seemed more relaxed.

"It's best that she's in Geneva," Apolline said. "Not only did we need to get her out of the limelight, we also had to get her away from my mother. She was sending our little girl to Titus's house, knowing all the time that he was a pedophile. To this day my mother doesn't acknowledge what she did. She said she was protecting her."

"Can I ask a question?" Victoire asked. "Whatever happened to Claudine Montzulac? We haven't heard a peep from her. It seemed like she fell off the radar in the middle of the investigation."

Alain Jemestre chuckled. "Well, as you know, she was conducting a parallel investigation. And she was making considerable headway. You solved the case first, but her hard work didn't go unnoticed. I think her friend Francis Béard had something to do with that. She's been bumped upstairs. In fact, she may be the capital's next police chief—and not for a day or a weekend."

"I'm glad to hear that," Victoire said. "She was a highly capable detective."

Jemestre put his arm around Apolline and smiled at John, Victoire, and Luc. "Now that Béatrice is safe, I can tell you that we've been able to reestablish ourselves in Southeast Asia. I had a frank discussion with the president of the United States. I won't let his country lay claim to this crucial part of the global economy. And I wanted to tell you this in person, because it wouldn't have been possible without your intervention. Thank you, and I hope our government can count on Fermatown's services if—and when—we need you again."

"We'd be honored, Mr. President," John said. There was a pause as he looked at Victoire and Luc. "But as a father, you'll understand if I ask for more assignments on French soil. You see, my little boy's counting on Fermatown's services too.

Fermatown's bottle-feeding, diaper-changing, and story-telling services. And I'd like to be at least one of the people providing them. Right, Victoire?"

He took his wife's hand.

"Right, sweetheart."

Thank you for reading Rare Earth Exchange.

Please share your thoughts and reactions on your favorite social media and retail platforms.

It's not too late to read The Greenland Breach, *the first book in the* Larivière Espionage series.
www.thegreenlandbreach.com

We love feedback.

About the Author

Bernard Besson, who was born in Lyon, France, in 1949, is a former top-level chief of staff of the French intelligence services, an eminent specialist in economic intelligence, and honorary general controller of the French National Police. He was involved in dismantling Soviet spy rings in France and Western Europe when the USSR fell and has real inside knowledge from his work auditing intelligence services and the police. He has also written a number of prize-winning thrillers, his first in 1998, and several works of nonfiction. He currently lives in the fourteenth arrondissement of Paris, right down the street from his heroes.

About the Translator

Sophie Weiner is a freelance translator and book publishing assistant from Baltimore, Maryland. After earning degrees in French from Bucknell University and New York University, Sophie went on to complete a master's in literary translation from the Sorbonne, where she focused her thesis on translating wordplay in works by Oulipo authors. She has translated and written for web-based companies dedicated to art, cinema, and fashion as well as for nonprofit organizations. Growing up with Babar, Madeline, and The Little Prince, Sophie was bitten by the Francophile bug at an early age, and is fortunate enough to have lived in Paris, Lille, and the Loire Valley.

CPSIA information can be obtained at www.ICGtesting.com
Printed in the USA
BVOW08s0353220616

452983BV00001B/1/P